CHILDREN are DIAMONDS

Books by Edward Hoagland

Essays

The Courage of Turtles
Walking the Dead Diamond River
The Moose on the Wall
Red Wolves and Black Bears
The Edward Hoagland Reader
The Tugman's Passage
Heart's Desire
Balancing Acts
Tigers and Ice
Hoagland on Nature
Sex and the River Styx

Travel

Notes from the Century Before
African Calliope
Early in the Season
Alaskan Travels

Fiction

Cat Man
The Circle Home
The Peacock's Tail
Seven Rivers West
City Tales
The Final Fate of the Alligators
Children Are Diamonds

Memoir

Compass Points

CHILDREN are DIAMONDS

DIAMONDS

An African Apocalypse

A NOVEL BY

EDWARD HOAGLAND

Arcade Publishing • New York

Arcade Publishing books may be purchased in bulk at special discounts for sales promotion, corporate gifts, fund-raising, or educational purposes. Special editions can also be created to specifications. For details, contact the Special Sales Department, Arcade Publishing, 307 West 36th Street, 11th Floor, New York, NY 10018 or arcade@skyhorsepublishing.com.

Arcade Publishing® is a registered trademark of Skyhorse Publishing, Inc.®, a Delaware corporation.

Visit our website at www.arcadepub.com.

10 9 8 7 6 5 4 3 2

Library of Congress Cataloging-in-Publication Data is available on file.

ISBN: 978-1-61145-834-3

Printed in the United States of America

For my mother, and my daughter, and for Trudy

Map of Africa circa 1995

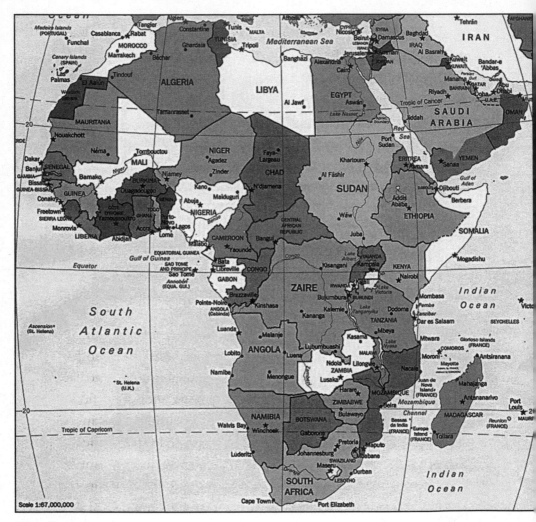

Courtesy of the Central Intelligence Agency

Chapter 1

• • •

IN AFRICA, EVERYTHING IS AN EMERGENCY. YOUR RADIATOR BLOWS OUT and as you solder a repair job, Lango kids emerge from the bush, belonging to a village that you'll never see, reachable by a path you hadn't noticed. Though one of them has a Kalashnikov, they aren't threatening, only hungry. Eight or ten of them, aged eight or ten, they don't expect to be fed by you or any other strange adult. Although you know some Swahili, you can't converse, not knowing Lango, but because there is plenty of water in the streams roundabout, they are fascinated that you choose to drink instead from bottles you have brought. Gradually growing bold enough to peer into the open windows of your Land Cruiser, they don't attempt to fiddle with the door or reach inside, seeing no food or curious mechanical delectables. The boxes packed there white-man-style are cryptically uninformative. Meningitis and polio vaccines, malaria meds, deworming pills, Ringer's solution, folic acid, vitamin A, and similar famine fighters. However, they will remain as long as you do, and you don't dare leave to take a leak because this fabric of politesse would tear if you did, as it would have already if they were five years older. You wish you could ask them if mines have been laid in the road recently by either the rebels or the government forces. Their fathers, the men of the village, haven't emerged because they're probably off with the guerrillas, and the women would not in a time of war—even the nun you are going to visit (a lay sister, although to all the Africans, a nun) has been raped, judging from what her radio message to the order's little villa in suburban Nairobi appeared to convey. That's why the footpath to their *tukls* is maintained indecipherably. The problem is your diarrhea. To pee in front of the children would be no big deal; the boys themselves pee in front of you. But diarrhea might amuse them enough to demystify you. They could open the car and loot it if you did that, or if you disappeared for a few minutes to relieve yourself. It's a balance you must maintain as you work on the engine: friendliness and mystery.

Disasters can swallow you in Africa, and yet the disasters, too, get swallowed up, which may be why we rolling stones roll there. Visas are fairly informal and the hotels wildly variant, so you can live awhile on almost nothing if you need to, as your troubles seem to piffle in the face of whatever else is going on. To shuffle tourists around on a safari route or manage a bunch of Kikuyu truck drivers who shuttle loads from Mombasa up to Nairobi or on to Kisumu and Kampala takes no special skill. I'm nominally a teacher (when I haven't had some kind of contretemps with an individual on the school board) and originally came over from America on the Salvation Army's nickel to work in one of its schools for the blind. It went well. Needless to say, I cared for the kids, and supervisors who live beyond their selfish interests I don't quibble with. But I did feel, over time, as if I might be going blind, too, which becomes a bit absurd when you are under these skies, in the midst of landscapes such as Africa's. I went to Alexandria on a business venture but returned to Africa.

Tourists want to be good guys in roughing it, and I can cook over an open fire, chauffeur a Bedford lorry, and recognize the planets or make a rainy evening more interesting by telling yarns, while keeping the Samburus from taking advantage of the Ohioans, and vice versa. Goodwill is not the problem; mainly just incomprehension. The former are living on a dollar a day. But expats in a stew like

Nairobi's may also barter for their daily bread—clerk in a store that caters to Europeans, selling fabrics, carvings, baskets, masks, with a crash pad in the back for that extra pair of hands boasting New England English and a whitely reassuring smile who's been hired for a stretch. Helps discourage robbers, in fact, to have a lug like me bunking in the place. Then there's always the blond Norwegian girl who arrived on an international internship of some sort but is staying on for an indeterminate number of months because an Ismaili merchant of advancing years but local wealth (gas stations, an auto agency, an office building and adjoining mart) is loaning her his garden house for the pleasure of her company occasionally at the dinner table, presided over by a portrait of the Aga Khan. The gent just likes to see her beauty in the room. He has a plump, swarthy wife as old as himself, so he doesn't intrude upon her privacy after supper or object if she accepts within the villa's high brick walls a presentable Western freeloader of her own for fleeting visits. The Masai watchman has been clued in—it's Kukuyu thieves he is hired to deter—but of course will turn away a *mzungu* like me, as well, if her nod turns to a frown.

But when you get a gig with a safari company, they will have a barracks to put you up in for the couple of days between the Amboseli and Serengeti trips. A schoolteacher like me probably "plays well with others," so you may meet richer clients who, after the Tsavo and Masai Mara jaunt, will want to hire a knowledgeable companion for a solo expedition west into Uganda's wilder parks, or south down the Indian Ocean coast, and not just to Malindi and Lamu, where everybody goes. This freelancing may then piss off an employer, but we're speaking of a city splitting at the seams with squatter camps, swollen by an enormous flux of displaced refugees from within hungry Kenya itself, not to mention all the illegals from the civil wars afire in the countries that surround it: Somalia, Sudan, Ethiopia, Congo, Rwanda. Look on a map—dire suffering—need I say more? And if you can drive an SUV or a Leyland lorry or ride herd on the Africans who do, and have the say-so of that Salvation Army major behind you, another do-good agency will have an opening in relief work for you pretty soon.

I do that, too. From gorillas right to guerrillas. I've chaperoned a perky Japanese fellow with binoculars hanging around his neck to eyeball the silverbacks in the Rwenzori Mountains; and next I'm venturing—or pussyfooting—slowly through Lord's Resistance Army rebel territory in northern Uganda with tons of corn and sorghum for one of the refugee camps up in the war zone of southern Sudan. But, between those ventures, there'll be the new San Francisco divorcée I ran into on the terrace of the Casino Club or the Thorn Tree Café, who has deplaned in Kenya to do the Karen Blixen, Isak Dinesen, *Out of Africa* thing in the very suburb—Karen, verging on the Ngong Hills—named for Blixen. Nearing forty, like me, she's just bought a villa from a South Asian or an Anglo-colonial former grandee at a fire-sale discount. It appears to have everything: the tamarind and flame trees, passionflowers and bougainvilleas, the leopard foraging in the garbage cans at night, killing the cat and dog if they go out, and the faithful Kamba manservant, Mutua, who accompanied the house but now is becoming nearly as fearful of staying in it as she, with no white man in residence who knows how to handle a pistol. Her first car, a romantic vintage Land Rover, has already been hijacked from her at a stoplight at terrifying gunpoint; and bandits armed with machetes boost themselves over the neighbors' walls, but when she tries to call the police—if the phone line does connect—they will ask her if she has "any petrol," because they don't. "Can you come and get us?" Wonderful colored tiles, crafted doorways of mahogany, teak beams, an inherited library of all the appropriate books—Adamson, Kenyatta, Lessing, Moorehead, Soyinka, Paton, Cary, *Things Fall Apart,* etc.—and a fairy-tale, gingerbread roof, but some nights she goes to the Norfolk Hotel to sleep, when she can't raise a friend closer than America on the telephone, if it works. She hasn't had time to find many of these in Nairobi yet, or an escort to take her places where she might begin to. So a "middle school history teacher," from America, no less, but who knows some

Swahili, and about motors, firearms, and the general East African maze, might be welcome to move in rent-free, after a look-over, if her long-distance harangues with her lawyer in California didn't bore me to tears, once the novelty of the stage set wore off. She had pals in the Bay Area who, like the lawyer, told her she ought to have sunk her settlement money into Napa Valley real estate instead of this. Now nothing could be renegotiated.

She also liked my name—Hickey. I escorted her to the Carnivore nightclub, where harlotry and brutality acquired new imageries for her, and to croupiers' tables at other places where the bouncers have you lift your hat to show them that no pistol is concealed underneath, but a white man who doesn't score can solace himself with the little girls and boys waiting outside at three A.M. to offer him a blow job for the equivalent of twenty cents. Also, however, to the Leakeys' marvelous National Museum, and the slightly swank dog show at the old racetrack, where the *West with the Night* lady, Beryl Markham, used to hang out; plus the fabled patio of the Muthaiga Club, which Beryl had already managed to join—Beryl played tennis and golf— and where divorce, according to legend, was the primary sport. Yes, Beryl was my landlady's name as well, although she wasn't a pilot, a horse trainer, or an author, like B. Markham. But she could brush her ash-brown tresses without the services of her Russian Hill hairdresser, glad to forgo being a bottle blonde for this cleansing period, while in Africa, she said. Quite a nice woman, she missed her therapist and paid for regular sessions on the telephone rather than trying our local quacks. Her son was a sophomore at Andover, so her trips home were going to be timed with those of his vacations that weren't slated to be spent with his father.

Once she had rendered it crystal clear that my position as a temporary live-in did not entail conjugal rights, she granted me some, if only because it was so much easier to vent her feelings in dishabille. She enjoyed tantalizing me at cocktail hour, and I didn't need to flatter her; she *was* wenchy as she mixed the drinks. I did tease her, though, because she'd finally bought a handgun for protection, when there were plenty of macho unemployed white hunters and former mercenaries around—now that shooting elephants was out of style and the apartheid wars were over and African dictators preferred black thugs—who could have run interference for her in an emergency much better than me. I wasn't beefy, red-faced, and recognizable around town as the type that, if bandits broke into their girlfriend's house in the dead of the night, could leap from a sound sleep, grab her ornamental six-foot Karamojong spear off the wall, and hurl it through the first of them. (A Frenchman, a Foreign Legionnaire, had actually done that—what a boyfriend!) But those guys, being even more downscale than me, were less presentable in the circles she aimed for or felt comfortable in. What in fact they were mostly doing for a living, now that no more Mr. and Mrs. Francis Macombers were seeking tutelage on the veldt, and in order to expiate their numerous sins, was lie behind sandbag emplacements in the desert heat defending U.N. and NGO enclaves in Mogadishu and other bad spots in Somalia that Hemingway would not have enjoyed either.

I couldn't go to visit my Norwegian damsel at her Ismaili pasha's villa in Thika and keep in Beryl's good graces, but since she, that damsel, didn't care, neither did I. Yet we were tiring of each other, nevertheless, Beryl and I. Beryl was used to computer innovators, grapevine splicers, or still whizzier, glitzier men with inherited capital to live on—even a polo player, whose photo, in whites, graced her coffee table. Politely, after a couple of weeks, I began to pack to leave without needing to be told; then was delayed because my glasses were stolen off my nose by a thief who reached in through the car window one noonday while we were stopped for a light, Beryl driving, which made it seem more stupid, since I didn't have the excuse that my hands were gripping the wheel. We talked about our poor parents: how what had looked apathetic or shortsighted or lackadaisical to a kid now appeared more throttled, and of course you feel sorry for them anyhow once they're safely in the ground. Her father had made his money as a go-getter, until he'd been shelved, after which he'd sat home for a year or two, running a comb through her hair every morning before sending her off to school. Earlier, I had noticed she liked me to do something resembling that, while she perched on my knee. But if she was mainly playing Meryl Streep, I wasn't an adequate leading man.

More important, the neighborhood had changed. Our faithful Kamba houseboy, Mutua, cooked and served our meals on Irish linen and Spode plateware with cut-glass fingerbowls from checker-boarded, fine-wood cabinetry. Yet one block down, an elderly white woman, a lifelong Kenyan resident and the widow of a coffee rancher from the highlands toward the Aberdare Range, who had chosen not to decamp in the general white stampede after independence but to live out her last years alone in the outskirts of Nairobi with five or six African women as companions—defenseless, penniless Kikuyu crones, with no villages or relatives of their own, they said, to go to, and whom she offered protection in return for some few services, in their penury—was smothered in her bedsheets. It had supposedly been a charitable arrangement. Not having quite outlived her money, she'd taken them in, one by one, in exchange for the house being kept reasonably well dusted, behind its shrubbery, and being served breakfast in bed and perhaps other minor amenities. She could have hired more energetic retainers, but two or three of these wrinkled ladies had known her husband, and how she and he preferred their tea and scones, plus Scotch in the evening. A gentle presence—a thread of continuity on the wooded street—she simply disappeared from view: not puttering in her garden or looking in her mailbox. No housekeepers were visible around, although taxis were seen entering, and an unfamiliar young man opened the gate. She was stiff and decomposing in her bed when her accountant and a security bruiser from his office forced the back door. No autopsy would have been performed on such an individual, snugly tucked in, with no untoward marks on her skin, if the house hadn't been stripped of whatever movables could possibly fit into a cab on a series of trips and the help had all vanished. Nobody really knew who they'd been.

But they must have possessed plenty of relatives and a web of villages out near Mount Kenya to flee to for a comfortable old age.

Nairobi's beleaguered, superannuated white community remembered other suspicious, inconspicuous deaths and looked at their own impassive retainers—not that they would have wanted to risk hiring any young strangers as an alternative, however. Few pensions existed for old people. Without an extended family, they starved. So you continued to take somebody in, with no wages necessary, if you happened to have run through your own resources and just had a roof and rice and beans to offer. The bewildering sheer size of this new megapolis, with fetid, unmapped shanty-town add-ons, its eclipsed police force carrying rifles on foot patrol through the downtown avenues to try to shoot the car-thief gangs, since there was no other way of stopping them, scared the old hands as well as Beryl. Pickpockets were simply kicked to death by a mob of civilians, when anybody managed to grab one. I myself had seen it happen to a whimpering little boy not over ten or eleven—all those polished, sharp-toed, office workers' shoes; you couldn't have squeezed through the tightening circle of fifty or more middle-class men in suits to save him. I tried—it was iron—and left. The joke, if you can call it that, among us expatriates is that if you feel a hand grope for your wallet, the second thing to do is try to save the life of the pickpocket. This is a city veering into calamity, where transient whites like me still dribble in because it's a hub for aid groups and yet a traditional wash-up spot for Anglo ne'er-do-wells who try to define themselves by where they have been and, more fleetingly, those parents who want their children to see wild animals before it's too late; they are sometimes my bread and butter. With the AIDS pandemic, it will soon be too late for a number of things.

Chapter 2

• • •

I AM A GUIDE, NE'ER-DO-WELL, AID WORKER, WHAT-HAVE-YOU, BUT A nice guy and I'd been supplanted at Beryl's trophy house by a natty English newspaperman (I can't blame her) who'd been brought in by the Aga Khan's business organization to spruce up the daily tabloid it owns in Kenya. Apart from making a few design changes and feature additions, his job was really to hearten the idealistic employees who wanted the illusion of a free press in this country that's so stuffed with corruption, as well as a Fleet Street veteran to witness and even help them stand up to the intimidation they are often subjected to. He was energetic, conscientious, supple, and when working-class Fleet Street met a San Francisco divorcée burning through her alimony, I didn't stand a chance. Being packed, as I say, and having given Beryl in her chic Land Rover a tour of Tsavo Park she would always remember, with the hippos at Mzima Springs particularly effusive, and where we'd glimpsed rarities like African wild dogs, hartebeest, oryx, while camping by an elephant herd's watering hole, with no schedule to follow—for both of us it was an idyll, and she'd ceased being ironic about making love for that half a week—I was content to go back to my hotel downtown. It's a hole-in-the-wall, owned by an Arab but across the street from the New Stanley, a famous old hostelry with a swimming pool on the roof and bulletin boards tacked to a thorn tree in the café patio, where Euro-American travelers traditionally leave notes for each other. I'd registered at the New Stanley earlier because they give you a free safe deposit box when you do, then never check on whether you've actually left. Living cheaply just across the street in my Arab's seedy brownstone (these are the tatty details of a roamer's life), I was a frequent figure on the Thorn Tree's patio, or at the glass tables beside the swimming pool, up twelve stories, where the black kites and vultures sail and scud, and where I'd met both the Norwegian and Beryl, for example—my valuables secure behind the New Stanley's desk in the meantime.

Even at the Arab's, with less than ten guest rooms—and as in many Third World countries—the barman, like the doorman at the New Stanley, would let in local university students who had bribed him or maybe were related to him and trolling for adventure or a foreign sugar daddy. Though I had pals in various flats around the city, if I was otherwise unoccupied after a day of trolling for a new job myself, or temporarily filling in at an NGO's office, I could wiggle a finger (by which I only mean to suggest how easy it was) and be joined by one of these anxious, rather pretty but thin young women, who'd sit down obediently at my table but scrutinize me carefully to size me up. I'd make it plain that I was not an ogre, only lonely, and offer to feed her if she was hungry, which she usually was. Even on a scholarship, some students need to skip a meal or two per day. Yes, she could have the chicken, instead of the measly bean dish (might not have tasted chicken for a month), and a soft drink; she was not required to get drunk. This was not a prelude, in other words. There would be no after-cost, so we could relax and ease our mutual solitude; then possibly a night or two later, as well. I'm not suggesting we were now on terms of equality—a man with hundreds in his wallet and thousands in the money belt he was wearing underneath his clothes, around his waist, with more in the hotel safety box across the street, facing a college girl fifteen or twenty years younger in threadbare clothing who lived on a dollar a day—but that I generally had the decency not to ask for a quid pro quo.

What she wanted wasn't really the meal so much as either a visa out or an employment opportunity right here in Kenya when she graduated; and the power of the white stranger from abroad was not just the beefsteak and green salad he could provide but the implication in his presence that he must know executives in the office buildings that cut the paltry skyline of Nairobi who could find a slot for a stenographer in a city where ten university graduates needed such a modest boon immediately. Although her chances of achieving that result with me were almost nil, our conversations would not be value-less; they would add fluency to her English, and insight into how to cultivate a European, her grip on reality, and how she fathomed the mentality of older men from northern continents, or perhaps become a sort of low-rent therapy if she poured her heart out. The classes she was enrolled in were huge, the professors aloof, the families the students came from often racked and shackled by grief and hardship, even over and above the threat of AIDS. Five extra dollars could pay for a doctor visit and medicines that were needed for a sister who was sick. But on the other hand, there would be girls who strode past my table, eschewing my relative sobriety and the proffered French fries and drumsticks for a drunken construction engineer from Rotterdam who wanted to haul her upstairs across one of his shoulders and fuck her in three ways in exchange for enough cash for her whole family to live on for three weeks, even after the bartender and elevator man grabbed their cut as she left, past midnight, in her brother-in-law's heap.

The city turns so risky after dark that, much as with the pick-pocket, you need to take responsibility for her life if you keep one of these girls chatting with you over beer and pretzels till closing time. Hire a taxi, sure, but even the taxis become dangerous, or the drivers too frightened to leave the downtown area for the wildlands where the girl lives. She may not get safely home, so you tip a bellhop to allow her to sleep in his broom closet until dawn, or take her into your room under whatever terms you dictate, which in my case would be her call. These fastidious girls, with their four-year degree in hand but still underfed, delicate, fit for an office career, though no employment is in sight because of the stove-in economy—no husband either, because of the AIDS tragedy—they panic after a year of walking the streets, trying every agency, bureau, and store, cadging tea and a cookie perhaps at the interviews, as their good clothes wear out.

—∞∞∞—

I'm alone, hunched over rice and a goat kebab, the generous helping at supper that paying guests get, when a girl sits down at my table. Her aunt is a cleaning woman at my Arab's establishment, so, while pretending to visit her, she spotted me over her shoulder.

I crook my finger and scrape half of my dinner onto my butter plate, give her my spoon to eat it with, tear my roll in half, pour half of my Tusker beer into my glass and hand her that, drinking the rest out of the bottle. Having noticed that day that music is advertised in a club window down the block, I say we're so close we could sprint back here at one A.M. without getting mugged. Okay? Tears glisten in her questioning eyes as she nods. So we go. There, I buy her a pizza to fill her small stomach some more, as she tells me that her mother died of appendicitis not long ago, as the cleaning woman, her aunt, already had told me. Her father is becoming disabled with arthritis. She has siblings with HIV. I change the subject to what she studied in school, to avoid hearing more unsettling details. Economics, history, art. She is of the Kalenjin, a tribe allied with the Kikuyu, who control the government at the moment and flaunt their power in public places by speaking Kikuyu instead of Swahili or English, which other people could understand. The music is Afro, on handmade instruments, so we dance and gradually feel a rapport. I ask her if this purple blouse, flattering in color but with a hole in it, is her best. She says no, her second best; she didn't know she was going to score on this particular evening out. Her bra strap is also frayed, but I observe without comment and assure her that she smells good when, sweating, she confesses that her family has no running water. I say I do, and we laugh. I wouldn't have come here without her presence at my table to save me from the assertive importunities of the muscular Kikuyu prostitutes.

We ask the bouncer please to watch us from the door as we run back through a sudden rainstorm to the Arab's building from the club—where I have my key ready to quickly get in. The girl must have had some bad experiences, however, because her face dissolves into a beseeching fear: Will I just mumble good night and leave her outside, at the mercies of the muggers? She opens her purse on an impulse, not like a prostitute asking for payment but like a girl showing that she has no money to go anywhere. Hugging her with one arm, I lead her upstairs, start the tub in the bathroom, and wave her in. I then sit on the bed, look for CNN on the tube, after hiding my wallet and money belts (yes, I have two, because my regular belt, the one that was holding up my pants, has a secret zippered section that you can also fold twenty hundred-dollar bills into), and watch a snatch of an Indian movie dubbed from Hindi into English instead. "Take your time," I reassure her through the door. "Enjoy yourself. Please. No hurry."

I hear her fill the tub again to rinse, or perhaps to double-suds herself. Then I hear her at the sink, washing her jeans, blouse, and underclothes, I suppose. Finally she emerges, saronged in a towel.

"I did my wash so you couldn't kick me out," she explains. I smile. Her face is pretty, winsome, and small; I wonder whether her breasts are, as well.

"Can I see you sometime?"

"You mean sometime tonight?" she asks.

"Yes, sometime tonight."

"Are you an art student? I was an art student," she says.

"Yes, I'm an art student. I promise."

"Sit where you are," she instructs me, then drops the towel, her arms upraised in a classic life-model pose, which she holds for my edification as if this were a class, while watching only to see whether I think she is exquisite.

"Exquisite!" I exclaim. When I move one hand very slightly, she turns round very slowly to display the small of her back and her buttocks. Her color is different from mine, but that distinction has vanished.

"Do you want to violate the code?" she asks.

"Yes, whatever that means."

She lowers her arms and comes to me, kneels, and puts her hands on top of my thighs, as I sit on the edge of the bed. I cuddle her, fondle her, bury my hands in her hair, while figuring what we could possibly do with no risk of AIDS. I carry condoms, of course, but with an African woman, just thinking of the odds can distract and unman you, even if you theoretically have protection.

She remains in that supplicant position, not playacting like a college student anymore. Her mind is not on sex.

"I want you to take me to America. Sponsor me, please. I know I need somebody," she elaborates bluntly, pleadingly, ignoring how my hands are cherishing her breasts. "I could be your maid. I'd work to repay you and go more to school."

Raising her up, shutting off the TV, I move to the little table, where we can look at each other. "In other words, go bail for you? I'm your friend, not your father," I answer, masking my confusion with unjustified irritation. "Do you know what it costs to guarantee somebody for a visa? What they would make me sign as an indemnity?"

Naked across from me, crossing her arms now, Leli, as she wants to be known (Nyawera is her African name), who just wants to escape from her country, nods. She has done her homework, been to the Western embassies, tried for student visas.

"You hurt my feelings," I complain again, a bit selfishly, as though the poor girl had picked me up more from calculation than straight, impromptu necessity. Waitresses in restaurants, who don't know you, will ask to be your "maid" also, occasionally. But, glancing at Leli's sadness, I have to soften and repeat that I am her new friend, and that in fact I am looking for work myself, and wave her close to me, to begin to cherish her again.

In the morning, as she dresses, the contrast is so poignant between how pretty she is and her threadbare underwear and outerwear that I take her shopping for inexpensive clothes that aren't incongruously ragged. Afterward, she surprises me by declining to go to a storefront I am temping at, where we feed street kids and treat them with skin ointments, antibiotics, inoculations, minerals, vitamins, whatever we happen to have. Powdered milk, powdered eggs, surplus soups or porridges that another nongovernmental organization may have given us.

I say bye-bye. She gets on a bus.

We have a basketball hoop up, and soccer balls, board games, playing cards, a tent fly hooked to the back wall in the courtyard with cots arranged underneath it, as a shelter where the children can feel some safety in numbers at least. What makes you burn out are the ones dying visibly of AIDS. Yet you don't want to banish them again to the furnace of the streets or, on the other hand, specialize merely as a hospice, where salvageable kids aren't going to want to come. Many of them wish to go to school but have no home to go to school from or money for the fees. So I'd scrounged a blackboard and taught addition, subtraction, geography, the English alphabet, when I had a break from refereeing a gritty soccer game or supervising the dishwashing or triaging kids with fevers or contusions who ought to go to the hospital (not that this Dickensian trip was often in their best interest). We had artful dodgers eating our fruits and sandwiches, between excursions into robbery, drugs, peddling, or the pederasty racket—knives, guns, money, fancy sneakers, or the other wicked chimeras that adults around the corner might be offering them—but also earnest tykes, plenty of them, who your heart absolutely went out to. Yet triage isn't teaching, it's frustrating, and I switch back and forth between such street work and the safaris and far-flung aid deliveries to conflict regions I've sometimes specialized in.

The girls were housed in a church anteroom nearby, spending the daylight hours with us; but I'd been surprised that Leli had promptly shook her head, from an antiseptic distance, with her new panties and bras in a shopping bag, much as Beryl might have done, and said she'd maybe see me at the Arab's another time. We *were* rather a rattled crew: a couple of dumbstruck interns from Swarthmore College in Pennsylvania, plus me, presently a little distracted by the red tape of renewing my Kenyan working papers, not to mention by Beryl's recent summons to return, since her Oxbridge yet working-class Fleet Street newshound had begun to be unfaithful to her with a fellow Brit with high cheekbones whose brown hair hung down to her coccyx, instead of promising to go home to the Bay Area land of milk and honey with Beryl.

Our boss at the shelter, Vernon, was a kind of born-again hangdog with a tolerant wife who was admirably cool during berserk emergencies, and those hundred young souls wouldn't have been fed without the two of them—would have been out purse snatching, jism swallowing, courier running, and pursuing other deathly gambits as dangerous as walking a parapet. I used to suffer dreams of doing that whenever one I'd had a chance to come to care about would vanish inexplicably. Our funding originated with an umbrella relief organization called Protestants Against Famine, financed by Baptists in the States and run by a friend of mine named Al, who was married to a Dinka woman from the southern Sudan, whom he had met during a stint of working in the war zone there.

So, intermittently, I'd freelance on one-shot contracts with Al's or another agency that found itself short of personnel to shepherd a fleet of trucks from Mombasa's port to Kakuma camp, in northern Kenya, which hosted thirty thousand Sudanese and Somali refugees, or to deliver half a year's food and supplies to some man-and-wife evangelical outpost spotted almost off the map in the outback. If you are genuinely feeding and medicating the locals, authorization for such missions will not be withheld. And that's how I'd met Ruthie the year before.

Chapter 3

. . .

Ruth's station, at an abandoned church on the hairy periphery, had been temporarily vacated after somebody had a nervous breakdown or underwent a flameout and nobody else could fill the bill. But before the structure was pillaged inside out, a new communicant, Ruth, rather shaky but fervent, volunteered to reestablish it. Her intentions were of the best (who else would imaginably come?), though she was ordained as neither a doctor nor a preacher. The closest authorities, who were rebels of the Sudan People's Liberation Army, accepted her, and that was all that mattered, apart from Al's say-so.

You don't have to be a doctor to help people who have no aspirin or disinfectant or malaria, tuberculosis, dysentery, or epilepsy pills, no splints or bandaging, and no other near facility to walk to in the bush. Kaopectate, cough suppressants, malnutrition supplements, antibiotics for bilharzia or sleeping sickness or yaws: if you were a nurse, patients would be brought to you for these or with hepatitis or broken limbs. The old stone-and-concrete ruins of a Catholic chapel that had been forgotten since the colonial powers had left could be reoccupied, if you chased the leopards and the cobras out, because joy is what is partly needed, especially at first, and joy, I think, is, like photosynthesis for plants, an evidence of God. Whether it, like photo-

17

synthesis, provides evolutionary advantages is arguable. People may have sexual intercourse out of boredom or simple hormonal pressures or vaguely sadistic motives as often as in love and joy, and so human nature is reproduced in all of its continuing imperfections. But joy, like beauty, is a continuum, too, and in temperate climates it waxes with the sun, somewhat as plants do.

What I'm explaining is that, even if I'm not of their exact denomination, directors of small missionary programs in a pinch for personnel may see fit to hire me for jack-of-all-trades assignments. I can do the basic mechanics if we break down on the road, and I know when to speed up or—equally important—slow down when figures with guns appear to block our passage. (If it's soldiers, you never speed up, but the decision is not that easy, because every male can look like a soldier in a war zone, and the soldiers like civilians.) The big groups, such as Doctors Without Borders, CARE, Oxfam, and Save the Children, have salaried international staff they can fly in from Honduras, Bangkok, or New Delhi to plug a momentary defection or a flip-out—dedicated career people, like the U.N.'s ladies and gentlemen, with New York, Geneva, London, Paris, Rome behind them, who've been vetted: not much fooling around. But there are various smaller outfits, whose flyers you don't receive in the mail back home, that will hire "the spiritual drifter," as Al put it to me, to haul pallets of plywood, bags of cement, first-aid kits in bulk, and sacks of potatoes or bayou rice, cases of your basic tins, like corned beef, tuna fish, salmon, peas, what-have-you, and trunks of medicine to provision the solo picayune apostle out doing Christ's appalling work in the hinterlands. ("Wouldn't you get a little picky, picayune, washing dysentery doo-doo off of cholera asses, with toddlers with blowfish bellies staggering around? The marabou stork stalkin' about, too," he added, "waitin' for his meal?")

You draw up lists of refugees, so no one gets double their ration by coming through the corn queue twice. Use ink stamped on the wrists if you have to—if their names are always Mohammed or Josephine. And you census the children, as well, and weigh a sampling of them in a sling scale, plus measure their upper-arm fat, if they have any, with calipers to compile the ratio of malnutrition in the populace, severe versus moderate, and so on. I've helped inject against measles, tetanus, typhoid when not enough licensed people were there, having been a vet's assistant at one point in my teens. I've powwowed with the traditional clan chiefs and tribal healers, the leopard-skin priests and village shamans and elders, and hard-butt young militia commanders, and have delivered babies when nobody competent was around. I've squeezed the rehydration salts into babies' mouths when they were at death's door, and mixed the fortified formula that you spoon into them, and chalked the rows of little white squares in the dirt where you have them all sit individually at their feeding hours so that every one gets the same amount of protein, the same units of vitamins A, C, E, B, calcium, iron, out of the fifty-five-gallon steel drum you're stewing the emergency preparation in. *Hundreds* of passive, dying children sitting cross-legged in the little squares, waiting for you to reach each of them. You don't think that breaks your heart? Chalk is never gonna look the same, even when you're teaching sixth grade again.

So, I'd met Ruthie one time the previous year, when her group, Protestants Against Famine, received a shipload of corn at Mombasa and needed to distribute it fast because of limited warehouse space. In fact, the sheds were full of other organizations' beans and sorghum and corn, storehoused for Somalia, and it was expensive to guard outdoors, against the nightly pilferage, or protect from the rains. Better to have the pilferage going on close to the refugee camps than in Mombasa, anyway. I was hired to supervise part of this hasty dispersal. PAF had eight or ten small splinter missions in eastern and central Africa, all serviced from Nairobi, and I took the overnight train down to the coast, getting a compartment easily at the last minute because of tourist cancellations after a washout and a wreck two weeks before, in which a lot of people had been killed. A hundred and seven bodies were trucked back to the capital and displayed for identification on open tables, naked or practically so, in the Nairobi morgue. I'm ashamed to say I went to stare, like every other rubbernecking lout in the city, because, along with the zaftig Africans laid out here and there among the less intriguing corpses, was a Nordic-looking white girl, as if at some dirty peep show. Her passport, in her purse or baggage, had washed downriver like everybody else's after the crash, so the authorities, instead of sensibly turning her remains over to the Swedish or British embassy, decided, perhaps with relish, to treat her just as bad as everybody else. That was before my phone call. So, on the same railway route, after enough jerry-built repairs had been performed to get us across that particular river where it joins the Athi, I felt doubly regretful, as if I were going to be lying on that selfsame slab myself pretty soon, and serve me right. Not to mention, coincidentally, the news from the PAF office manager, Al, that I ought to be forewarned that one of their mission women, Ruth Parker, had recently been captured at an isolated clinic in Sudan by a rump ("no pun intended") guerrilla group of the Sudan People's Liberation Army, which had overrun the clinic in order to seize the supplies and medicines. But eventually they'd turned her loose to walk naked ("as is their wont") twenty miles south to the nearest outpost that had white people at it. Whether she'd been raped, like the Maryknoll nun I'd mentioned earlier, he didn't know. ("Couldn't ask over the radio, could I?") But since she was refusing evacuation, he asked me to try to evaluate ("Yes, I know you're not a therapist") her state.

What with the sudden cancellations, I got a roomette for the rattling rail trip across the lion-colored gamelands of the Athi Plains— wildebeests, zebra herds, tommy gazelles, and a cherry sun when it sets—down to the sisal farms, sugarcane fields, and coconut palms on the coast. I thought I might have the adjoining accommodations to spread out in, too, on account of the scare; but no, just as the conductor was about to hoist the steps, two German business types came huffing-puffing along the platform toward my sleeper, hauling wheeled suitcases, with two brawny, blowsy African women keeping up with them, panting and hollering bye-bye, who were obviously going to stay behind. The Germans, in German, appeared to be amused by, but at the same time now wished to be well rid of, them. And just then one did turn back, as if giving up the hope of wangling a parting tip for her services performed, muttering as much in Kikuyu to the other. But the bolder woman, after hesitating, pressed ahead. The Germans were wrestling their bags up the stairs into the vestibule, but she called out, "Please take me! I've never been to Mombasa. I'm a Kenyan and yet I've never been to Mombasa!"

It's a refrain I hear often in Nairobi. Americans will be standing around in safari togs—twill pants, brimmed hat, open-collared tan shirt—and the desk clerk, bellhop, taxi driver, or restaurant greeter, recognizing me as a regular, will say with more than a twist of irony: "You know, I've never seen an eland or a leopard." So, speaking again in English, which was apparently their lingua franca, she pleaded: "Save money! You can fuck me there instead of new people."

The laggard of the Germans, who looked more sensual in the shape of his mouth, was tempted. He let her mount the steps, though motioning to the conductor please to wait until they'd made their minds up. He glanced into the compartment their tickets had paid for, then at me for a reaction, because their side door opened into my own space.

"Save money. You can fuck me there instead of new people!"

"Are you broad-minded?" he asked me. I nodded, so he nodded and turned. "Must go back on the bus. We fly to Europe," he explained to her—the bus of course being joltier and cheaper. Probably about thirty, she'd never ridden on a train before and was so eager that she promised him she'd sleep on the floor. She opened a window so she and her friend could squeeze hands and exchange purses because the other woman's was bigger and had more inside.

Otto, the German who was her champion, told me he was a vintner, his pal a hydraulic engineer. As the train began to rollick and roll, he pumped his arm like his joystick. "Ava, maybe," he said to her, "the rocking will make me come too fast."

Ava—as she called herself, she later told me, because a customer who liked Ava Gardner had dubbed her that—assured each of us that

he was "very strong, very strong." A tall highlands woman from the
Nairobi slums, she was excited to be speeding along in this famous
Mombasa sleeper train—not just a jam-packed, plebeian, pothole-
bumping bus—and on the same railroad roadbed where we could see
thousands of her fellow citizens traipsing home at this evening hour
from their jobs downtown. I asked her where she lived, whether she
had walked beside the tracks innumerable times into or out of the
city herself from Mathare, a railway-siding slum, to save the bus fare,
like all these countless men in office shoes and shabby, respectable
suits using the cinders as a thoroughfare. She smiled and waved her
hand, only vaguely agreeing. I didn't ask whether she'd told the
Germans about the crash, or mention it myself. The lower and upper
berths where they were going to sleep fascinated her, and the
windows, with a cooling, exhilarating wind, despite the muddy fetid
slums going by and people in torn jerseys shitting in the open—until
the limitless horizons of the veldt began.

"I want to see a lion," she said, when I pointed out how each
railway section master's bungalow was fenced high for protection.

The dining car had spacious windows, too; they complemented
the table linens, crystal glasses, and silverware, although we kept them
closed so our soup and rounds of beer and plates of fish and beef
would stay clean. Sunset bled into dusk as Ava ate a Herculean meal,
reaching over exuberantly to finish the leftovers on each of our
plates, even to the last string bean or sliver of fat and strand of carrot
or dab of mashed potato. This was a banner trip, and she wouldn't
deny herself any of its perks. The attitude of the waiters and other
diners didn't faze her. Yes, she was going to be able to handle all three
of us who were at the table with her tonight, if I was given to her as
well—though of course I didn't intend that.

Sitting next to her, facing the grinning Germans, with their vacation fares (this jaunt was part of the advance package for them, Otto
said, and Ava's company was only costing them an extra coach ticket
because she was going to sleep on the floor), I was only nonplussed
when I tried to ask her a serious question, such as what she thought

of Daniel arap Moi, the nation's president, or if the accent of the Mombasans, when they spoke Swahili, would be recognizably different. She apparently thought I was patronizing her. Bristling, she stared at me as though to say *Do you think I'm an African?* But, realizing I meant no offense, she would then put her hand on my knee and slide it to my crotch, to reassure me that she was competent to handle everything.

Munching cake, after Ava had finished the trimmings off the steak on their plates, Otto and Hans kept talking about getting inside her after supper, pistoning their fists. Should we rename her Betty, after Grable? We could decide when she was naked, during the gymnastics, when they could see her legs. Meanwhile, outside, a maintenance shed occasionally provided a bulb or two in the darkness, where a generator had been placed. Our twenty yellow-lit railway cars coiling raffishly around the curves behind a black-plumed engine was a more glamorous spectacle, and we might hear kids faintly shouting from a hovel beside a campfire. At first I'd be alarmed on their behalf—they sounded as if they were dashing toward the train (was their mother dying in childbirth?!)—till I realized they were only wildly seeking to register their existence on our consciousness.

We had three hundred miles to go in about ten hours, from the relatively recently British-built city of Nairobi (previously a Masai watering hole) to the Arabs' eleventh-century port settlement on the Indian Ocean, which had been conquered by the Portuguese five hundred years later. Ava's English was better than that of Otto and Hans, and she knew a smattering of German, too, so she could translate a bit when we talked European politics, besides quizzing the waiters for us in Swahili or Kikuyu while reaching out to finish off a rind of cheese or scrap of cake frosting on anybody's plate. She took my mind off the train crash and rested her hand on my knee rather pleasantly whenever she fathomed that I might be on the point of mentioning it. Although she ate like a survivalist, she drank watchfully, clutching her purse. No one could have snatched it.

Later, however, as I fell asleep, I could hear them fucking her in the adjoining compartment like an athletic event. Having told them that Ava could sleep in my extra berth whenever they were through with her, I hoped they wouldn't actually wake me up, it began to take so long. And they didn't. But I felt guilty in the morning, she looked so bedraggled from slumping on the floor through the wee hours. Didn't even go to breakfast. Napped on a bunk disgruntledly, complaining that she missed her children; her auntie was taking care of them. Her first train trip was ending badly. "Good jig-jig," Otto complimented her, handing her enough money for the bus ride home. Hans told me they'd decided that they wanted to find themselves new women in Mombasa who had "some India in them. The Goa eyes, the Bombay brown."

Barefoot toddlers waved at the train, and older kids were running to register their presence on us from the huts they lived in on the citrus plantations. It was tropical here at sea level, with vegetation rioting for any foothold along the roadbed, as I leaned out the half door of the vestibule to feel the warming wind. On the causeway to the island, Mombasa-bound workers were hiking to their jobs, much as they would be in Nairobi just now. On my last trip down, I'd picked up the companionship of a Canadian professional woman with a heavy knapsack full of asthma medications who was on the touching mission of trying to meet an English boyfriend who might resemble the one she had suddenly lost. He'd broken off with her, and from Toronto, she'd flown to Nairobi and gotten on our rattly train, and from Mombasa I soon put her on a bus for Malindi. Not that *they* had met in Malindi, but her beau had talked about this string of Indian Ocean beach resorts, and she believed a man like him might be found vacationing there. It was a slender and forlornly different agenda than mine, but we went together to the massive stone watchtowers of Fort Jesus and climbed into a high, snug cranny to gaze out toward the crinkly bay. She was haggard from her asthma seizures and the loss of her love—inaccessible to me, of course, when I'd knocked on her hotel room door the night before—but another of the gallery of lovelorn whites you meet in Africa who at least have the grace, I suppose, to try to do something about it. I still remember her grim, plaintive face, battling for breath, when she opened to my knock. "Don't you think it would kill me?" she said.

Hungry Somalis sail down the coast from Kismayu, and hungry Tanzanians drift up from Dar es Salaam, to make the warren of Mombasa's Old Town a dangerous place. No more so than a dozen others on the continent, but its flavor combines Islamic complexities with the Hindu and the Byzantine; plus, it's prostratingly hot. I found that our smart local fixer had already preloaded PAF's corn onto trucks to keep it dry and had loaned the rest of the grain to other organizations, like the Lutherans' and Catholics', that could use it quicker and later pay us back. So we got started.

One delivery was headed up into Turkana and Toposa country, past Nairobi (where they picked up Al), into northernmost Kenya, past Lodwar, Kakuma, Lokichoggio, to Chukudum, in Sudan near the Ethiopian border area. Another, including my own bunch of trucks, turned northwest from Nairobi, through Gilgil, Nakuru, Kisumu, and Jinja and Kampala, in Uganda, continuing from there on into the Congo, via Fort Portal. I was going to turn north, like the Nile, from Lake Victoria toward Masindi and Gulu, in Uganda, and then Equatoria in the southern Sudan. But first I accompanied the Congo trucks to Kisangani, which I always take the opportunity to do, even though my French is bad and it's scarier than anywhere else. Thus a couple of weeks had passed before I did meet Ruthie at last: altogether a couple of months after her ordeal.

———— ⚬⚬⚬ ————

Wiry though round-shouldered, with a short torso and wide hips, and quite sputteringly electric, as if plugged into a faulty cord, Ruth did not greet me as placidly as Dr. Livingstone had Henry Stanley. She walked in a half-rotating manner because of hip trouble, which made her look older than the color of her hair, Airedale-brown and cut short for the climate or to reduce attention to her gender, as did the unbelted smocks she wore.

Her feeding station at Loa was in a moribund church school, built of fitted stones with a sheet-iron roof. We could imagine the stones being rolled laboriously into place a century ago by the Italian priests or monks and their convert crew; then, the original rats' nest of a thatch roof proudly replaced later on. This section of the Nile had been delegated to the Italians to Christianize, whereas the Anglicans were granted more northerly and southerly pieces of the river, and the Belgians, needless to say, the Congo and its watershed.

Not that the rats disappeared with the thatch. Along with a new medicine chest and personal staples, Ruth and her Aussie assistant had asked for traps, which she now set strategically, as men unloaded the bags of millet and corn and little boys collected whatever kernels spilled—as they would the rats. Except for one truck to bring me back, I let the drivers stay only overnight because they were being paid per diem, but I could report at once in a note to Al that it was Ruthie's Aussie assistant who was having panic attacks, more than her. Yet neither was quite ready for evacuation. I had no right to raise the "R" question in so many words because a war was under way, with no one to complain about a crime to. Her captors had been Nuer—enemies of the Dinka people we were feeding, and who they themselves might be surrounded by. The Dinkas were no doubt committing comparable daily crimes up the road toward Juba a ways. Her limp did give me an opening, without being personal, to ask if they had kept her shoes when they let her go.

"Sure," she said. "Anything and everything."

I'd been primed to extract either of them chivalrously from their precarious position, but they didn't leap at the offer, not even the jittery Aussie, who I should have perceived was cracking, and stuck into one of the trucks when they departed the next morning. I was still preoccupied with my trip into the Congo because my bad French had been a disaster. In the complexity of a "mission of mercy," and a tribal web that is extravagantly hallucinatory, with Lendu massacring Hema, or vice versa, I also buy diamonds, frankly, when I'm in the Congo—which, unlike Sudan, has them—whether stolen rough from an open-pit mine or from a streambed. In your hotel room, or to your restaurant table, a guy comes sub rosa to present you with a pouch you can sell afterward to a Ganda in the Chinese hotel in Kampala, who also knocks on your door, once you've registered, and gives you a three hundred percent profit for defying death, going through those roadblocks on the track back from Kisangani or Bunia to Fort Portal and Kampala.

I'd been primed, too, by Al to flinch at the hunger. But we'd arrived soon enough to prevent these skeletal scenes. I'd had a companion on this last leg north, a CIA guy, as it turned out. Three passports spilled out of his luggage when we roomed together in Ruthie's parsonage, as he unpacked. One "Herbert" had been born in Ipswich, Massachusetts, and another in Tunis. He grabbed the third away from me before I could look at it. "Are you with Mossad or our own spook?" I asked. I'd made him travel in the cab with another driver, not to be squeezed for many hours against his professorial chest on the bumpy road. But he insisted he was a genuine Baptist preacher and preached at me like an Anabaptist to prove it until I said uncle: "You know your Bible."

"Do I look Jewish?" he joked. He was a funder, he claimed, out to "witness firsthand" how the money being generated in church collection plates in the U.S. was being spent by Ruthie. Just as the spooks do, in fact, who fund the Sudan People's Liberation Army guerrillas, who we were feeding, and who were fighting Khartoum's army and militias. Mossad arms them, too, off and on, when we don't, in order to bleed the Arabs.

Herbert kept calling us Baptists Against Famine, instead of Protestants Against Famine, but he prayed like one of those missionary pilots you have to fly with, if you can't go by truck. My friend Ed prayed very loudly before he took off, and he flew his Cessna with one finger on the map in his lap, peering downward to see if the lakes that the plane's shadow crossed were the same shape as the cartographer said they ought to be, being fresh out of a flying school in Iowa where people who feel called upon to become missionary pilots train.

"Shortest name you can pick," Ed liked to say of his. "Been to the Holy Land, but not Africa before this. But it's more biblical here. That is, Christ would surely have his work cut out for him." Ed, with an Iowa Adam's apple, who sometimes flew Al to Ruthie's, was flabbergasted at how "biblical" this setting could be. The ancient illnesses, like polio—people crawling around on all fours right into adulthood as a result—and yellow fever, bladder prolapse, and the numbers of the blind, each one led about by a small child with a stick because there was no cataract surgery or treatment for glaucoma or trachoma. And leprosy: grandchildren caring for grandparents with hands or feet eaten away. Babies dying simply from diarrhea. He'd been dumbfounded at how any corn kernels that leaked from the floor of a truck or the seams of a GIFT OF THE AMERICAN PEOPLE bag onto the dirt road were snapped up.

Herbert wasn't bogus enough to pretend to be surprised, but he admired how Ruth had strings of Christmas tinsel hanging in the wind year-round to twist and throw off reflections of a spectrum of colors. We sat underneath a banyan tree, watching how huge the stars grew after dark, hearing a hyena giggle, a lion grunt. Herbert was gray-haired, which the local people understood as indicating in a white man (a *khawaja*, or a *mzungu*, in Arab-speaking Sudan) power as well as age, the power demonstrated in obtaining emergency deliveries of food. With his fine boots—when they were barefoot—one aged man asked him the following day if he was a king, and maybe had he walked from America? Or was he the leader of the United Nations—because, I supposed, of his imposing, professorial bearing, due to shuttling from the Third World to Washington, D.C., which he hardly attempted to disguise. Could he therefore save their lives? Several told their children he could, and dozens soon ran to surround him, until tears filled his eyes. A mortar shell had gone through the roof of the defunct church in whose rectory we were sheltering, but this rendered it somehow more austere—did not detract from its dignity. In the right light, it was lovely, like old stone spiritually imbued. Herbert had not been told by either his office or ours about Ruth's ordeal, so that she could avoid gratuitous comforting, but when we were alone, I did ask her if she was okay.

"An old bag like me? A tough old bird? All right," she answered flatly, her challenging gaze not letting me escape the suspicion that my question was partly prurient. She wouldn't give an inch toward satisfying the office's curiosity as to what had happened to her when the Nuer seized her. The Nuer, who were former allies of our Dinkas, were now fighting them on behalf of Khartoum's Arabs, after, by their account, being betrayed by the Dinkas. And all three wore "biblical robes," as she pointed out, remembering our Ed, who amused her. "Over the shoulder, like Jesus and the prophets," she said. The Nuer had different forehead scarifications than the Dinkas and were being executed by firing squad by the Dinka commander at Loa when they were captured, which angered her.

My drivers slept late, before starting the mammoth drive back to the coast of Kenya. The Catholics had work for them next. But wherever they delivered it, they usually held out a little extra corn or sorghum for the women who slept with them on these overnights; and so they were likely to come to the trucks stretching and yawning luxuriously. Even a feminist like Ruthie worried mostly that they were bringing AIDS from the cities to camps such as this one, which were so isolated the new diseases were slow to approach. What you had to remember before yelling righteously at them was the chance they ran of being blown up by a mine, machine-gunned, grenaded, mortared, shot, or just pistol-whipped, or having their arms deliberately broken at a rogue roadblock when passing through the territories of guerrilla groups that we weren't bringing any food to, like the Lord's Resistance Army, which Khartoum armed in exchange for the Lord's Resistance Army's attacking our relief convoys. The Nuer, in fighting our Dinkas, were being fed, oddly enough, by the U.N., though armed by Khartoum. And then there was the so-called West Nile Bank Front, in northern Uganda, which was fighting Kampala and didn't mean to attack us but sometimes mistook our trucks for the Ugandan army's, and who were supplied by dissidents in the Congo.

In the dispensary, at sunrise, laying out her replenished supplies, with a line of patients already waiting outside, Ruth glanced at her watch ironically. "Long night for your boys?" Hunched, obsessive, workaholic, she'd touched me from the start of our acquaintance, and, seeing my softening expression, she softened, too. They had a dangerous drive ahead of them. After we'd been tending the ailing side by side for a while, and after our pale, brainy Herbert had woken up, breakfasted, and then mysteriously been escorted off to meet with the Sudan People's Liberation Army's military folk, she took a break and led me out a side door and to a basketball court-sized patch of elephant grass into which—I hadn't noticed—she'd tramped a continuously whorling, puzzling path. She needed to explain it was a labyrinth because I'd never encountered one before: a helix, or a double helix, or an earlike, snail-shell scroll to walk assiduously around during a crisis or merely a meditative time. "The archangel" had helped her plot its nine levels, she confided to me. "It saved my life."

I nodded as well as shook my head to indicate a promise not to blab about her in Nairobi. She must have sensed I had no intention of doing that, because she also showed me that she kept a regular Roman Catholic rosary to help her out, and Greek worry beads, as well as a North American Indian "spirit stick," chest-high, that she'd scratched angel or Celtic figures on, with a crescent-shaped quartz crystal suspended in the wooden circle at the top, plus a "gazing globe" of a blue mirror material, set on a pedestal, that witches supposedly couldn't look into. It all seemed quite as logical as the cruel anarchy hereabouts, with the Dinka and the Nuer tribes split apart from an effective alliance that had previously been winning both of their homelands back from Khartoum's army, and some of the nearby hill-country Acholi tribesmen fighting alongside the Dinkas but others joining the lunatic Lord's Resistance Army—who specialized in kidnapping children and who cut people's lips off if they'd ever bad-mouthed them. The similarly disaffected local Baris were now enlisting in what they called the Equatoria Defence Force, to protect themselves against our Dinkas, and the Arabs, and everybody else. (The Kakwas, who were interspersed among the rest, sometimes got the West Nile Democratic Alliance to fight for them.) And, piercing this dismaying mess, Ruth's duty was to do her best for the hungry children, the civilian injured, the helpless bystanders, of which I saw more complexities later on. If she was cranky about keeping to her office hours, it was mostly because to work round the clock wouldn't have answered the immediate needs. The kids were trawling about for minnows, insects, rodents, songbirds—three or four would light a twig fire under a tin can to boil these, with leaves and grass, to share out the fluid. Ruth splinted bones and bandaged gashes, peered at earaches, festering sores, malarial sweats, and gravid bellies.

Meanwhile a large Arab garrison was being besieged by the Dinkas in the city of Juba, the regional capital, about an hour's drive in peacetime up the road from where we were. The siege was a loopy one, however, because the Arabs were equipped with tanks and armored personnel carriers and the Dinkas were not, and the Arabs held the airport, too, for resupply, so they could probably break through at will; they were probably biding their time. Not for the first time, they could blitz through to the Uganda border, then withdraw to the bastion of Juba once again, because of the constant sniping along their supply line. No doubt Herbert and his masters in Washington would keep the Dinkas undersupplied for real warfare.

Cryptic Herbert returned from his meeting and we bade Ruth good-bye and got back to Nairobi safe and sound, except that I had to tell our Kenyan driver, halfway, that I'd heard over the radio from headquarters that a brother of his had been shot in a political quarrel, Luo versus Kikuyu, in Kitale, his hometown, and killed. Herbert soon flew on to Joburg, and I returned to my storefront, with some side jobs occasionally up at Lokichoggio or Kakuma, or down at the port facilities in Mombasa, for World Vision or Catholic Relief Services, whose country directors were acquainted with me. I could have applied for a regular post, but I preferred the knockabout role—bringing authentic Congolese masks across the border and through Uganda to the classier specialty shops that high-end tourists stop at after their fly-in safaris. I did some fly-ins also, because sometimes the outfitter has to hire a personal guide for each family for them to feel catered to. "That is a giraffe," I will say. "Oh, how graceful!" they remark. "I didn't know they were so graceful." Then the gap-toothed Masai spearman who is hired to come along, in his warthog-hide sandals and red toga, with a sword in his scabbard, ocher makeup, beads, amulets, and neck bands, tells them that giraffe flesh is "the sweetest" of all meats, to add a frisson of life's ambiguities to the trip.

As before, I stayed at the Arab's otherwise, paying him a reduced weekly rate, and resumed tipping a few key service people at the New Stanley, across the street, so I could frequent its rooftop swimming pool, street-level café and bar, etc., as if they really belonged to me. When my Arab landlord happened to hear I'd been in the southern Sudan, I told him I'd worked for the Lutheran World Federation, who were known to be flying food to the populace of Juba, on the Arabs' side, and over the Dinkas' siege. That pleased him.

You meet many travelers in a venue such as the New Stanley— businessmen with attaché cases full of banknotes to persuade the bureaucrats in Government House to sign onto a certain project scheme; ecologists on a mission to save the chimpanzees; trust-fund hippies doing this route overland, now that you can't go from Istanbul into Afghanistan; specialists from one of the U.N.'s many agencies studying a developmental proposal or transiting to the more difficult terrain of Rwanda, Zimbabwe, Somalia, then resting for a spell on the way back. The New Stanley's taxi stand was busy from sunrise to pitch dark, and the pool on the roof was patronized by African middle-class parents, some of whom were teaching their kids how to swim, as well as KLM airline pilots and Swissair stewardesses, the Danish or USAID water-project administrators waiting for permanent housing, and bustling missionaries passing through. It was so spacious high up, overlooking the central city, with Tiny Rowland's few Lonrho skyscrapers standing about on the same level, while the savage street dangers were segregated twelve stories below—so terraced and gracious, with iced drinks, potted trees, a luncheon grill, umbrellas over the tables to buffer the midday sun—that I could retreat there for a respite whenever I had ten or a dozen dollars to burn.

Nonetheless, I didn't forget Ruthie: her exposure, of course, yet especially because she had trusted me at the end, not with the secret of whether she had been physically abused, but her solace in the occult Labyrinth, and with the spirit stick and·witch-foiling gazing globe, which would have been anathema to the Pentecostal preachers employing her, if they had known. I remembered her at poignant moments at the storefront, when a particular bony child seemed as baffled as her hungry Dinkas were and we were salving his skin sores. Even at the pool I was reminded incongruously of her by an unusual scene. A customer had brought a prostitute up for a sandwich and a drink after transacting their business below: a kid in her late teens, and he seemed like a decent fellow—blond, Dutch, fortyish, probably in humanitarian work, treating her as a comrade, not a servant (and taking the chance of being spotted by a gossipy colleague). But the girl was so enthralled by the sumptuous buffet and lofty view, the light, the sky reflecting in the blue seductive pool, that when he had to leave, she wanted to stay, and couldn't unless someone else official-looking took her under their wing. So I let her shift to my table, while she watched not just the airline stewardesses swimming laps, then rubbing sunblock on their legs, but Kenyan white-collar fathers teaching their small daughters how to swim. *This,* she could hardly bear: not to participate, like a girl, and have it happen to her. After watching her frustration, I did get in the shallow end with her, in her underwear, when the respectable lunchtime crowd had mostly departed, and held her up, at the middle, just as a father would have, while she hooted and flailed. It was a precious moment to her—not least because she'd never been in a swimming pool before, but also perhaps to pretend she actually *had* a father. However, the waiters were displeased because she was in her underwear, not having brought a bathing suit, which mildly scandalized their white customers who remained, and their black ones were more seriously worried because of the notion that AIDS could spread through sharing any water. I'd have had to persuade her to get out, except she already knew the game was up. It was too late to pretend she had a prosperous father who was teaching her to swim. God knows if hers had had more than the fifteen children he acknowledged, living in Kibera, which, by rumor, is the largest slum in Africa. She toweled herself, pulled on her blouse and skirt, and wolfed down the chicken fingers left on my plate before she needed to descend again to the boiling street. Wistfully, holding the menu in front of her face, she bluffed for me that she could read and was only deciding that she had had enough.

Moments like this, on the roof of the city, when you did want to teach this poor girl—who deserved so much better—to read, made me think of Ruthie, who, out of the blue, I'd heard, had lost her assistant, the Australian lady with the panic attacks, who'd remained in her room a good deal while Herbert and I were there. She'd finally gone bonkers, been evacuated by Ed in his shaky Cessna; so Ruth was holding the fort alone. I thought of her when guiding hot-air-balloon safaris for Japanese magnates or Swiss honeymooners, as one of Nairobi's Euro-American floaters. Because Africa is more interesting than America or Europe—substituting geography for personality—we feel more interesting, too. And newcomers do depend upon us, pump us for excitement, information: the size of the crocodiles that live under Victoria Falls; how dangerous is Zambia for a backpacker; and do we know Jane Goodall? Or else you go out with somebody's clients to the game-viewing lodge at a water hole and lecture them: "We're lucky, we're seeing an aardvark, or an aardwolf. And here come the small fry, the duikers and the dik-diks. Yes, elephants are matriarchal. Will you have another gin and tonic? No, the bandits only hit the campgrounds. There are soldiers in back of this building guarding us."

But you have to pay your dues, and I ran into a couple of gaunt, drained Maryknoll nuns, who had trained on the Hudson at Ossining in New York, recuperating on a two-week Christmas holiday from their current post at Chukudum, in the Didinga Hills of borderline Sudan, where a pretty waterfall burbles down the rock bluff behind the garden of the priory and Khartoum's Antonov bomber wheels over every morning looking for a target of opportunity, although they mostly dealt with emaciated refugees, not rebel fighters. These nursing sisters, in civilian clothes, were lunching at the Thorn Tree Café but reminded me of Ruth—who, they said, was about a week's walk west of them. They knew the distance because an X-ray technician, a Dinka, after Ruth's machinery had broken down the year before, had walked all that way, crossing Acholi, Latuka, and Dodoth country, to their dispensary, hoping for work in spite of their having told Ruth over the radio that they had no equipment either—a measure of his desperation, and he'd traveled carrying only a stick. The Didingas disliked the Dinkas as much as they did the Arabs, now that the two sides had fought over their fertile valley several times and the Dinkas driven the Didingas onto the ridgelines. But he wasn't killed because Dinka forces were in control, and simply drafted him to carry a rifle.

The Maryknolls are seasoned heroes. They're deep-dyed. You meet them on the hairiest road, coming from or going to a posting, and they don't wilt. They actually don't believe that God is dead. In Nairobi, too, they were wary but unflappable. We didn't chat long because they didn't permit it, but as if by telepathy, the phone at the Arab's soon rang and it was Al, sounding me out about another trip to Ruthie's to resupply her with medical kits, toddler formula, corn-soya blend (CSB), her Christmas mail, and spare treats like chocolates and canned crabmeat. The bad news was that a World Food Program delivery of bulk grains was going to be late, and she might like to think about either leaving temporarily or else keeping me for protection and company till it came.

"Put your money where your mouth is," Al joked when I hesitated, being, like me, a sort of knockabout—a specialist in drilling boreholes for far-away pastoral peoples like the Kababish, a low-salaried idealist "watering camels in the desert" before he'd married an African, had children, and settled here in town, still was low-salaried, of course.

"They have gold there in the Kit River, near Opari, you know," he added, as if that should be an incentive to me. I was startled—glad we were on the phone so he couldn't see my face. Had one of the drivers told him I was smuggling a few diamonds when I had the chance?

When I went to visit him the next day, we struck a deal about direct deposits to my bank account if I stayed awhile (I tried to wangle some term life insurance as well), although Ruth, on the radio, deferred her okay to my extended presence till she met me again. I didn't expect to stay anyway, but we loaded the Protestants Against Famine Land Cruiser with the standard fortified nutritional preparations, as well as spare stethoscopes, blood-pressure cuffs, tourniquets, penlights, tongue depressors, tendon hammers, antimalarial amodiaquine, acetaminophen, antibiotics such as amoxicillin, co-trimoxazole, ciprofloxacin, and doxycycline, mebendazole for worms, water purifiers, tetracycline eye ointment, paracetamol and ibuprofen, bandages in quantity and tape and nylon strapping, syringes and needles, scalpels, antiseptics for sterilizing, insecticide-treated mosquito netting for many people besides ourselves, IV cannulas, stitching needles and thread, umbrellas and tenting for the sun and rain, white coats for each of us to wear to give us an air of authority, and as much plastic sheeting as I had room for to shelter families in the coming rainy season.

Al is a sandy-haired Scotch-Irish Bible believer, but funny (he'd now begun calling me "a diamond in the rough"), who said that children are diamonds, too, and knew so from the front lines, having witnessed the successive Ethiopian and Somali famines and the Sahel droughts of the Kababish country in northern Sudan; he knew that you can be nearer my God to Thee without sectarianism. One Christ, many proxies. In fact, he'd snatched his beautiful wife from the Somali furnace and adopted the starveling child she already had, shelving his image of himself until that time as a semicelibate free-lance man of the Lord, for uxorial piety.

Chapter 4

• • •

ONCE THE LAND CRUISER WAS LOADED, EVEN BEHIND THE PAF'S compound walls it was a sitting duck for robbers. Since we couldn't leave it long, I got in at dawn and set off, steering for Limuru, past streaming crowds of people walking to work, with buses and *matatus* swerving over to pick up those who had any extra money. That momentum carried me along for many miles, past Longonot's little mountain and Lake Naivasha, to Gilgil and Nakuru—looking down at the flocks of pink flamingos and the pretty acacia forest, where the tourist vans turn off. But the Mau Escarpment rises behind Molo and Londiani, the traffic sporadic but perilously fast, with hell-bent lorries and crusty pickups, while herders switch at zebu-horned cattle and nosy goats in a different time frame alongside. A brief swatch of industry appears at Kisumu, with railroad sidings, a bus station, outdoor market, manufacturing and office buildings of minor height and consequence, two hundred miles out, plus the sweetening scent of the Kavirondo Gulf of Lake Victoria nearby to moderate the tempo of violence implicit in such a place, if you stopped. As per my usual custom, though, when driving toward Uganda and Congo, I continued without pausing to an empty resort hotel on the shore a little beyond. Lovely spreading mango trees, an unmown grassy lawn, a large, wraparound, white-columned porch, and the lake's grand skyscape and glistening waters, plus delicious crispy fish and rice and curry the Indian owner's wife makes herself, because so few guests stop by anymore. Although their property is on Kenyan soil, when Idi Amin kicked the Asians and Europeans out of Uganda it wrecked their business for a while, and they haven't advertised aggressively along the road to try to snag some customers back. They seem a little too old and disheartened by the terror of the Amin years, but, on the other hand, unfretful, as if they glean enough income elsewhere, maybe by assisting the tobacco smuggling that goes on by boat across the international boundary line. The lakeshore breeze, so savory, reminded me of that gambit as I dawdled, giving myself a headache from the noonday wine.

Maseno, Luanda, Butere, Mumias, Nambare, and Busia. At the border at Busia, I got a visa without the sort of dragging wait that would have been required at Uganda's consulate in Nairobi, or even paying a bribe, because the elderly immigration official in the little tin hut had a soft spot for "missionaries." He just came outside to confirm that the contents of my vehicle jibed with my story. Then I hired a young college-educated fixer to speed my paperwork through customs so that I could get clear of the crowds at the barrier and on through Bumulimba, Buwaya, Bugiri, Busowa, Iganga in time to reach the city of Jinja, at the falls that launch the Nile and power Uganda's industries, and then twist on through wicked Mabira Forest, which expands in the imagination because it's still the haunt of bandit gangs and rebels, as well as the memory—the ghosts—of thousands of tortured corpses who were dumped there by Idi Amin or his bloody successor, Milton Obote, and finally reach, by dusk, the security and greenery, of the lush, red-soiled, hilly outskirts of Kampala.

Traffic is not crazy to thread through in Kampala, or the crime comparable to Nairobi's, with all the banana trees around to eat off of, nor people terrified by their current ruler, Yoweri Museveni, and I moseyed past the university, the general hospital, and the Bugandan king's palace, over various humpy hills, to my hotel, where I'm known, and enjoyed an immediate drink out on the terrace, with much of the winking city spread out below me. I'm not widely acquainted in Uganda, so seldom bother phoning anybody if I'm leaving early next morning anyway. The Sheraton, the Nile, the Speke, the Fang, the Fairway, with their bars and terraces, are where you go to chat up the passing parade of World Bankers, Monetary Funders, agricultural and AIDS experts, and business hustlers, if you have some time. I did call the offices of a couple of NGO groups that have outposts within striking distance of Ruthie's place in the Sudan—the Catholics', the Norwegians'—but they were closed for the night, and when I phoned our trucker's local dispatcher, he could confirm the sorry news that no delivery of foodstuffs was in the pipeline for either them or our agency as yet.

Food is so central that you can't exaggerate the issue. My waitress, for example, was hungry for protein even though she worked in an expatriates' hotel. There was a pot of gruel in the kitchen for the help, but it wasn't nourishing enough for a lactating mother, and the chicken parts and fresh fruit, meat, and vegetables the guests ate were exactly inventoried each night to compare what remained in the refrigerator with the restaurant's orders. Nor did she eat leftovers off of people's plates, because she'd heard that AIDS could spread by saliva. And, although she wouldn't be robbed at night once she reached her bus station, she said to get to it she needed to use her tips to take a taxi because men with clubs waited next to a corner between here and there. The other waitresses, not being nursing mothers, could sleep on the floor behind the bar until broad daylight. They hadn't a lot of customers anyhow because of an Ebola scare up near Masindi—northward, on my trip tomorrow—so that the tourists and other nonessentials had been clearing out of Uganda altogether lately. I'd paid no attention to that matter except for planning not to pick up any hitchhikers along my route. But I felt a pang of startled grief because that Bible-preaching pilot, Ed, who flew for missionaries and had trained in Iowa and justifiably prayed so very loudly on takeoff, following the scrawl of lakes underneath his wings with his finger on the map in his lap, had just crashed, they'd told me at the desk when I arrived. The news was raw. In the Congo. So what I did now, after I finished supper on the terrace, was order a room-service chicken platter to go on my bill and, when she delivered it, had her eat it then and there, as if perhaps in Ed's memory, which she did with evident, unsmiling, quick, efficient hunger. Then I handed her the equivalent of a couple of bucks to catch her bus safely, at least tonight, while she wiped her mouth with the napkin and prepared to return the tray to the kitchen.

"Thank you so much," she said, waiting watchfully for a counter-request. But I shook my head and opened my palms to indicate that she could go. She wasn't sure of the signal, however, pausing, then coming quietly to kiss me good-bye. At the same time, feeling lonely, hardly thinking, I regretted my generosity and changed the signal by wiggling my fingers as a summons. She wasn't going to stay and keep me company, with her six-month-old waiting to be fed, and so we stared at each other. Quizzically, still poised to kiss me on the cheek, she decided I wanted proof she hadn't been lying and uncovered her breasts, wetting each of my forefingers with her milk and moving them to my lips.

"Tastes good?" she teased, buttoning up again, leaving me to get to sleep as best I could, though after a bit I began to wonder if AIDS could be transmitted through a mother's milk.

I slept late, after waking first with the hadada ibises that roost in the trees in the courtyard and cry their name a hundred times at sunrise before they flap away to feed. Then I pigged out on fresh eggs and melons—last chance for that—and checked with a Kampala office or two that might know the latest conditions up in Ruthie's particular neck of the woods, as well as Al in Nairobi again. No good reason to cancel my trip?

"No, no. She says she's baking a banana pie for you guys!" Al laughed.

"Who?"

"You and the spook," Al told me. "You have a party going up there with you, like last time. From Gulu, probably. He flew there from Kinshasha or Kigali or someplace to see what's up. Was supposed to go in to Ruth's with Ed, but Ed was flying the Ebola people from the Congo to Masindi, the poor guy, to investigate the outbreak. He doesn't sound as dorky as the average minister, when I talked to him on the phone, so I suppose he's a spook. I get my funding and my orders from America just like you."

I said okay, not really sorry about having company on this particular bungee jump. Mine was the hair-shirt hotel, for the nonprofits, and several gangly young Caucasians of both sexes in the dining room were en route to study the disappearing bongo antelope or dispense hearing aids and tuberculosis drugs to the destitute, with nary a Herbert type with many passports in his fanny pack among them. *He* would have stayed at the landscaped Sheraton, up on the president's own palace hill.

I cleared the string of tatty, red-dirt, banana-plantation villages surrounding Kampala, where no one looked either rich or hungry because the equatorial abundance of rainfall and vegetation meant they probably had something to eat no matter who they were. But there weren't the roadside truckers' fleshpots, either, like those decorating the east-west route, because this was no longer the fabled "Cape to Cairo" artery from South Africa toward Khartoum and Egypt—a jaunt that had been throttled first by Idi Amin and now choked off again by the war in the southern Sudan. Beyond the city's suburbs, indeed, signs of human occupancy almost disappeared in the elephant grass and regrown jungle, because for the next eighty or a hundred miles all of this had been a triangle of death, incinerated in Uganda's own civil wars: Amin's eight years of butcheries, and then when he was overthrown, Obote in an ostensibly saner manner had killed just as many, till Museveni upended him. So many clanking tanks, half-tracks, and fearsome assault platoons had crawled up this road, mowing down anything that moved, that even in the peace

Museveni had established, nobody wanted to take the chance of living anywhere that might be visible in the forest. Sunbirds, bee-eaters, secretary birds, reedbuck, dik-diks, spitting cobras, and black mambas were about, but the people who had somehow survived on-site or returned afterward were not going to trust the neighborhood of the road, except for bicycling quickly along the asphalt. And then the trick was to vanish imperceptibly when you reached your destination: with no visible path to a hidden village that soldiers rumbling by in a grisly truck would notice. Settlements had been scorched, torched, eviscerated horribly, the skulls piled up from the massacres. And women still sometimes flinched—broke into a run for the woods—at the sound of my motor.

Near Lake Albert and the quarantined town of Masindi, nervous soldiers manned a checkpoint. But they were nervous about catching Ebola, not shaking down a traveler. Since I was headed north toward Gulu, not turning into the epicenter of this minor epidemic, they waved me through with no inspection. I thought of Ed, with that Iowa-flying-school Adam's apple but less than a year in the air in toto, because he had crashed while landing just across the lake from here, at Bunia in the Congo—his passionate, tenor-voiced prayers, as you sat next to him in the cockpit—who had probably questioned God in his last moments because he wasn't solo, being that kind of man. But no wonder Al said Ruthie's poor partner, the Australian lady with the panic attacks, had been hard to fly out. Ed had been sent to collect her, and made it safely back to Nairobi, "and no strait-jacket!"

Past Masindi, the countryside had been less blasted during the seventies and eighties. In the hamlets there were shops, canteens, and wide-boughed village conference trees in whose generous pool of shade everything from school to market day to court proceedings and old folks' confabulations could be held. Consequently, I sped past thousands of pedestrians (the luckiest had bikes) with basins, baskets, or bundles on their heads, and sticks in hand. Cassava, sesame, yams, millet, groundnuts, and oil palms grew. There was commerce, or simply a relative to visit—all the usual hubbub and bustle. Last time, going with Herbert, we'd ridden in the trucks, so for this trip I would have filled the passenger seat of the car in Kampala with additional goodies for Ruth's clinic, if I hadn't been warned about the spook. Traveling at a mile a minute, passing countless individuals trudging, the empty space beside me felt funny, until the crowds thinned for another war zone around the roar of Karuma Falls, where the Victoria Nile swings west to join Lake Albert and become the Albert Nile. A machine-gun emplacement and five jittery soldiers guarded this bridge. I had to stop, but they were correct and polite. West Nile Democratic Alliance guerrillas (Obote holdovers) operated in the national parklands close by; and I drove even faster. Then, nearer Gulu, the landscape opened out again, with cultivated plots, and old folks under a banyan tree in front of provision shops built of sheet metal or thatch and mud. I stopped at one such, the Happy Hour, at the town of Bobi, which had once belonged to the family of a friend of mine in Nairobi who were now Canadian citizens, after Idi Amin had kicked all of the Indians out of Uganda. He made his living drawing wild-animal T-shirt designs that were sold in Vancouver but had asked me to look in and find out what was left of the place, what it might be worth, and whether he should chance the risk of coming back and filing a claim for its return, as the new government permitted "Asians" to do, as long as they were physically present, not merely acting through a lawyer. Would he be a guinea pig if he did, and get macheted?

What could I say? The African family who, through no violence of their own, had taken over lived in a wattle shack adjoining the establishment and had created a tiny center for gab and pleasure—of which there is little enough in northern Uganda. Nice, conscientious people: what happens is you then feel sorry for them. I looked in on the proprietor without revealing my mission and bought a bottle of banana gin from him. My friend's father similarly had not been a counter wallah in a spotless tan safari suit but, rather, a down-to-earth man who loved traveling the side roads on buses as a peddler, for the adventure of it, besides running this store at Bobi—and he had died as a democrat, crushed underneath a bus that he was trying to help the driver fix. It had broken down in a dry streambed near Atura, and the jack calamitously collapsed.

Sharing a drink with the Acholi gentleman who owned the store, to brace myself for encountering the intelligence operative just ahead, I listened to him complain, as other Acholis did, that the troops billeted upon them in Gulu were Ganda from the capital region who disliked northerners such as the Acholis on principle, and especially so since both Idi Amin, a Kakwa, and Obote, a Lango, had been from tribes here in the north. But the Lord's Resistance Army, multiplying the problem, was itself an Acholi rebel movement that had gone completely bonkers; it kidnapped children and turned them, by terror, into robots, he said, who ran out on the flanks during a battle and rattled the bushes to draw the fire of Museveni's troops, so that their bosses, in safety, knew where to shoot.

At the Gulu Hotel, always half empty, I was remembered, given my same room, with no one else's bags in it or messages. Maybe I could just go on alone tomorrow. I rested, then sat outside by the paddleball court with a Pepsi watching some officers' kids, privileged teenagers, whack at the game. There was also an exercise bicycle, with a white man, well-knit, well-kitted out, pumping on it, timing his sprints. Good pecs and abs. "God bless!" he called after a while, and I knew I'd found my man.

When I asked if he went to gyms much in the States, he said he had "tried out for the Steelers once, but they flunked me. They gave me five thousand dollars for signing—which was a helluva lot to me right then; I had debts—and flew me to Arizona. But they put the starters against us, wearing shorts and sneakers, and us candidates all suited up for training camp in full uniform, trying to outrun, outfeint them, and catch a pass. No contest! Round-trip ticket!"

Not faceless like pale Herbert, who could be in academia, Craig grinned, introducing himself. He showered; said he was "church-affiliated," when he came back, "a consultant on delivery systems.

Angola. Burundi. Goma." Didn't mention where he had flown in from, or who with. No, hadn't known poor Ed, or Herbert. "Maybe a voice sometimes on the radio."

"You consult for the Baptists?"

"I have my divinity degree."

Al could have quizzed him on theological matters if he'd wanted to, but my knowledge of the Bible is spotty. Craig agreed that his accent was Texan, when I asked. The town of Liberty, in the oilfield salt marshes near Houston: so heat and bugs were not a problem for him, and the cattle here were similar, he noticed, to the Brahman breeds that could survive in that hardship country. Texas Tech, in Lubbock, had educated him.

"I thought you were from Mossad," I said, to startle him out of pretending to be a hick.

He laughed. "You're giving me more credit than is due. I don't even have an Uzi."

"Well, you're with somebody. They used to fly in Kalashnikovs, not Uzis. Herbert had three passports."

"I don't know who Herbert is. I'm with the Baptists."

"Great. You'll see what a fine job Ruthie does. She ought to get a medal or a million dollars."

"From Mossad?" he said, teasing.

"We do a good job, but I'm a temp, unlike Ruthie, and I meet a bunch of people. Even CIA."

"That must be titillating for you."

"I'm a temp," I repeated, more disarmingly, not wanting to jeopardize his view of Al and Ruth or make our trip unpleasant. "A soldier of fortune."

He laughed. "Bully for you. And I'm a Bible-thumper."

Over supper, in a chesty soldiers' joint that Museveni's troops frequented, with rifles stacked in the corner and a wheezy jukebox, Craig—no offense taken—tried to get me drunk on Kampala's Nile beer. But he mentioned with genuine concern that if the Ebola epidemic at Masindi grew any worse, the road our food trucks followed might be blocked by the quarantine—it had climbed toward thirty deaths now. Both Gulu and Juba had had their own Ebola emergencies in the past, I said, and people died so fast the virus didn't fester. Unlike AIDS, it burnt out quickly.

The do-gooders, whether gimpy or gaunt, I usually traveled with seemed to look for signs of malnutrition wherever they were, even in a bar; they'd notice rags on a rib cage, as if on automatic pilot. But Craig, in his "BAPTIST FELLOWSHIP" white T-shirt, had a sort of military bearing. Or was it just that he had better gym machinery when he was at home? The soldiers loafing around were noticing his posture or physical conditioning, suggestive of a SEAL or a "security contractor," perhaps, in civvies. He wasn't aggressive, though, even when a jolly, antic sort of fellow tippler, an African, began snapping "souvenir" photos of us.

"I sell 'em to you," he explained. "When I develop them. For your scrapbooks. When you come back."

Of course we hadn't said where we were going or if we were going anywhere. Craig waved his hand in front of his face, halfheartedly attempting to cover it. "You wait till you're in Khartoum next time, in some dungeon in a ghost house, with your hands tied behind your back, and they show you those," he muttered, finishing his supper of fried potatoes, chicken, boiled beans in a few efficient gulps. "See you later, alligator."

Two officer-looking types in civilian clothes sitting at other tables stood up to join him, and soon I heard the grating engine of their jeep recede. Since it was not important that we hang out together, after checking on the PAF's Land Cruiser, I went to sleep. A guard had the hotel parking lot under surveillance.

The streets of Gulu, a garrison town, were orderly, with clusters of barracks, a motor pool, a quartermaster's warehouse, a prison, and off-duty soldiers strolling—an island of short-hop traffic in contrast to what had otherwise been for me a solitary drive—when we got under way bright and early. We sped through more deserted forests, in a free-fire shooting zone. Uganda's guerrilla wars pale only by comparison with Sudan's, and I asked if Craig's new friends last night had told him who our photographer represented.

"I guess they don't mix business with pleasure," he answered, without disclosing whether he himself might have. I said I'd noticed that the plainclothes police circulating in Kampala had crueler faces than the ones in Nairobi. So even though Museveni was a much more civilized dictator than his predecessors, he must not have cleaned house. They looked like torturers; the humor inscribed on their faces was blistering.

"It's not something I know about," Craig answered again. He missed Houston's shrimp dinners, he said, the scent of the bayous, and the cosmopolitanism of Washington, D.C., where he'd once taken a couple of courses but no parish assignments, he told me.

Northward toward the village of Atiak, we saw sparser hamlets, fewer footpaths or human disturbances of any kind, and only a single straggly infantry squad patrolling, at one point. But it was lovely broken scenery, often wooded and hilly, Africa at its lightest, if you like the short brushy views that maintain the mystery: eight-foot yellowish thickets that would conceal guerrillas (or "Charley," as Craig put it) until the last minute—or a lion, for that matter. Somebody had run over a python, but nobody had eaten it. Speke and Stanley, Grant and Burton had traversed a similar terrain, and rather as in that simpler era, white men were not a special target in these quarters. You could be shot by accident or mistaken identity or because of your own reckless behavior, but not for a calculated purpose.

When I asked Craig about Vietnam, he said he'd "found his faith there"—which, if you doubted whatever else he claimed, was mildly funny. But he didn't act like a war junkie, or the gunslingers that private companies hire to protect their installations in Africa. He talked about airports—Amsterdam's duty-free shops were the best—and the British parliamentary system, where you could change your government's leadership more swiftly, and how Khartoum's relationship with Libya's Muammar Gaddafi, which fluctuated pro and con, had been the determinant of America's attitude toward Khartoum: something any newspaper reader knew. Although I wanted to test his knowledge of the Bible, I hadn't enough myself to do so. How mid-level was he, I wondered: this product of the evangelicals who sent us our money but were also glad to oblige the agency in any way they could? I didn't want to offend him, having no desire to be catechized, myself, or to rattle the cage of anybody who, come to think of it, might possibly be able to access Interpol on his laptop. I had indeed been a middle school history teacher when in New England, but I'd also left Alexandria, Egypt, for Cyprus one time in a great hurry with my girlfriend's leotards stuffed with greenbacks because we'd just been watching, to our surprise, on CNN, several ships of the international transportation company we worked for being bombed to smithereens in Umm Qasr, Basra's port, during the 1991 bombings of Iraq (the Iraqis had embargoed them). And so, realizing that our outfit was going to go bankrupt very shortly, we'd emptied the local bank account we had signing privileges for. And from Cyprus via British Airways to the hospitality of Heathrow, never so cash-rich before or again: I can't go back to Cairo—big deal.

Atiak had a police station, where we had to show our passports and permits for the paperwork we would display at the army post ahead, on the border with Sudan. It was a bare-shelved town, built for trade as the last village in Uganda on the road, but the war had obliterated those opportunities. While stretching our legs, we bought candy, pens, notebooks, soda pop, and other odds and ends to cheer up Ruthie's people a bit. Also nine live chickens with their feet tied, to stow underneath the front seat. Two civil servants, a teacher and a cultivated customs man, begged us to intercede for them with the bureaucracy in Kampala when we got back. They hadn't been paid for six months—were they forgotten, or was their money being stolen? The teacher at least was a local Acholi, being fed a daily bowl of *posho* by his pupils' parents, but the inspector, painfully frail, with crispy white hair, a Tororo from far away, and marooned at this defunct crossing point—but who wanted us to know that he had read Charles Dickens—was not so lucky. He had neither pupils nor grandchildren to take care of him. More beggar than patriarch, he tentatively, then righteously, tried to wheedle a bribe out of us, in order to "clear" our load, but the police chief laughed at, then roared at him. I felt a twinge on his behalf, driving away. How did he eat?

Craig had jogged through Gulu early this morning with one of his military friends from the night before, a tour during which the guy had lent him a few useful names to drop with this police chief as well as at the army post ahead. He'd arrived in Gulu "by crop duster," he said, "the same as your Ed's." And "the Pearl of Africa," he quoted Churchill on Uganda, though Tororoland, where the customs man came from, *was* very pretty, he said. But we'd entered a no-man's-land without settlements—primeval after a few huts at Pabo—and I spotted one of those super-sized eagles nobody sees anymore, ripping at the mongoose clutched in its claws, as it flapped toward a bluff. A trotting jackal looked up enviously. The vegetation, too, was moving significantly, not from a breeze. It was a savory-smelling, dry-season jungle, with elephant grass as tall as an elephant and zigzag bluffs of distant relief. At one point we saw six dispirited foot-soldiers, with bolt-action firepower, resting under an umbrella tree; but no civilians. Later, what I thought was a waterbuck, or one of the other meaty antelopes, crashed away. This was the center of Africa, choppy, leopardy, where an infinity of species go at it for sunlight and space, but emptied by war of the creep of modernity.

The army post, once we reached it, was encircled by wire but not trenched for combat, as if the soldiers and guerrillas roundabout were engaged in a live-and-let-live charade. Nevertheless, a handful of gingerly hangers-on had congregated outside the fence to be near the soldiers' protection, but took pains not to offend them. I noticed, for instance, as we waited beside the gate after submitting our papers to the sentry, that locals who passed had to remove their sandals and walk by with footwear in hand as a sign of respect or be beaten with clubs. Nor were we allowed to enter, though our shoes could stay on.

After keeping us waiting for the requisite half hour or so in the heat to prove that whites received no special consideration from him, the commanding officer stepped to the door of a cabin fifty yards away and waved us toward the real no-man's-land. Ten miles or more of forest stretched to the international boundary, and appeared to have been abandoned to the elements long ago: where you truly wouldn't want to meet anyone. For safety's sake, in our cream-white vehicle, we were unarmed. That's how you don't get shot, because if people stop you, they know you're always unarmed. To cut the tension, I joked about traffic driving on the "British side" in Sudan, so we might as well switch to the left lane now. Finally we rattled across a rickety-rackety pilings bridge over the Unyama, a tributary of the Nile, and its swamp bed, into Sudan People's Liberation Army territory at the town of Nimule. This was a sketchy, streamlined checkpoint, and we were quickly cleared by a bookish clerk. We'd each obtained a "visa" earlier at the rebels' office, back in Nairobi, and there was the brusque sense of discipline of a war zone. It was not only a hamlet but a supply point for the rebels; and a firing squad here had recently executed twenty-two of their own soldiers for the sin of being Nuer, not Dinka, after the tribal split had occurred. Ruthie had sounded apoplectic over the radio about this.

I was interested in whether they were expecting Craig as more than just another aid worker. His visa—a cardboard placard six inches by eight, like mine, with a passport picture stapled on and the signature of the revolutionary cadre, "Jane," who had validated him—listed him as being a pastor, the occupation he had given her. So the Dinka lieutenant, who in age and attitude resembled a university graduate student, asked noncommittally if he was "going to preach at all." Craig responded genially, and we continued on, although I did remark upon not having seen his Bible.

"The little gray cells. The gray matter," he answered, tapping his head.

I'd shifted to the left side, from Uganda's right-hand driving, but of course there were no other cars. Yet one sensed more of a belt of military control on the road than in slipshod Uganda, whose anarchic areas were exhausted, spotty, disillusioned. Bandits wouldn't kill you where we were, or even a lion; though, on the other hand, the SPLA entry officer—that studious young man who'd looked up from his novel to clear our papers—had pointed out his window to a tiny herd of five elephants at the bend of the bank down below on the purling Nile and told us they were being preserved to draw "ecotourists," once the rebellion had established their new nation. Nimule had been the scene of other ugly internecine episodes at the time of the split that had broken the momentum of the SPLA's offensive against the Arabs, but now he wanted peace.

I asked what Craig knew of the course of this war, as we bounced north, trying to guess what must be a wider experience of conflicts than my own. Central as well as Southeast Asia? Ethiopia and Angola as well as the Congo? Here they had martial law but starvation. We could smell the burnt grasslands where rodents had been rousted out of their burrows to be eaten; see skinny boys with slingshots after the last bush birds or grabbing a grasshopper.

"Our focus isn't on the war," he said, although I didn't know which employer he was pretending to sound sanctimonious about.

"Do you have family?"

"Yes, high school age. My wife's a nurse. They're in good hands."

"Has she ever been over here to work?"

"No, no," Craig murmured, as if that were absurd. Politely, he asked my own status, which was divorced. "Are you sorry?" he asked. When I shook my head, he asked about Ruthie.

"She's the salt of the earth," I said, so he could judge for himself. Maybe the rebels would cut her more slack the more visitors she had.

A few wattle-and-daub, straw-roofed, round *tukls* of the local Baris had shown up by the road—settled abodes, by the look of the small gardens in back for millet, cassava, peanuts, sesame, and the three or four flourishing banana trees. It was hard to know if they'd been left unstripped by the Dinka soldiers for appearances' sake, since they were alongside the road, like the little collection of elephants left at Nimule, for future tourists, although tusks bought Kalashnikovs, just as surely as bleeding the Arabs procured them from Mossad. When Craig asked where the camps were, I said farther on. "So they'll be too far to walk to Uganda without getting caught."

He didn't reply, and I didn't either for a while.

"Cynics say they're 'farming' them for food," I informed him, "because we or the other NGOs have to bring it in for the civilians or they starve, and the fighters go to each family at night and take half."

"And what do *they* say?"

"That they're building a black-African, non-Muslim nation, instead of being peons to the bigots in Khartoum, and everybody should participate. Women and children, too, should remain on the soil."

"Not just the shooters?" he remarked with amusement. "It's an argument, isn't it? Starvation instead of sharia."

"Yes, but some of the folks would rather be allowed to get to Kenya, where the U.N. would feed them. Have you seen a lot of camps?"

"I've been around the block," Craig said. Not the glassy type who might be smoking a pipe in a faculty club next year like Herbert, he didn't have a brutal air, either, like a former "shooter" detailed to a CIA consultancy.

"The Catholics have an operation near us—and some Norwegians. Plus, the publicity you've read goes to the Bible Belters who buy slaves back from the Arabs for fifty dollars apiece. They fly over us because they need to reach the front for the exchange to take place. If there is a front. The front moves."

He knew that the U.N. had already pulled back to Kenya after four of their people had been killed by the SPLA, as had a mainstream Protestant group, also. The Dinkas' commanders were controversial. He said his exit wasn't planned. He would charter "a crop duster" to pick him up if I wasn't going out.

We fell silent because we had begun seeing devastated women by the roadside, and I noticed Craig's lips moving, possibly in prayer. Maybe he *wasn't* an Agency bruiser. By devastated, I don't mean they were living skeletons, but these were people who'd been moving—walking—for years. May have had five or six children altogether, and been carrying the small ones who had survived for hundreds of miles, seldom finding enough to feed them. Walking from a home ground like Wau, Aweil, Rumbek, or Gogrial, west of the Nile, across the savannah and then the swamps of the Sudd, to Ayod and Waat, on the Jonglei Plateau, east of the great river, gradually losing their cattle herds to the enemy or by attrition all the way along, cattle being the traditional axis of the Dinkas' culture. The cattle shot or rustled, by a MiG from the air, or on horseback (the Arab tribesmen rode, the Dinkas walked). Harried on into Ethiopia, hassled and chased to Gambela, where the army and Arab militias couldn't follow because Addis Ababa was aligned against Khartoum. That was the first half of the story, and, depending on when they arrived, they'd had a year of handouts before Mengistu, the dictator there, was overthrown and the SPLA and its refugees were chased out of Ethiopia, too. Then they had to walk back, under fire off and on much of the way.

Where the Aswa River flows into the Nile, the first of these new camps was laid out, and Ruth, on the radio, had asked me to swing through for a survey because her jeep was up on blocks and she couldn't. Hunger, not discipline, is generally the problem in this revolution, so a looping track was laid out with orderly mud habitations, the people in front of them hoarding their energies. Children who hadn't died of dysentery during the trek back from Ethiopia were playing with a saddening lassitude, the mothers looking haunted by the toll of the ones not alive. It's not a sexy sight, such gaunt and lackadaisical grief. Wartime rape is motivated by unexpended adrenaline and sadism, not because there are any "dolls" around. A war correspondent—a Brit who runs with the rebels in several countries—once told me in a bar how you're so pumped up you have to do *something*.

I didn't slow down, in order not to precipitate a rush on the car by people thinking we had food to distribute. Even so, the kind of boys who will run out from the brush with their last strength at the sound of a motor to represent their families showed up. Not that they were that far gone today; but I'm speaking of a type of boy who would die to bring food to his mother and little sisters and brothers and will brave the Nile's crocodiles after water lilies you can eat or to find a frog or fish. I told an old man who I knew spoke English that, alas, no trucks carrying corn were behind us: not to wait anticipating them. But we did have medicine for an epilepsy patient in one of these huts, and malaria medications, if they came to Ruthie's during office hours.

Five miles up the road, Ruth in her sun hat was "talking to the line," as we used to say, telling them in fractured Arabic that unless somebody had just broken his arm, she was through at the clinic for today. Attlee, the Kikuyu from Nairobi, glowered like a bodyguard beside her—small protection, really.

"Fire me!" she exclaimed when she noticed this new man, Craig, dragging his duffel out of my Land Cruiser. "It's the only way I'm going to get out of here." She groaned with impatience as I fumbled to find her small packet of Christmas mail, overdue by a month. Tears welled in her eyes, but she didn't forget to yell suddenly to the parents of a little girl who was being led away.

"You have the stuff for her? I'm out," she asked. I had forgotten this particular girl and what meds she required in the time I'd been gone, as anybody not a doctor would have, but for Ruthie, her emergencies, and therefore my presence in them, picked up as though from yesterday. "Insulin," she prompted, clutching the letters and magazines I'd located next to the chickens and between the seats, while curtly greeting Craig with her free hand.

"Sorry to drop in on you. Did you know I was coming?"

She flipped through the envelopes she'd received, looking for what to expect, almost ignoring him.

"Part of the cost of doing business. It's called donor dinners in the States, isn't it? You'll find we're pretty basic here. Life and death."

Then she laughed to dilute her rudeness and nodded her thanks to both of us as the squawking birds were unearthed and handed to the Acholi cook, whose name was Margaret. The whole load being uncommonly precious, of course, Ruth was torn between wanting to supervise the unloading of the dispensary's supplies, checking special items she had radioed for, and going off immediately to pore over her holiday cards and letters, already offended that a stranger had seen her on the verge of weeping, and bristling (as I fathomed) that there might not seem enough of them.

I mentioned how sorry I was about Ed, and how remorseful he must have been that passengers had died in the wreck. Was it quick for him, or in the hospital at Bunia? She said there'd been a fire, but no one knew whether he'd been alive in the fire. Al's idea was that Ed's "finest hour" had been evacuating Ruth's helper who had flaked out after I'd left. Both of them high-strung and devout, they'd bolstered one another; he'd met the Cessna in Nairobi and stuck her directly on a plane legging toward Australia. "No, no," said Ruth, scanning a hand-drawn Christmas card from her niece, proudly showing it. "What he did at Ayod was braver." A Catholic lay sister had lost her leg during a food drop—hit by a sack, out on that spongy plateau where planes couldn't land, trucks couldn't reach, where the famine was most constant and most cruel, the vultures most insolent and overfed. A two-engine plane would buzz the drop zone once a week and guys inside kick fifty-kilo bags of grain out of the tail, before zooming off to the next site. She was a famine expert, new to Africa and so urgently invested in the food's arrival—that no more kids would die—that she left the sidelines, her arms raised as if to signal the plane: that it not skip her people and pass overhead. And every nun in Nairobi was waiting to give blood for a transfusion if someone would extract her. Which fell to Ed, based in Gulu for that week, to pick her out of the largest swamp in Africa, a hamlet and an airstrip where he'd never been, and no surplus fuel for a mistake. There were scenes at Ayod worse than ours. Even a news photographer, after the assignment of tracking her, had killed himself.

Ruth badgered me to find the insulin in the piles of supplies, also a box of powdered milk, before we were shown to our room by Attlee, the brusque Kikuyu, whose virtues included the fact that he felt no kinship with the locals. Then we were presented with a pitcher of water and a metal basin to wash in by Margaret, who was from Gulu but a sophisticate, having been married to a man from Entebbe and learned English and amenable Western ways, before he left her and died of AIDS. She'd returned to Gulu with her three children and now was supporting them, plus the orphans of several cousins, on her salary from Ruth of sixty dollars a month, which I'd delivered on my last trip down to the man who cooked a daily bowl of gruel for all of them. Guiltily, I couldn't meet her eyes because yesterday, in Gulu, I'd been too preoccupied with Craig and other tensions or errands to remember to look him up for news of how they were doing to pass on to her, or to advance him more money. She had no way to get down there. Apologizing, "I will, I will," I promised, thinking Ruth should have reminded me over the radio. But Ruth and I were childless. Tears glistened in Margaret's eyes. I told her I hadn't expected that she'd still be here, but I didn't believe that myself.

Attlee had families scattered about, in the polygamous tradition, but appeared more protective of Ruthie at present than conscious of his paternal responsibilities elsewhere. Being named for a British prime minister afforded him acerbic amusement. He was not unduly pro-white, but since Ruth was an underdog on the Nile, why not look out for her? He and Makundi, her Kamba houseman, were watching her mix the powdered milk, when I noticed a toddler clinging with both skimpy arms to her ample hip, malnourished, malformed—his head disproportionately large, because skulls can't shrink—but closely watching the cup she would soon feed him the milk from, and her eyes, hands, and face.

"My addition," she said. Father Leo, the Maryknolls' priest, had dropped him off. "So, meet little Leo."

After a nap, I wandered out and found myself staring upward inside the holey old church, reinforcing my memory that the mortar shell through the roof had not reduced its solemnity. The light let in was rather ennobling, so I knelt and prayed in this deconsecrated house of worship of a denomination none of us belonged to. It wasn't even Irish, like Father Leo, but built by long-dead Italians in the era when this region was "the white man's grave."

"Craig," I hollered when I saw my companion walk by. He took a couple of seconds to turn, as if reminding himself that that was his current name; or was I too suspicious? He said he had tipped Attlee to walk him around the paths while I was asleep and had been "sobered and stunned" at the maze of children's graves alongside many of them, each small mound of earth decorated with a scrap of clothing or a torn toy, for the life cut short to be remembered by. His lips were compressed and, being a doer, after only glancing inside the church, he fell to examining Ruth's jeep, up on blocks. I'd brought a tire at her request, and we put that on the wheel that was flat, using a bicycle pump on the rest. Working together, out of breath, made us relax.

"She shouldn't be stranded," he said, and asked about the waves of starvation that had swept through here, though not a neophyte who needed a lot explained to him. In the sixties, after independence from the British, it had been mainly these local forest tribes, such as the Baris and Acholis, who logically should have been part of Uganda to begin with anyway, fighting the Muslim government. Then in the seventies a new president of Sudan had made peace with them, with regional freedom of religion and cultural autonomy, until the eighties, when a fundamentalist sharia swing reignited the war, led now by the big plains tribes, Nuer and Dinka, pastoralists living between these mountains and forests and the vast Sahel of the Arabs. It was a more serious insurrection, with the southern black army officers defecting to command the rebels, and on the government side, the Baggara Arab tribes armed for lethal, devastating cattle raids against their neighbors, the Dinkas. The U.S. was allied with Khartoum for strategic reasons at the time—to harass Gaddafi on Libya's flank—and discouraged transporting even food aid to the southerners.

"So a quarter million starved; died," I reminded Craig. "The survivors got to Ethiopia." He nodded noncommittally. It wasn't less humane than current American policies with regard to Mobutu in Zaire, or in Angola, but when the refugees were driven out of Ethiopia in 1991, with cannons firing behind them, the government having changed, Khartoum's had also, in the sense of cozying up to Libya and other radical Arab states, and Washington began supporting these rebels it had shunned before. "So they starved, getting back to the Nile."

By his expression, he knew that, too. His question was about these past three years, when the revolutionaries were shrugging off the Marxism they had adopted when the West was neglecting them, or when the food in the pipeline was interrupted by ship delays or pledges not met or diversions to half a dozen other crises, like Somalia's, more publicized and just as bad. "I'm like you," I said. "I'm not familiar with everything that went on. They killed some U.N. people along the way, these guys, which didn't help their cause."

He nodded. The jeep had mechanical problems and Ruth hadn't known which spare parts to ask for, so she was still stranded. He leaned under the hood, under the car. My Land Cruiser, packed to the roof with medical replenishments and food supplements, had been unloaded, and what was left were bundles of church-collected clothing we'd wedged in between. People at the post-and-wire gate, in the luscious twilight, were asking for that. I gave out an armful—Indiana barbecue smocks and incongruous suchlike—but when the crowd grew, Ruth and Attlee emerged, angry telling us to come to supper.

"These guys aren't angels either, these warlords, just because we're helping them to bleed Khartoum. They torture and kill."

"Oh, I know," Craig muttered. By a shaft of telepathy, I asked if it was like being in Vietnam. "I was in Laos," he said, walking away.

Supper was subdued, except that Ruthie enjoyed having her three-year-old on her knee, sucking the juiciest tidbits off the chicken bones, and we had a bottle of South African wine. The contents of her mail, or perhaps its scarcity, had not pleased her, but the little boy, still in starvation mode—wobbly-necked, not blinking much or twisting on her lap, and mainly drinking milk out of the cup in preference to solids, but imitating the grown-ups' rhythms with their wine, because he was watching us—certainly did. Snatched from the crucible, Leo was going to live, and see Ohio someday.

Father Leo had been radioed and managed to show up, livening us before it got too late. A shambling, white-haired Dubliner, he explained humorously as he wolfed a taste of everything that he was in Africa because he had "tired of counseling drunks." He agreed to stay the night so he could speak with Craig, but in the meantime he enlightened our curiosity about the orphan, whom he had found on his last legs beside a foothill track near an Acholi village, Palotaka, whose inhabitants were in such straits they had decided not to feed him. He was not Acholi—his words probably Latuka. His parents, fleeing through, had been killed.

"Leo's a neutral," I explained to our spook. "A man of the cloth. He and the Catholic bishop of this region were put under house arrest in a straw hut for three months because the Dinkas thought they weren't favoring the Dinkas enough."

Craig glanced at Ruth. She said, "In the hill villages they'll sometimes go ahead of him so if a mine blows up it won't be *him*."

Leo changed the subject to Ruth's jeep. I asked him what was wrong with the world. "The world is broken," he said with a rueful chuckle, and reached to dandle his namesake.

"Leo, the Lion!" I toasted. And then: "To Africa, our future and our past!" The baby gripped his milk.

Craig asked about the calisthenic shouts we were hearing from a nearby rise.

"They do it before they let them go to sleep," Ruth said. "It's a training camp. I block it out. They take a new batch up to the front every other week."

"But it's some protection for you?" I suggested.

"Nothing is a protection. They either draw the Antonov or they, the officers, get drunk." She suddenly remembered that she ought to grab a flashlight and show Craig where the bomb shelter was, a short trench with log lumber laid over half of it, so he'd know where to jump in case of a raid. He knew Antonovs, the Soviet freight planes bought surplus by Khartoum for the purpose of bombing the south, since they had no regular bombers. It droned overhead, looking for targets of opportunity from eight or nine thousand feet up, and the crew might kick bombs out of the tail, much as the U.N.'s food plane crew kicked grain sacks out of their aircraft's rear end for the food drop, only without worrying about a Stinger.

The moon was rising, and we heard drumming and singing from the civilian quadrants of the landscape, as well as the drill sergeant yells in the military camp, with recruits chanting patriotic slogans as they did squat jumps and push-ups. Craig grinned.

"Are you going to be able to help her?" I asked, after he'd chatted alone with Leo and was preparing for bed in the monastic cell we were going to share. He'd warned me to fall asleep first, because he snored.

"How about you, if I were to ask you the same?"

"Well, I'll try. But we're not in the same position."

"In war; yes. If a bullet had come through the windshield today, who would it have hit?"

"I mean money."

"Can I raise some? This war has created four million refugees and two million dead. I'm a pastor from Bissonnet Street in Houston, and I can't even fix her jeep."

I smiled, repeating how Herbert, in this same room a month ago, had opened his overnight bag and three passports from three different countries had tumbled out, and we'd then listened unwill-ingly to the poor Australian woman weeping in the next cubicle, through the plaster wall, as if she, and not Ruthie, had been captured and raped.

"Five minutes," Craig insisted. "I'm like a band saw."

Chapter 5

. . .

CRAIG AND FATHER LEO HAD GONE THEIR SEPARATE WAYS WHEN I woke, to a lovely morning sun and boundless rolling perspectives, after I climbed a viewpoint behind the church that overlooked the modest gorge of the Bahr al-Jebel, the "Mountain Nile," flowing under the Imatong Range, Sudan's highest, behind the ridges behind me, all downstream from the Victoria and Albert sections of the Nile, in Uganda's lake country, but not yet joined by the Bahr al-Ghazal, the "Gazelle River," from the west, and the Sobat, from the east, near Malakal, to form the White Nile. Then, at Khartoum, the Blue Nile from Ethiopia joins the White to constitute the famous Nile that flows to Shendi, Atbara, Wadi Halfa, Aswan, Luxor, Cairo, and the delta close to Alexandria: nowhere, though, more beautiful than around here. Beyond the gorge sat endless savannah grasslands, woodlands, parkland in tropical, light-filled yellows and greens, where, although the hartebeest, kob, buffalo, and reedbuck may already have been eaten and the rhinos and elephants shot to buy guns with their horns or tusks, the vistas remained primeval because for decades civil war had prevented any other kind of development, like logging, tourism, or mining.

I had a spear-length stick in hand, to defend myself afoot or keep the wildlife at bay, and to more appropriately remind myself of how the Dinkas, as a cattle people from time immemorial, had been able to protect their herds and pasturage from the Baggara Arab tribes whose homelands adjoined theirs, even though the Baggara domesticated horses as well as cattle and rode into battle, instead of merely running. A Dinka, who could run for twenty miles with six spears in his free hand, attacking from the reeds and rushes of every river crossing, every hyacinth swamp, was not a foe whose cattle could be rustled and women stolen with impunity. What had skewed the equilibrium of spear versus spear was when Khartoum had given the Baggara guns and sent its army in motor vehicles and helicopter gunships to mow down the lumbering cattle who escaped the horses, driving the surviving herdsmen off of their beloved prairies, steppes, and swamps and plains.

Earlybirds had lined up at Ruth's already, as we ate our oatmeal and Craig completed his customary jog. He was borrowing Attlee again, but I told him I hadn't enough gas to let him take the Toyota. Ruth, when they left, called him "Captain America." Sleeplessness had masked her eyes like a raccoon's.

"Is he or Herbert going to do more harm than good?" I asked.

"No, no, they won't harm a hair on his head." She did an imitation of Makundi—who was laughing—mimicking the rotor blades of a rescue helicopter swooping in. "He's not to be messed with, unlike you or me."

I mentioned the four U.N. relief workers the rebels had killed—and one of whom the Dinkas had also held under "house arrest" earlier, like Father Leo, but for trying to census their civilians to regulate the feeding program, a Filipino woman Ruth had known. She groaned.

"More good than harm, though?"

"I want them to have their bazookas," she answered finally. "I want them to have their land back, and everybody else." The problem being, of course, that these river villagers had been displaced by the refugees. She couldn't stomach the firing squads, the killing of every prisoner on the battlefield, the torture of dissenters, who were kept in holes dug in the ground with a log laid on top and taken out once a day to be whipped and fed. She therefore didn't encourage the SPLA to bring her soldiers with wounds or fever; they had Dinka doctors who had trained in Moscow or London for that. Also, closer to the Juba front, a Norwegian NGO operated a medical station where Scandinavian surgeons cycled in and out for three-month stints, which was about as long as anybody could stand the gaff: that is, eleven operations a day, often no electricity or window screens, no airlifts, ambulances, maybe no anesthetics or antibiotics. The patients might have been transported in a pushcart or rolled along on a flatbed truck empty of fuel or burned their final energies in stumbling along, hit several days before. You didn't give transfusions or much food, and the scalpel was the principal anti-infection agent—just scraping with it before you sewed the patient up. The gatekeeper was a fierce young Irishwoman who seemed to think the SPLA was an offshoot of her own country's IRA and had enraged Ruth when her nursing assistant had had to be invalided by Ed from the airstrip the Norwegians controlled—the Irishwoman asked whether she had obtained an "exit visa" from an SPLA commander "authorizing" her to leave. That a woman could become a "war junkie," like a man, and so suspicious of "spies," Ruth thought absolutely heinous.

Our wire fence, though any strong man could have lifted each post out of the ground, functioned as a sort of magic barrier. So, unafflicted by the begging that might occur outside, I used to pace its dimensions for exercise. Ruth predicted that the next time the Arabs' tanks decided to break the siege of Juba, with extra infantry flown in from the capital to flank the armor, they would clank clear past our church at Loa all the way to Nimule with no effective opposition. The Dinka troops would run into the higher forests of untankable terrain, as they always did, but the civilians, in their panicked tens of thousands, would be tearing down the road in front of us. As a mote in the mass, it could hardly matter whether your jeep worked or not. Unless you'd gotten a head start, with no particular malice, but their spear points flashing like fireflies, they would strip you and the compound in a quarter hour.

We were inoculating babies against measles, before the dry ice that kept the vaccine fresh was gone. But an elephantiasis sufferer was in the line. How could she have survived this long? We gave her cephalexin, for whatever that might be worth. The queue was checkered with people with rag-fashioned bandaging on, and blue robes for one clan, red for another, or body paint, headcloths, loincloths, tribal scarifications on the person's forehead, and possibly a giraffe's scrotum as a carryall on a rawhide strap from his shoulder. Yet he was wearing a garage-sale apron from Peoria to cover his family jewels. Having never lived in a trading town like Juba or Malakal, rubbing shoulders with Greek or Lebanese storekeepers and Africans of half a dozen alien tribes, they were amused by the church-basement, Wal-Mart froufrouerie somebody like Ruth was able to hand out from the bales of clothing she received, without finding it demeaning. She made sure no school-age child lacked clothes who wanted them, even though they had no school to go to, and every woman was as covered as she wished to be.

Some hadn't walked from the Nile to Ethiopia and then endured the harrowing escape back from Gambela, through Pochala—with hundreds drowning in the Gilo River, crocs in the water, but being shelled on the bank, or while swimming the Akobo after that—toward Boma; then Kapoeta, two more weeks from Boma; and Torit, two weeks from Kapoeta, the question continuously how to fuel the walk. In the Kenamuke Swamp, the local Murle and Toposa tribes, freelancers who were neither allied with the government forces nor against them, robbed or killed stragglers from any side.

But we'd get naked Dinkas who hadn't seen that much of the world or all this miscellaneous cruelty. They'd plunged instead into the Nile's own infinite braidwork of papyrus swamps, when the Arabs had attacked their cattle camps, surviving on bush pigs and river perch as their cows were stolen or died, and had gravitated here by the grapevine afterward, or to join the fight. Not having experienced the catastrophic reversal in policy of the Addis Ababa government, which had cost so many thousands of Dinka lives, followed by the loss of the Nuer as allies, costing thousands more, not to mention the government coups in Khartoum, whose vacillating policies had previously pretended to advocate a multiracial society tolerant of other creeds, they were less baffled. They hadn't attended college in the capital, worn suits in London, or maybe converted to communism when Washington and London shiftily deserted them, hadn't served in a ministry or as chums in the army with Arabs who now, after their mutiny, wanted to kill them, like the SPLA's leading figures. Barefoot, six-and-a-half feet tall, wearing a cape or just a kob skin covering their privates, they'd walked for hundreds of miles under duress themselves but could still negotiate with a lion until its behavior became reasonable, or bleed and milk a cow to make a balanced meal, along with *merissa,* millet beer, out of the mixture. They felt no inferiority to these uniformed Dinkas who had been to Cairo, Cuba, or Fort Benning, Georgia, to train. What had it got them? Their children, too, were starving, and if they yelled at you bossily, you could vanish again, naked or in your cape and kob skin, spear in hand.

Ruth was known along the river for not refusing to treat nude patients, as the Catholic nuns did. "I've seen other cocks," she said, not afraid to feel a man for a hernia, either. Naked folk, whether Dinka or Didinga, didn't understand English, so how could you explain your objection, as she teased her Maryknoll friends? "Just treat them!" On the other hand, you could "set your watch by" how regularly those women prayed; and she'd once witnessed "the faith which passeth understanding," when invited to an SPLA confab over at Chukudum, in Didinga country, beyond Torit, where the Maryknolls maintained another station, a little doctorless hospital near an empty church, like Loa's. The conclave was a military one, a number of commanders attending, as well as the more gung ho NGOs who supported them. The problem was that the Dinkas, having been brutalized and evicted from their homeland, had brutalized the

Didingas and burned their valley villages, driving them into the hills, and created a number of indigenous enemies or "spies." And when the Antonov droned over every morning, on the lookout for a target to bomb, somebody was signaling to it with a mirror from the ground. Probably a kind of Morse code or a visual parallel to what the Dinkas themselves had developed for their radio transmissions— whose best operators talked rapidly in sequences of pops and clicks that nobody not in the know could understand. Over coffee in the clinic we used to listen to these for fun; and then whichever Dinkas were present would grin at how smart their leaders must be to have invented a language neither the Arabs nor the Americans could comprehend. They didn't simply use Dinka on the radio because their old allies, the Nuer, now with the Arabs, knew that, as did the many Arab traders and army officers who had served for years in Dinka land.

Anyway, this spy—who was himself either an educated Didinga or embedded with them—was signaling to the Antonov's crew from a hillside when it cruised over every midmorning, as was indicated by answering mirror flashes originating from the plane. So when this splendid SPLA get-together with speeches was held on what had been a prewar parochial school soccer field, it wasn't the big, slow, noisy Antonov that came chugging over to try to kill the leadership and disrupt the ceremonies, but two of the MiGs based in Juba or Malakal—roaring out of nowhere to strafe and bomb. Soldiers, civilians, and NGOs like Ruth dived for the drainage ditches. Ruth was burrowing like a mouse in the high grass, and the bigwigs scrambling in mud. Two young nuns did also, but the old one, who prayed like clockwork three times a day, just stood there upright in the middle of the field, trusting God, while bullets kicked up spray patterns of dirt on both sides of her and the MiGs' bombs, too, exploded all about. After they'd made their second run, she'd suggested to her colleagues and Ruth, "This is over. Shall we have a cup of tea?"

"So, she won't know if you have a hernia! Big deal! They don't have a surgeon anyhow," said Ruth, recounting it.

In our own compound, a ten day's walk west, on the Nile, and closer to Juba, the new hub of the war, we had more shell-shocked, hungry refugees coming to our church nowadays than to those sisters posted in Chukudum, although not more than to the pair north of us, nearer the siege. The church was actually superfluous to most except as a relic where white people preferred to distribute food, but we did have a tamarind tree that was a natural gathering point, which Ruth had tactfully left outside her fence, and here a schoolteacher named Bol was conducting impromptu classes. He and I went and salvaged a blackboard from a building the Antonov had bombed, under the correct assumption it was being used by the SPLA command. Attlee, when he returned, helped us fetch and nail it up, saying Craig was on a tour and "in good hands."

Ruth's "equation with God," as she put it, fluctuated when the stubbornness that I thought was her saving grace reared up and fussed. Although she did not consider Him responsible for every famished child, the accumulation of outrages was undermining her faith. She prayed less, walked her Labyrinth more; and feeding little Leo every few hours helped a lot. "I'd wake up anyway," she claimed. Misproportioned, he wobbled when he walked, and fixed his eyes on Ruth with intensity, when awake, hugging her thigh and hip like an oak tree in a windstorm. She hadn't been aiming to serve in Africa since her teens, like the Maryknolls. She was a "wash-ashore," like me. In fact, I'd never told her that I'd heard from Al in Nairobi how she had found her mother floating in a swimming pool, in Toledo, when she was small, and then been handed around among indifferent relatives before being sent to nursing school, instead of to a regular college, like her cousins. Ruth was from southern Ohio, a pretty swath of bottomland her father had let go to seed. He was a jailbird, in fact, always phoning for bail, in Ruth's critical memory, or else born-again at the Pomeroy church, and she'd creamed him lightly with a frying pan on her last visit. Ruth was a lay sister and glad to feel those looser parameters, able to withdraw from the commitment if she wished to. She suspected that people like her needed crises for grounding, like the proverbial social worker whose job always surrounded her with clients plagued by problems more severe than hers. She was seldom tempted by conventional sins like avarice or sloth, only (as when no task lay at hand, when she went home on leave) suicide—which was insulting to the Lord: not to be infatuated enough with His world and its opportunities for service and love.

Bol could translate English into fluent Dinka or Arabic, as our Acholi cook and Kikuyu and Kamba assistants could not do, and wanted to practice his English, although he seemed adept enough already, having gotten a degree from Makerere University, in Kampala. In his skinny wistfulness he reminded me of the young women in that city or Nairobi who wanted to make friends, pretending to offer sex but really after money for the bare necessities or a chance to earn an honest living or carry on a wider conversation than in the claustrophobia of where they were. He was in charge of a *koi,* a group of a hundred or so underfed orphans, or Unaccompanied Minors, younger than the regular recruits but being trained by the cadre to dig a trench, attack a gun emplacement, and as a schoolmaster, he felt used like window dressing, because they were going to become cannon fodder and studied almost nothing else. Nor had the military people trusted him enough to let him translate for Craig, for example. Ruth and I, comparatively, were of no importance. It was not that any Dinkas opposed the revolution—some Islamists being so extreme they still tolerated slavery—but what they thought of its leaders. But if you were a Dinka and didn't disguise your doubts, you might find yourself digging one of those pits in the ground with a log laid over the top that would serve as your prison cell. All of the black Equatorians had been supposed to rise up and drive the Arabs back to the Sahara, but instead you had the Zandes, Baris, Madis, Mandaris, Morus, Kakwas, Acholis, and Latukas lukewarm in this area, or entirely withholding their support, not to mention the Murles, Toposas, Didingas, Anuaks, Nuer (a true misfortune) and the Kingdom of the Shilluk, in the eastern regions of the south. The

Nuer, ancient foes if only because their cattle-centered culture was so similar that they shared a basin of the Nile, were killing more Dinkas now than the Arabs were: foes historically so tough that the Nuer used to like to boast, in the early years of the century, that they needn't bother carrying shields on a raid against the Dinkas. Only their spears would be enough.

It had become a mess, but noncombatants in particular couldn't say so, and Bol's idealism had trapped him, because now there was no leaving. If he had stayed in Uganda after Makerere, or sidled to a nearby country such as Tanzania, or returned elsewhere from the scholarship he'd won to Moscow during the SPLA's Marxist phase, when Khartoum was allied instead of at odds with the U.S., he would have been all right. Elsewhere, he could be regarded as a sympathetic neutral, not a traitor, if encountered by the rebels' enforcing cadre outside their narrow band of territory. Like the other Dinka professionals—physicians, veterinarians, bureaucratic paper shufflers—who were being protected until the fighting ended, schoolmasters were scanted, yet tolerated, by the warriors for now. They had to tiptoe in advancing a proposal to improve conditions for their kids, however, because the kids were supposed to be undergoing a hardening process.

"Studying is for later," a sector commander remarked, glancing at our blackboard sessions under the tamarind tree. With a face severely lined, he wanted to be sure no one of soldiering age was there, and he noted my presence as mildly complicating. Once a teacher, always a teacher, you do find yourself haranguing in your mind's eye a classroom of upturned souls even where they no longer exist—and especially when the alternative is the wetter work of a health clinic, like swabbing throats, incising pustules, changing compresses to poultice a festering wound. But nothing is cost-free in Africa. If I appeared within sight of the gate, Bol would inevitably turn up accompanied by several of his Unaccompanied Minors needing tutoring. (He may have kept one on duty as a lookout all the time.) A bomb from the Antonov at ten thousand feet had killed Bol's wife in Wau a year ago, when that town, way northwest of us, kept changing hands. His in-laws were sheltering his children, under occupation, in Malakal, and we talked about them, or London and New York, where he'd never been and wished he was, while showing the children where they lived on a map of the world.

Since Bol was an unassertive fellow of about my own age and inclinations (skeptical, secretive, prudent), I withheld judgment on whether this new commitment was going to be such a sensible idea. Ruthie, who hadn't an ounce of the executive in her personality, expected to have to do everything herself anyway. When she put her foot down, it was to my suggestion that we invite him inside the fence to help. That's why she employed the two Kenyans, and Margaret from Gulu, she said. If you took in adult employees of the country, you might have to save their lives. One of the Nuer men who had been seized, lined up, and shot in Nimule after the tribal split had worked for Ruth. It broke her up. She had been trying to sneak him out, but they ran into a roadblock and there was no disguising the tribal insignia incised into his forehead. Up in Juba, she insisted, when Khartoum's politics reversed within the Arab world and the Americans hastily closed their consulate, *they* of course got out all right, but not two Sudanese employees, who were tortured to death.

I'd instituted a sort of hospice under a sheet of canvas on the opposite side of the church from where our quarters were. On about a dozen cots lay aged people with no families to care for them, some mission-educated, who had not sought a more animist sanctuary for their death throes. Makundi, the Kamba, helped when the few bowel movements occurred, or spooned porridge and bestowed sips of water. I happened to have volunteered one time on my travels at Mother Teresa's death house in Calcutta and knew about scratching the scalp to lend distraction, ease the passage, if you lack morphine. You couldn't manage a hospice during a famine, but this was a respite between famines; the pace of death had moderated. Nor did I need to know what they were dying of. There were no death certificates to fill out, no cholera epidemic to report, and few children were dying, to wrench your heart.

Craig showed up after supper, after three days, but Ruthie said good night abruptly when she noticed he'd acquired a hand grenade—"protection," which pleased him but flew against the NGO principle of no weapons inside a compound. He seemed played out but quite invigorated by his investigations or whatever he'd been up to. A bald spot glistened hot as he lay on one elbow on the bed next to mine, in our monkish cubicle, jotting notes in a shorthand that was unreadable to a snoop and grinning at my furtive attempts to do so.

"Have they got an obstacle course now over there? Did you show 'em how to build one?" I asked, because the shouts from the training camp on the next hill already had a different pitch, more strained and breathless. Bol's boys had been warned of something precipitous ahead of them. "Or did you interrogate anybody?"

"Perish the thought. You've got to be kidding," Craig murmured good-humoredly.

"But is it different from Laos?" I asked with genuine curiosity.

He hesitated, surprised I'd mentioned that.

"Yes."

"The warlords?"

"Oh, everybody's a warlord. Oliver Cromwell. Alexander the Great. Ethan Allen."

"But are these lugs different from in Laos?"

He didn't answer for a couple of minutes while writing in his notebook—he had a miner's headlamp on—or squinting at the bugs that consequently circled him or were burning their wings in the candle we also had.

"I heard they pounded nails through one guy's feet who they were torturing. One of their own. One of the dissident Dinkas, up on the Opari road, where my blackboard came from."

Craig shook his head without undue reaction. "No, I would know nothing about that." I didn't want to alienate and shut him up;

but, no, he received the information as imperturbably as though inscribing it in shorthand for his report. I asked if he would like to lecture Bol's collection of kids about world history.

"My cousin does that at Rice," he said, smiling at my effort to soften him up. "But you want a warlord story, so you'll know what a warlord is? Okay. I was in the military: try this one. I was a corporal, and we had an airfield at Longcheng that was controlled by this anti-Commie, anti–Pathet Lao chieftain named Vang Pao. They were Khmu, a hill tribe like the Hmong—Plain of Jars stuff. And we had the runway fenced, because of course they were pouring in for help or resupply—food, ammo, meds, or wanting to get the hell out of there to Bangkok on the Hercules. If we couldn't hold the field we were going to have to abandon them. That is, their fighters needed to hold it with what we gave them to hold it with. But so this general, this clown, comes back from a battle and hears that a girlfriend of one of his commanders has been sleeping around, and he has her spread-eagled naked upside down on the fence for people to put their cigarettes out on, et cetera. That could happen in Liberia, yes?" Craig added. "But not yet in Sudan. Neither Islam nor these guys would do it."

I didn't speak.

"And, no, we didn't stop it. She screamed slowly, there all day, hundreds of us Americans in the area, and the officers saying, Oh, Vang Pao would kick us out if we cut her down, knowing that his resupply wouldn't be stopped just over an incident like that."

"You were a youngster?" I asked.

"I was. I went to seminary after that."

When I asked if he had later dropped out, he shot me a look.

"Five minutes," he reminded me. "Sweet dreams."

Back when her jeep had been operable, Ruthie left the vicinity of her compound only once a week, for the ten-mile trip to another compound she maintained, when possible, for chronic patients at a refugee camp up the Juba road: beyond which the route became more dangerous and led to where she had been captured. Father Leo traveled it more regularly, as well as to the troubled towns of Magwe, Obb, Parjok, and Palotaka, to the east of Opari, and Kajo Kaji, across the Nile.

He shambled into our kitchen, when he drove by Loa, always bringing a dab of food to replace whatever he ate from our dwindling larder. Ruth kept a room vacant for his use. Her Leo's progress in gaining weight and coordination were a pleasure to him, since he'd snatched the boy from being "recycled into vulture," and he enjoyed the blunt-thumbed, dig-in-the-ribs bantering celibate men and women sometimes engaged in. He had been informed that he had bone cancer but considered staying out here a better treatment than going back to the doctors in Ireland, as Ruth later confided to me. So the perils of the road—the Mandaris' self-defense militia; the Acholi Lord's Resistance Army moving more into the mountains on our side of the border as the Ugandan army attacked them—fitted into a wider perspective for him. Nobody, not the Acholis or Mandaris, would want to kill Leo, per se. Like a leopard-skin-priest of the traditional Nuer, or a master-of-the-fishing-spear of the traditional Dinkas, he was not to be messed with by Joe Average and remained politically radioactive for a military commander, since one wasn't likely to kill a brogue-speaking, dog-collared Roman Catholic priest even to hide an atrocity. But that didn't mean it mightn't happen accidentally from a mine or ambush, intended perhaps for the commander himself. He saw whip marks on people, mauled corpses, and panga cuts on the survivors, and bottomless grief for deaths that had occurred purely gratuitously during a raid to steal a cache of grain, much of which was burned, for lack of means to carry it off.

Over a glass of wine, after giving Margaret, whose Acholi name was Atta and who was a Christian, the comfort of Communion, Leo shared opaquely much of what he'd seen—polite to Craig but more indulgently oblique with me, as a partial colleague, although religiously squishy. I found his shamble disarming, as it was so often in passing him through bristly situations where the potential for villainy was palpable; and then he'd leave the next morning as early as he woke.

He'd delivered another child, this boy older than Ruth's inseparable appendage, and not abandoned by unfriendly neighbors, like the toddler, Leo, but an escapee from the Lord's Resistance Army's herd of kidnapped children: sex slaves, soldiers, porters. He had been eating leaves and caterpillars while walking away as fast as he could for several days, he told Margaret in their common language of Acholi, which was the only one he spoke. Ravenously hungry, forlornly posted beside a scarcely-ever traveled jeep track, he hadn't run from the sound of Father Leo's motor because he knew the Lord's Resistance Army had no vehicles. They chased you down on foot instead and tied you into knots and slowly beat you to death, which always took a while because the other children were assigned the task.

Otim was his name. We didn't immediately invent another but set a pillow on the floor of the kitchen for his head, put a pot of rice next to it for him to dip from if he woke during the night, and showed him the outhouse and what it was for. His extraordinary scrawniness did not appear to result from dysentery or any fever Ruth and Margaret could detect by candlelight, although he would certainly need worming, and his jaundiced eyes showed their yellow color better in full-spectrum illumination, after the sun rose. The brutalities of the Lord's Resistance Army did tend to isolate its conscripts from epidemics that might have hit a normal village or refugee encampment. In the morning, there he was, occupying his corner of the kitchen, cross-legged on the floor with a conspicuously full tummy and observant eyes. He told Margaret that since he knew no white people were members of the Lord's Resistance Army, he'd felt safe for the moment. The night before last, hyenas had circled the tree he had slept in, after all day trying to make his ten-year-old legs travel quicker than any fifteen-year-old's who might be trailing him. He had dreamt of that, and heard the chanting songs of recruits marching or else, crammed into stakeside trucks, being ferried from the training camp up to the siege lines surrounding Juba. What was *that?*

They were our protection, Margaret told him. He believed her, knowing to begin with that the Dinkas were enemies—to be either attacked or avoided—of the bunch that had grabbed him, and were located along the Nile, which he had seen from Leo's car for the first time. Margaret next pointed at me, to my surprise, and informed him in Acholi that I would be his future helper. We peered at one another dubiously, unknown quantities, and I wasn't of the gentler sex, nor did I understand his language. Without standing up, he reached for her skirt. She laughed and reassured him. The usual protocol was for these children, who had been force-marched for hundreds of miles through the bush, to be returned to their own country's army at the Ugandan border, when they escaped or were freed during a skirmish. The Ugandans then eventually repatriated them to a collection point in Gulu, if they weren't drafted for menial duties in the meantime, or hadn't been, indeed, by the SPLA here first. That sounds cruel, but not all were fit to be shuttled home. Otim looked more like a gnome than a zombie, which is what the Lord's Resistance Army tried to create with its captured children. Zombies in the sense that the ritual was that they should help kill members of their own families or neighbors in the village before being allowed to survive, so that they couldn't think of running home, and eat a piece of their parents, to sever them forever into pliancy.

I would be driving him to Gulu was what Margaret meant, so no soldiers would be involved, and no orphans' "holding pen," as Leo had expressed it: Leo, who had told me he was glad for his lifelong celibacy in the burned hamlets he went into, when consoling the raped widows left behind. Saint Brendan, the peerless sixth-century traveler from County Kerry, Leo's own birthplace, and his boyhood hero, had explored Limbo, too. Leo's gimpy, rolling gait made me wonder whether his hipbones hurt him. Otim's sister, Margaret said, was still a prisoner, and he had seen her frequently raped, or "bred," one purpose of that group being to repopulate the earth with right-eous offspring.

Ruth took care not to mention our acquisition of Otim over the radio, lest the sister be punished. The Lord's Resistance Army had radios, furnished by Khartoum. Margaret could translate their Acholi, though they were "madmen" to a person such as her. And we listened to the Morse code vocalizations of the two Dinka operators, and to the Arab officers' frequency, and to Al and another NGO adminis-trator warning of a looming shortfall of food. Ruth returned to work, with her toddler accompanying her because he cried so desperately if she was out of sight, and Attlee to help. Craig had paid Margaret to wash his clothes for him because he was leaving tonight, presumably in a dilapidated rebel truck and via their route, which we were not allowed on, through Kitgum instead of Gulu, toward Lira and Tororo, to the airstrips in Tanzania where they got their weapons. They excluded us from all the roads at night.

Craig was touched by Ruth, bothered that her jeep remained disabled, in fact stuck his head under the hood again, then agreed with me that we should siphon her gas into my tank before the Dinkas took it. He was antsy on her behalf, as if from what he'd learned while with the SPLA chain of command, but let no hints slip. He did point up ironically at the brazen drone of an airplane, not the Antonov we feared but the "Lutherans' plane," a Buffalo, which flew three times a week from Kenya to keep the two hundred thou-sand souls trapped in Juba fed, while under siege by the rebels we were feeding: just as the U.N. folks were feeding, by air, the Nuer, whose bands of militia were thrashing "our" Dinkas. So, from their angle, you couldn't blame the SPLA much for their suspicions of visi-tors. The French, for instance, they believed, were surreptitiously helping Khartoum through the Congo, in retaliation for Anglo-Saxon interference in Rwanda.

"See you again." He left on foot at sundown for his rendezvous.

We rarely heard firing because the SPLA didn't have enough bullets for live rifle training. They let their recruits learn how to shoot by sniping directly at the front. So we were flabbergasted, a few nights after Craig's departure, to hear shouting at the gate and the voice of Attlee, the Kikuyu, who was on duty as our watchman at the time, shrieking with fear, a pitch I'd never heard before. With my flashlight I ran out and found him twisting on the ground, bleeding at the ears and head, and soldiers with clubs milling around. They told me—the officer speaking English—that they were searching for deserters from their boot camp and he had tried to stop them.

"He's right. You can't come barge in here like this, you bastards!" I yelled. But they pushed past, looking for conscripts who had run away, as if nothing had happened, while Attlee lost consciousness and bled and jactitated quietly. Ruth was speechless, banging her fists on her hips, tears blurring her eyes, when the lanky officer in charge shone his light at her.

"You are in our country," he stated, in good Khartoum English— where so many Dinkas had attended the national university, in the capital, during the decade of truce they'd had. "And we are doing a police search. If I was in America and the police were searching for a criminal, I would not complain."

"They wouldn't beat a bystander to death!" I interrupted.

"They wouldn't beat a black man?" He laughed. "Did you ever read a newspaper? Besides, he was interfering with our duties; he wasn't a bystander. You don't like us? The Norwegians like us better, and the Irish lady at the airstrip, so that's a comfort," he remarked sarcastically.

It was true that the Norwegian NGO, run by a retired military officer who had never been able to fight in a shooting war in Scandinavia, was very partisan. He often took a video camera to sites where Dinkas had been massacred to show the armchair journalists back in Nairobi, or hurried to witness mortar skirmishes himself. The brutalities the Dinkas themselves inflicted that Ruth and Father Leo agonized about were not in his purview. Married to a willowy one, he was for the Dinkas rain or shine, and so this officer looked at us unlovingly in my flashlight beam, as Attlee died—Ruth squatting beside him.

I wanted to leave at dawn; we certainly didn't go back to sleep. But Ruth dug in her heels. First, we'd have to bury the poor man, once his family, via Al at headquarters, had been notified. We couldn't transport him anywhere, although Al and Ruth had known him and his family for a couple of years. Offices had to open in Nairobi, a driver go to his house, while the body waited on a pew inside the church and job seekers who had heard the news collected around the gate. Ruth sent Makundi to size them up for grave diggers as she mused over the choice of a grassy site, near to but not disruptive of her Labyrinth, her toddler clinging to her because her change of mood had terrified him. Attlee was "not replaceable"—that acrid sophistication you could almost lean against: white being his "lesser of evils."

Al was so mad for a minute he was glad to tell us that the corn delivery for these camps was going to be further delayed. A low-keyed, curt assent was radioed from Kenya when the sun was at about quarter height, and a few petitioners were permitted to excavate a coffin-shaped trench, though we had no coffin. Ruth skipped her clinic in order to wash him, except for chronic patients who were receiving amodiaquine or amoxicillin or Cipro for fevers, or meben-dazole worm treatments or eye-ear ointments for crying babies. She used her best sheet to wrap him in, and kept checking the grave to be sure it wasn't "heaving," then smoothed the soil by hand, may have thrown up once or twice, walked distractedly, and took to her bed. I had diarrhea myself and lay propped in an improvised deck chair under a fig tree reading a mystery set reassuringly in San Francisco. Nevertheless I peeked at the site repeatedly, remembering turning the first shovelfuls of flowers, thinking we shouldn't kill flowers, before giving the implement to somebody else.

Ruth sent away an apologetic lieutenant, not the same individual who had supervised Attlee's beating, but wanted to lodge a protest when we could gear ourselves up for it. Fashioning a cross would be another priority.

Makundi was close-mouthed except to wonder if Craig had "displeased them": Was it a message? I didn't think so, but from his perspective this was a natural guess. He said Attlee had supported at least two families, and the one we'd informed would not tell the others, lest they needed to share the death payment. Attlee's "temper" had served him badly when the posse stormed in. Was it courage to stand up to them, or should he have recognized that they weren't going to hurt Ruth? "Maybe because she was raped," Makundi murmured: another explanation that hadn't occurred to me.

Joining my new friend, Bol, near evening at the blackboard underneath the tamarind tree was a relief, although I just sat at the side while he sounded words the children could repeat. They had no pencils with which to write, but until his ration of chalk ran out, he could show them what a sentence should look like—the lessons slow because, since they were underfed, they were accustomed to husbanding what energies they had.

Ruth and I got high on wine, watching egrets fly toward roosts upriver and sunbirds flitting, wheeling, in the crescendo of the Nile sunset. She had set a broken arm, dusted somebody else's gash with antibiotic powder, and inoculated two new babies but suggested we burn a little of the gas she'd given me to confront the higher-ups tomorrow. I would have wanted to invite Bol to join us on the terrace—we even missed Craig's ambiguous presence—but knew it might not be in his best interest. We were "rinky-dink" as an NGO, she said, to be bludgeoned that way or, indeed, to lend ourselves so transparently to the convenience of an intelligence agency. I was wondering whether she might not pack it in and go back to Nairobi with me for a break, but in fairness, not to stack the deck toward that outcome, reminded her that the rebels had killed four U.N. employees recently and imprisoned the Catholic bishop. "Not just us," I said.

"Indulge me," she replied. I was fidgeting, thinking of clearing out when I decently could. She followed me into the room Craig and I had shared, as if to talk more privately, and then sat on my lap when I sat on my bed, as if to cry and seek a bit of comforting. I was surprised, but not *too*: not enough to be rude. I remembered that around Otim's age she had found her mother floating in the swimming pool and that the coroner had inadvertently used the term "suicide" within her hearing. But she hadn't described the episode in detail to Al—whether there'd been a lap to sit in—since her father had been in jail at the time, in one of his periods of incarceration.

I was game; but she surprised me again by moving my obliging, limp, and neutral hands from the back of her head, where I had placed them as if to comfort a hospice patient, to her breasts, which were quite ample, as the saying goes.

"I'm an old bag," she punned, and began to wriggle on me with her conception of a lap dancer's technique. "You can squeeze."

I soon hardened, whereupon she laughed in triumph and stood up—"Aren't you forward!"—but told me ceremoniously that she would see me tomorrow, "If you can handle it."

Tomorrow I'd hoped to consider taking off again, with my eligible passengers, such as little Otim—the traumatized Lord's Resistance Army boy, who had indeed been forced to "eat his parents," Margaret said—and perhaps Margaret herself—who, as the breadwinner for that baker's dozen of related children in Gulu, wished to check on them—and even Ruth and her toddler, if she quit resisting. But now I was committed to a visit to the commander's compound near Opari.

Outdoors, from Aswa's civilian camp there was drumming that night, celebrating some clan or family affair, and the sky overhead tingled with stars, the air womb-warm. Ruth asked if I was all right, like a pal, her gamine face scrunched concentrically by the hardships she had witnessed.

In the morning I blushed when we raised our coffee mugs together.

"We need doughnuts, glazed doughnuts," she said, smiling, two nervous eyes and a serviceable nose peering out. "Got a nix on the food, on the radio, for another day." The light was buoyant, clean and clear, opening out toward the intricate landscape, and the prospect of bugging out on Ruth immediately because of Attlee's murder seemed less defensible.

Chapter 6

• • •

THE BUNGALOWS SCATTERED AMONG THE SPLA'S COMMAND CENTER were colonial-era but hard to find in the grown-up forests near Opari, so that the Antonov would have difficulty as well. We were fobbed off at first, only our white faces permitting us access at all. But abruptly Salva Garang, the Number Two, appeared. He'd been a colonel in the regular Sudanese army before the revolt and, with that air of authority, asked how much foodstuff we had for distribution, as though this were the point of the conversation we'd requested and would determine for him how important we were. In fatigues, rangier than the average Dinka, but with a face that indicated he had executed many prisoners, he was impatient.

Ruth stepped forward so close to him that he stumbled backward slightly, losing the advantage of his military panache.

"Why did your goon squad kill our man? Outrageous!"

"I'm sorry about it. They must have lost their cool. They weren't authorized."

"You bastards!" I exclaimed.

"Murderers," Ruth said.

Irascibly he bridled, adjusted the holster of his pistol, then glanced at me dismissively, knowing I was just a temporary hire. He had contemplated enough corpses that emotional outbursts alone wouldn't make him flare up.

"This is a war. It was a mistake. I've sent the men who did this to the front. You think I haven't lost my friends to stupider mistakes? You think your revolution didn't kill people who didn't deserve to be?"

I pulled in my horns—not being his cup of tea—except for reminding him that Americans knew one another, even an insignificant cipher like me, by asking whether he'd liked Craig. Then his stare was what a prisoner must see, as Salva decided how long he ought to live.

"The children you are feeding," he said to Ruth, "We are going to give them their own country. They will be very happy to have their own country. Not to be slaves, but citizens." He stopped, not used to eloquence, or to people who might not know that the words for "black" and "slave" in Arabic were the same. "I hear you on the radio," he added approvingly, placatingly.

Ruth was silent, before needling him: "I don't see you at the feeding stations."

"What else do you want? You want us to give up?" he asked. "I'm sorry about what was done to you. That was not us." He now meant her capture by the raiders at the outrider clinic. "We are fighting them."

"You don't need to be. You should be on the same side," she insisted: which must have disgusted him, because he agreed.

"They should be on ours!" Loud, exasperated, with military brusqueness, he turned, time a-wasting.

Ruth was finished with him but not with me. After letting me poke my head into the two shops functioning in Opari to ask about gold nuggets, which nobody would admit knowing existed anyway for fear that the rebels would seize them to sell for guns, she stopped to greet the Maryknolls, Elizabeth and Nancy, who gave us tea and their sense of life paced not in sprints but as a marathon. Their clinic was less hectic but more hazardous than Ruth's, being nearer the front but farther from the camps, and was the post she'd walked to naked after her release. They fathomed, in fact, before I did that our present errand was to revisit the scene of that crime.

"He's leaving," she explained, which unaccountably sufficed for them. Like gears, they appeared to fit together as a team for peace and continuity—fiftyish with thirtyish; pragmatist with idealist; morning person, afternoon dynamo; magazine reader, watercolorist—and they loaded a modest packet of the one's drawings and both their outgoing mail in my Land Cruiser to be delivered to Nairobi. Another chapel of the White Fathers in deteriorating condition was located here, but Father Leo had reconsecrated it for their use. We looked in, knelt, and prayed for Attlee's welfare in the afterlife. I didn't balk when Ruthie disclosed her further plans, partly because the nuns weren't astonished. She had patients to see, her jeep was out of commission, I could transport her. A long, popish view can be comforting. She told them little Leo had been sleeping when we left but would be crying now, at their first separation. He was lopsided, as his body stacked on belated muscles and fat in irregular form. God bless!

Our drive north from the Maryknolls' was blessedly uneventful. Not only no mines; not even a roadblock. The people walking were sparse, and mostly from the local Madi or Bari tribes, a foot shorter than the Dinkas and thicker-set, scrambling along like forest-and-mountain folk, not striding like cattle herding plainsmen. As food got shorter again next week, they would disappear into the woods and gaunt Dinkas take over the roads, stalking, famished, for something to eat. Instead, we saw a burly man with a bushbuck slung over his shoulder that he had snared; he started to run when he heard the motor, till he realized we were aid workers and not about to steal his meat, as guys in an SPLA vehicle would have done. Another man, two miles on, was squatting on his heels, quietly collecting wood doves one by one every few minutes, when they fluttered down to drink at a roadside puddle he had poisoned with the juice of a certain plant that grew nearby. He, too, was frightened that this clutch of birds he had already obtained might be snatched away, until white faces in the window proved we weren't hungry. He showed us the deadly root, and how pretty his half dozen unplucked pigeons were, as well as a pumpkin he wanted to sell.

Close to the rope ferry from Kerripi to Kajo Kaji, we passed several Dinkas with fishing nets, and spears tall enough to fend off a crocodile or disable a hippo—which was what they were good at, when not embedded in the intimacies of their cattle culture, with five hundred lowing beasts, and perhaps a lion outside the kraal to reason with, the rituals of manhood to observe, the myriad color configurations and hieroglyphic markings of each man or boy's specially selected ox or bull for him to honor, celebrate, and sing to, and the sinuous, cultivated, choreographic eloquences of its individual horns, which he tied bells and tassels to. The colors were named after the fish eagle, the ibis, the bustard, or leopard, brindled crocodile, mongoose, monitor lizard, goshawk, baboon, elephant-ivory, and so on. Like the Nuer, who were so similar, they had been famous among anthropologists but were now shattered by the war. Adventure, marriage, contentment, art, and beauty had been marked and sculpted by the visual or intuitive impact of the cattle, singly, and in their wise and milling, rhythmic herds—as bridewealth and the principal currency, but also the coloring registering like impressionistic altarpieces, the scaffolding of clan relations and religion. A scorched-earth policy by the Arab army and militias needed only to wipe out their cattle to disorient and dishearten them.

In our white man's bubble, we tooled along, noticing women balancing baskets of plants they'd collected for food, the minutiae of woodcraft that smaller tribes who'd always lived off wild things on the shelves of the mountains had. A man was carrying a black-and-white colobus monkey three feet long, plus the three-foot tail, that he'd shot with an arrow and could provide meat for a family. This was the defunct Juba culture, with an occasional charred tank hulk to go around, and I was anxious or suspicious that Ruth was taking us farther than anticipated. Footprints (at least not bootprints!) kept turning off at every junction, as if the ordinary joe had been trying to clear off to Karpeto, Fagar, Kit, or wherever.

"You're leading me astray," I protested.

"I'm getting you a souvenir. The Kit River has gold in it."

"How do you know who's in control?" I muttered, but startled also that some truck driver must have gossiped to Ruth that I smuggled, besides collecting souvenirs.

"I heard ours are again. It's a one-shot. When can I come back, even with a car?"

We'd met not a single vehicle for an hour. "The scene of the crime?" I complained. I had the jitters. "I hate macho men. I mean it; I wouldn't have come here with a man. Never. Is this like an exorcism for you?" At the same time my mind skittered back over the past twenty miles, where she must have had to walk. My respect for her fortitude was mixed with uneasiness that I was trapped in a foolhardy repetition stunt.

In a hardpan yard out of sight of the road we found a concrete one-story bungalow that had been gutted of its equipment and window sashes, the wooden roof burned. Hemmed in by thickets, the location was deserted except for airborne and crawling bugs, and a cobra prowling the veranda, where we then sat sweatily on the bare cement, munching our peanut butter sandwiches, joking about "No plague," because any rat carrying the plague would have been eaten by the snake.

"You'd think they'd recognize by now, with this war going on so long, that if you capture a place, you're going to need a hospital there, too," she observed, grimacing. She stood then and, with her waddle, stiff from the jolting car but energetic, paced, while waiting for us to be discovered. Not knowing who was there, you didn't simply blow your horn.

After a while she pointed out that people were emerging from the bush. One man was burdened by a goiter the size of a bagpipe's bladder; another with a hernia bulging like an overnight bag. Breathless children had run to find out if the rumor was true that Ruth had returned; they spun around to carry the news. They were Madis, Baris, the so-called Juba peoples, displaced by the war and siege, and she put on her nurse's hat and white coat, as emblems of authority, gathered her penlight, tongue depressors, a scalpel, tendon hammer, syringes, needles, stitching thread, bandages, her meds satchel.

"Our dog and pony show," she said. Not a stick of furniture was left in the room where she had examined patients—only scraps of a deflated soccer ball she'd once brought for the kids to kick around, which somebody had since cut slices out of for making sandals from, and wisps of tropic grass sprouting from cracks in the floor. She had palliatives 'like vitamins, chloroquine, acetaminophen, atenolol, mebendazole, metronidazole, Phenergan, Valium, co-trimoxazole, even some iodine pills for the goiter man, although, like the hernia character, he needed surgery.

There were perhaps patients with cataracts, VD, bronchitis, scabies, nosebleeds, chest pains, Parkinson's, thrush cellulitis, breast tumors, colon troubles, a dislocated elbow, plus the usual heart-breaking woman whose urinary tract, injured in childbirth, dripped continuously, turning her into a pariah, although it would have been as easy as the hernia for a surgeon to fix. Ruth could do the elbow, with my help, and knock back an infection tempo-rarily, but not immunize the babies or anybody else because our vaccines had had no refrigeration for so long. She bestowed her smile, having logs carried inside to serve as benches. The line that formed, the fact that she was going to finger and eyeball every-body, was reassuring.

"We can't spend the night. We have to leave before word spreads too far. But I wanted to look in on my old bunch. Picture a pebble dropped into a pond," she told me. "If the ripple reaches the far shore before we're gone, we could be dead ducks."

Employing the Arabic word for gold, *dahab,* and pointing at me as I waited like a chauffeur for her to complete her mission, Ruth produced from the crowd a frazzled though stalwart, furtive man who spoke to me in that language. I tried pidgin Swahili back, but we had few tools in common.

"Don't cheat him. You have all the cards in your hand," she warned as we walked into the brush. This was arguable, as easy as I would be to mug. But the scenery opened out into a parkland of copses, swales, and savannah, with plots of cassava, millet, or sesame hidden about where a party of fast-traveling raiders could miss them in moving through, and scattered banana trees, some damaged years ago by elephants, before the herds were shot. Because it might be death for him to be caught by the SPLA in possession of any gold, I could understand why hundred-dollar bills would seem safer. Yet if buried, they wouldn't keep as well, and were only marginally more portable. As we talked with our hands, he signaled that he had five children, none dead (or not counting whoever had died), and two wives. I hadn't seen people who appeared pathetically underfed; and yes, he agreed, here the civilians were surviving, unless they got shot in a firefight by mistake, or had asthma, or bloody flux. He mimed these different fates and showed me some Kaopectate tabs Ruth had slipped him. The bodies discovered by the wayside were strangers fragmented off from tribes far away and fleeing nobody knew where. Nobody of his group either harmed or helped them, except perhaps to strip their remains. They fed their own children and aged folk what they had, but not refugees.

In the privacy of these open spaces, sitting down underneath an acacia tree to be less visible, he showed me by circling his thumb and forefinger the size of the several nuggets he claimed to own. I showed him currency, in return, whose numerals and pictures he already knew—pointing to Benjamin Franklin with a grin.

I opened my palms and rolled my hands to indicate not "hurry up" but "what can you spend it on?" He then made his hands take off like a little plane, and specified it wasn't him but that a child or children of middling height might fly to safety, maybe on an empty aid plane if somebody—he indicated this by rubbing his finger and thumb pad together—was paid. So we now traded a Ben Franklin for every rough nubbin of bicolored rock he had: each of us trusting the other, via Ruth's okay, as, indeed, he would have to trust a pilot with his child eventually.

We were seated in scented elephant grass, seven feet high, under the umbrella of the lonely tree—lovely, but not entirely a good idea in central Africa unless you're trading in contraband. I could feel a leopard grabbing the back of my neck, or a mamba slithering close to measure me for a fatal bite. My companion must have had many questions corresponding to mine, which were how and where he or his friends had found the gold, and was it before the war or lately? And what was going to happen to this designated child, once he or she was in Lokichoggio or reached Nairobi? He himself had a disturbing cough. Had he caught TB? Had it spread to his family? How much longer, under these new circumstances of the Nuer-Dinka war, which was becoming worse for the likes of him, Ruth said, than the Arabs' war on the blacks, could this small Madi tribal band hold out without splintering? What had he witnessed? Centrally, maybe, that was what I wondered.

Ruth, although displeased at the length of my absence, had made the most of it. "And you're going to be a Good Samaritan," she told me.

"I thought I already was!" I waved at this dangerous cul-de-sac where we were lingering on borrowed time.

"No, no," she said, while dispensing the various capsules she had brought. "You've just been making money."

People had been summoned from farther off and were straggling into sight, one handicapped because his foot had been blown off, with a false construction attached in its place, jerry-built from wood and home-cut straps of hide and spongy padding. Another family included a girl who was walleyed, with the father or her grandfather above military age, like my gold prospector, and therefore not already conscripted by the Dinkas, the government, the Nuer, or the Madis', Mandaris', and Baris' own self-defense force, which had coalesced between the pincers of the rest.

Ruth was peering into an old woman's mouth, lancing abscesses, although the lady also wanted Ruth to pull her teeth.

"No surgery and no dentistry. I see people die of appendicitis, or tumors showing right on the surface, or a childbirth impaction that could be fixed but would be a bloodbath if I tried to. The midwives who could help with obstetrics have been scattered, too. These are the rabbits, the ones who ran fast," she said. "The rabbits are left—or the ones who would be a liability to anybody else."

"Which liability am I supposed to be a Good Samaritan for?" I asked. It had dawned on me that she intended for me to bring someone back. "I see plenty."

"You can guess, if you want. Ultimately it's up to you."

I said I knew that, but she didn't reply. It was like Father Leo deciding who to pick up—out of the untold number of orphans he had seen dying—to bring to our doorstep. Who would somehow get surgery—the man with the goiter? The one who had whittled his own wooden foot? The woman who was going to get blood poisoning as soon as we left, for lack of a dentist? The one dripping urine all the time from a fistula or prolapsed bladder? Triage is not my specialty and I'm squeamish, besides. Snobbish, perhaps, in favor of the young and the cleanly. Our excuse when turning down the veritable sea of supplicants along the roadsides of Africa who want a ride is the roadblocks. *Can't get you through the roadblocks.* But of course the man with the grotesque goiter could have passed through any roadblock in an NGO vehicle, if you just muttered the word "hospital." No one would want to unload him. He didn't know enough to ask me for transportation, however, and I didn't want him sitting beside me, smelling of death for hours and hours.

The clue would be found, I surmised, in Ruth's face. She was bustling to treat patients faster, as though running out of medications as well as time, yet probably our window of safety was shutting down. Her waddle seemed twice as endearing when her intuitions caused her to hurry at the same time as, while swabbing a gangrenous sore, her conscience kept contradicting and slowing her. Most everybody understood this was partly a sentimental journey, not a visit they could count on again. They were people she'd handled before and, like a doctor, you did for them whatever you could; whether they survived later on was in other hands. But her glance did light up when she looked toward the gangly girl with the wandering eye.

"That girl with the walleye," she remarked over her shoulder— after noticing my attention had turned that way at last, among the hundred or so spectators we had. "Figure out if you want to take her with you to Nairobi. Otherwise she's better off staying with her own people than just coming back with us."

"You mean for surgery?" I asked.

"Of course."

Yes, she was scrawny, yet not yet pitiable, still had her vitality, reaching for a rubber band that Ruth held out for her to do her hair. Because of the eye, she was likely to succeed at the roadblocks without being hauled off and raped. I sensed, astonished, that the karmic point of our entire trip might be this very moment, and I nodded, primarily because Ruth wanted me to. Quickly, she asked the parents and the girl, using the assistance of another aged village survivor, who had graduated from a mission school before independence and spoke English, if they would like to have her eyes fixed. Ruth was anxious that we be on our way but simultaneously panted ever so slightly, the way you do when you've been thinking about doing something and feel inspired.

Ya-Ya was her name; and she had no belongings to fetch. Although they obviously hadn't heard of the proposal before, her parents were not amazed so much as caught by surprise. The idea that two white people should descend upon this clearing and repair her eye problems, free her from the misery of being a freak, and turn her life around was not as astounding as that we *would*. Because they already knew Ruth and what she'd suffered from the Nuer raiders for trying to maintain the community's medical care, they trusted her. *Mucho manga-manga* was the term we heard for Ya-Ya's ailment, and though they didn't really know where America was, the translator said—they thought you could walk—would she be going there?

She was bouncing on her feet, faced with this fait accompli, and I wouldn't have turned her down for the world, but neither Ruth nor I was acquainted with any ophthalmologists in Nairobi, or Kampala either, for that matter, or a place to deposit her upon arrival for an extended preoperative or postoperative stay. Who would pay for it, and what would then be done with her between now and the end of the war? Ya-Ya inspected the Land Cruiser from the outside, circling on tiptoe—it would be her first car ride, the translator said— yet all wrapped up in the magic of maybe becoming like other girls. Her parents hadn't much chance to cuddle and reassure her, or debate and think through the proposal, because Ruth's sixth sense was reported to be accurate. Raiders were on their way on foot, said the Madis, who were melting away themselves.

Borrowed time, my mind chanted. I was almost less afraid of being shot than of being captured, stripped, and losing the agency's vehicle. When Ruth gestured "finished" with her hands, I waved at the girl to get in, as I helped Ruth pack up our leftovers. Her parents boarded, too, carrying their younger child. I was teasing Ruth that she must have planned this all along—"I bet you just came back for Ya-Ya" then smiled at the girl, since she had recognized her name.

"No," Ruth insisted, repeating Father Leo's mantra about his regular visits to places riskier than here: "You have to give them hope!"

Before the translator fled, Ruth made sure the girl and her parents understood that they couldn't accompany Ya-Ya to Uganda, or wher- ever else they thought she might be going. But the light of intelli- gence irradiated their faces and they were holding her hands, helping her gulp down her panic as the motor roared to life and, all together, we pulled out of the empty clearing onto the dirt road, heading upriver, south.

I wondered whether she'd be carsick. Courage wouldn't solve that. Then I was afraid her father might. But they were all exhilarated, like riding on a roller coaster, instead and, underneath the fun of jolting along, convinced that their daughter, touched by Ruthie's wand, might soon become a beauty—in any case, whisked out of the war zone. I thought how parents must have felt as their children were evacuated from Europe during the lead-up to World War II—so happy but sad, her mother patting her and crying. The other child, half Ya-Ya's age, was a comfort but also a limitation, because they were going to have to walk back from wherever they chose to be dropped off, using the honeycomb of trails they knew.

We had clear sailing for a while. Ruth assured them in her fractured Arabic that no soldiers had stopped us on the trip north. Too smart to trust that, however, they tapped me on the shoulder after ten or fifteen miles to stop. I let them out at a small runneled tributary, the brush impenetrable to eyes like mine. Mercifully fast, after wails, tears, hugs, and thanks, they vanished into a thicket. Mercifully, too, because around another few bends we did run up against a blockage of soldiery, who made us get out of the car while they searched for weapons or stowaways, scrutinized our passports and the big pasteboard visas "Jane" in Nairobi had signed for us, and at Ya-Ya herself, glancingly, who Ruth explained in English and Arabic was going to the "hospital." They nodded in approval, not bad guys, though you never could predict this in a civil war.

For her, it seemed to have been a rite of passage. We'd been tested—able to protect her, and not unduly frightened ourselves. So she began to enjoy the swell of unfamiliar scenery, the rising foothills and bulk of the Imatongs, the twisting, occasionally frothy, Nile below, and just the speed and bucking of our car. I handed her a stick of gum but forgot to indicate that it wasn't food. After swallowing it, she observed us gingerly but closely, and tasted with some amazement the tuna fish from a tin we opened. *"Na kima Bahrini,"* "like the ocean," I told her in my version of Swahili, which she didn't understand. *"Jogul baharr,"* said Ruth in Arabic. Despite the jouncing, she let us know that yes, she was ravenous and not about to be sick, so we bought her two baked ears of corn and a goat's rib, the last rib the owner had, at a *shamba* we passed. The children who gathered laughed to watch us drinking out of our jerrican rather than the nearest stream, but also at Ya-Ya's cockeye, which put me into a bad mood for changing a tire in the rainstorm that followed. Ruth snuggled an arm around her and nuzzled her ear to persuade her that a man's grumpiness was silly and meant nothing, however.

Having missed the curfew at sundown, we needed to drive exceedingly slowly in the blanketing dark, not just to avoid losing the road but in order not to draw gunfire. It was better that we appear humble and tardy, than like the sneaky spearhead of an Arab attack. Whatever gun emplacements had been laid in ambush let us pass without a challenge, and the church compound had never looked so cozy. We all fell asleep after sipping sweet cocoa and scrambling some powdered eggs, which made Ya-Ya laugh because she'd naturally assumed they were going to turn out to be some kind of vegetable porridge. Next morning, she wanted an exact repeat.

The next morning, though, she also took in the complexities of her new situation quite bravely—the towering Dinka soldiers and civilians all around, whom, along with the Nuer, her people had been frightened of; the skeletally bloated toddler, Leo, who'd cried all night, though allowed into Ruth's bed, because she'd been away during the day; Otim, the escapee from the Lord's Resistance Army, who clung to his corner of the kitchen like it was the one true star and was comparably jealous of Margaret's attentions but wildly preoccupied and traumatized. Yet Ya-Ya was hopping with curiosity. In fact, I taught her to hopscotch, after showing her the church, the clinic, the hospice, the flimsy boundaries of our little compound, she watching carefully because her parents had told her (the last time anybody had spoken her language) that, beyond Ruth's period of kindness, I would be the one carrying her on. She didn't want to miss spotting me slipping into my car in an emergency and wind up left behind. Her fugitive eye, by its jiggling leaps or tangents, expressed both joy and jitters, whichever was predominant, and you could learn to tell the difference.

She was considerate in her manners, which moderated her bottomless appetite at the table, as did Margaret's severity, whose Acholi was not comprehensible to her. But going along the fence, listening or talking through the wire without venturing to leave the protection of the yard, she looked for other Madis to talk to—short people like herself but not the Baris or Kakwas, whose languages were intelligible but accented queerly, and who constituted most of the short people about. Meanwhile, at Margaret's suggestion, she tried taking over Attlee's duties at my ten-cot hospice, tactfully spooning water or cornmeal into the mouths of the patients. In that survivorly pattern, nothing seemed to amaze her—no request or condition. Having seen deaths, thirst, and hunger, and as though to compensate for her unmoored eye, she appeared unusually focused for a youngster, inside her head, when I coached her about sponging the lips and forehead of a person who was dying and how to scratch their scalp to gently distract them from the pain. She'd never been permitted the margin for error other children got.

Word traveled. A Madi man, an Anglican deacon, who knew some of her clan, showed up at the wire asking for Ya-Ya. We went outside to talk to him because, after Attlee's murder, Ruth didn't want strangers inside the gate if they weren't patients. I was able to have him convey a promise to her, however, that I wasn't going to desert her. She needn't watch the Land Cruiser so nervously. And he confirmed for her that big-city surgery would be able to mend her eyes, although telling in English that he'd never visited a city larger than Juba himself. He needed glasses—begged me to find him some. His had broken. He couldn't read his Bible. In the sunset's afterglow he led us to the straw church he had built, quoting Isaiah, chapter 18, and Matthew, chapter 24. "For nation will go to war against nation, kingdom against kingdom; there will be famines." Ladoku was his name; and it's no exaggeration to say that his church was constructed mainly of straw, or that any big drugstore would have had ten-dollar glasses that would have helped him a lot.

I could promise my young pal Ya-Ya not to abandon her, but not Ladoku, her translator, that he might be wearing spectacles again anytime soon. Bol had joined us, because schoolteachers know ministers, and Bol was watching my moves in any case. He was unencumbered by Ladoku's scaffolding of belief—and flabbergasted disbelief at the scale of this suffering—compelling quotations from the Book of Zephaniah regarding desolation and destruction in the Land of Cush (Sudan) and the necessity of staying here right on until the bitter end in order to bear witness to it. Each felt a responsibility to his students or parishioners, but Ladoku's went beyond that, being scriptural and theological. Even if there were no parishioners, "like a captain going down with his ship," he said, his eyes ought to be the last eyes left. Bol, on the other hand, felt compromised: not truly "teaching" so much as monitoring a bunch of boys who might well be killed before they'd even learned to read and write. Ladoku, not engaged with cannon fodder in the war effort, could devote himself to his religious passions, and hadn't dreamed of walking the streets of London and Paris, like Bol, anyhow. He only wanted to walk the straight and narrow. But when people didn't have enough to eat, that didn't work out.

They both kept watching me for hints of when a food delivery was going to come, yet not trusting each other much—Ladoku because Bol was a Dinka, who ruled these camps with arrogance, and Bol because what he really hoped to do was clear out entirely, and if anybody except me learned this, he could be shot. The presence of the girl—springy with hope and curiosity and the sudden confidence of being with somebody who spoke her language—also put a damper on the two men's urge to speak frankly to me. How could this be happening? Ladoku's body language kept emphasizing, although he told Ya-Ya that she herself should expect all good things. And Bol, by contrast, was trying to plot an escape, of which I didn't want to know the details, because I assumed they involved cutting cross-country for umpteen miles and materializing beside the road at the Uganda border as I went by. Bol wanted to help his country from exile—something I could certainly understand, since I couldn't go back to the States at the moment for fear of being prosecuted by the American owners of that Alexandria shipping company. Instead, I was doing some good over here. And my heart went out to him; he was such a conscientious, lively teacher, who wanted to work in a refugee camp run externally: not by guerrillas, in other words, but by the U.N.

My girl might have to manage to bluff a bit at the Kenyan border, I explained to Ladoku, for him to translate. Without papers, we might have to be inventive and resourceful to get Ya-Ya across, and also exercise a mutual understanding in the big city after that. Did she realize there was to be no magic involved, just teamwork? Ruth was planning to adopt the starvation-stunted boy properly, with formal papers and all, and send him eventually to Northwestern University (whose nursing school was her alma mater) when he grew up. But *we* were going to need to be creative for her not to wind up in some high-fenced, catchall detention center for aliens in flight, such as Kakuma, in the northern Kenyan desert. Nor would the street children I worked with in Nairobi treat her kindly, since she didn't know Kikuyu, Swahili, or any other languages they spoke. She wasn't leery of me by now, or any of the other adults who had proven they weren't going to laugh at her, and was not callous to or revolted by people who were at death's door. In fact, Ruth bawled me out for letting her tend to a woman who coughed as if afflicted with TB. I'd come to my senses about that.

Civil war winnows out the nitpickers who dither on the station platform as the last train is leaving—people paralyzed by their own crabbiness or indecision. But Ya-Ya wasn't thrown for a loop by any unpredictable development, and enjoyed playing in the ruined church, that stone-and-beam labor of love of some long-dead Italian friar or "White Father," whose shaping hands had somehow enabled it to retain its eloquence and dignity. She delighted in gazing up, lying on one of the pews that remained, in this first playground she never needed to share with other kids. She had a bushbuck horn, hollowed out and pierced so she could blow notes on it with a trumpeter's lips, that her father had given her at the last minute, and she used to sit up on the altar blowing that, after watching Ruth's and my reaction to be sure this would be okay. She swept the church, to please me, and helped Ruth trim her Labyrinth with a trowel and clippers or shears.

Instead of leaving immediately, I took a few more long walks. In part, the beauty kept me lingering, where Africa had not been logged, mined, safari-ized, or industrialized. The human catastrophe hereabouts did not mar the vistas but, of course, was the other reason I stayed: that Ruth was refusing to leave. A food delivery still hadn't been contracted for, or whatever the bottleneck was. And no partner was en route from the States to help her—it should be a doctor. Maybe the powers in Little Rock were waiting for one to volunteer for service with the Lord. Margaret, the long-suffering woman-of-all-work, had shown me her Ugandan passport so I would be aware that she was eligible and wanted to go. Those children whose support she was responsible for in Gulu preyed on her mind, outweighing her loyalties here. Al, from the office in Nairobi, told her on the radio that he'd paid the individual who was supposed to be feeding them, but having been away for nearly half a year, she was torn. My ride would be the only one foreseeable, and with rumors of another offensive to be launched on us from Juba with armor—extra government flights from Khartoum landing at their strip with reinforcements—once she got home, she might find excuses not to return. I couldn't stomach turning her down; nor would Ruth have asked me to. Better to postpone leaving, with the excuse that Otim needed more time to adjust. The more you heard from him, the worse it got. He and his sister, still a sex slave with the band, had been forced to eat their parents' hearts.

As I say, not being a labyrinth type of person, when I wasn't teaching with Bol underneath the tamarind tree, I walked. Children might follow me a while, till the lassitude of undernourishment wore them out, but there was no scary wildlife left to worry about, just the shifting drama of the African play of light, the surflike tier of eastern mountains, green and blue. In a tightly military region such as this, you didn't risk much chance of getting mugged when you were by yourself but instead were watched by the occasional suspicious junior officer who couldn't understand that a tourist from the U.S. might be gazing at the loveliness. One said he thought I was "scouting" for a place where enemy parachutists could land. "You will be shot!" he warned, until his commander, less officious, intervened with a laugh.

We were located in sort of half a bowl. So at night they were burning brush off the slopes up where an attack by one of the militias opposed to us—Lord's Resistance Army crazies, or Equatoria Defence Force, or Nuer commandos—might commence, perhaps to coincide with the Arabs' tanks rolling down the road from Juba. It was important to clear a field of fire, offering no cover for a raid, and the crawling tongues of red created a pretty scene uphill—with shouts like Mardi Gras from all the young people chasing protein. Every creature fleeing the flames had more than one hunter after it, throwing a stone, swinging a club. But you couldn't see that, exactly. You saw controlled burning, heard revelry. Like so much in the landscape—the gorge of the Nile during the day, with the crocs waiting for somebody to get hungry enough to wade out too far after lily roots or with a fishing net—it was stunning. And never having heard a horde of white folk enthuse about their shimmering, supple, layered horizons or seen TV shows about New York, they neither wanted to be living among the skyscrapers nor conceived that New Yorkers might want to be here.

Ruth, indeed, wouldn't consider leaving. Eventually, sure, she was going to have to send that clinging little boy to Northwestern, but not during the emergency. She realized, however, that both Margaret and I were planning to. The nuggets in the money belt I wore under my clothes rubbed against me like pearls in a bed of oysters, and knowing this, Ruth would tell me to take my pants down for a hernia exam, which made Margaret laugh also, without being in on the secret. We had two girls living with us now, because as soon as word spread that Ruth had brought back Ya-Ya, with the wandering eye, to be healed by surgery in the big cities, a Dinka girl, Nyoka, stranded in Amei Camp, who suffered from the same ugly problem, heard about it and summoned the courage to walk the dozen miles and stand outside our gate in the subdued, straggling medical line. She might have sat there the whole night, but Ya–Ya spotted her first and agitatedly brought me over. This was a more bashful person, and even more afflicted; or it seemed so because, being taller, she was more conspicuous when trying to efface herself, and flustered when we waved her inside. There were women with week-old babies waiting, a boy with a sore throat and a cleft palate, an elderly blind man bent over in considerable pain, led by a timid child, and numerous other patients, though not the same numbers who had shown up when I'd arrived to replenish Ruth's medical supply. She had some Cipro left now for the boy's strep throat, for instance, but told him to come back each morning—mostly, I think, to shame me into taking him along so that his lip could be sewn up.

Ya–Ya had apparently never seen another girl with her own condition and hugged Nyoka in excitement, which embarrassed her. Nyoka remained reserved and tentative after I'd invited her to jump the line, whereupon Ya–Ya proudly showed her the expanse of the church—sweeping a few leaves out—and a folding cot ready for the next patient at our little hospice. Naturally this alarmed the Dinka girl, who assumed it must be meant for her, among these dying people. She and Ya–Ya shared no common language except a fragmentary Arabic, and not only was she still displaying her best behavior, but was more austere, cautious, or maybe bruised to begin with. Her parents turned up that midday to bestow their blessing on what was now another fait accompli and to give Nyoka an amulet to wear around her neck, some strings of beads and trinkets, and a small skirt, a cape, a smock, a water gourd, a rolled-up antelope skin to sleep on, and a forked headrest. They gave me a pipe fashioned from different calibers of brass shell casings, fitted together and framed in a reddish hardwood. Both of them and especially the girl were relieved to hear from Ruthie in broken Arabic and Dinka that she wouldn't be required to fly anywhere but instead would be traveling on the ground. Unlike Ya-Ya, she'd ridden in motor vehicles before, but her vision seemed worse, causing her to twist her head oddly back and forth to focus her good eye, and I guessed that one reason why she tried to minimize all of her reactions was to avoid attracting attention with this swinging motion and, therefore, mockery.

Her family (another wife of her father's had accompanied them, with three children) had brought along a plaited basket containing millet and mangoes for her to eat, in case we weren't able to feed her. Somebody must have watched at the gate to see whether we were going to take her in, then run home when we did. They said to Ruth that hungry times were coming again—right?—and when the hunger was at its worst the Arabs would attack. Yes?

Ruth shrugged and nodded. "We'll bring her back when it's over, with her eyes like a fish eagle's."

Instead of refusing the food, Ruth paid them for it and distributed the four precious mangoes to the two girls, Otim, and her toddler. The radio's chat that day had been bleak. No NGO had food deliveries in the pipeline. Even the U.N.'s own camps had had their rations cut to fifty percent of minimum requirements. Their cash flow hadn't matched the pledges. But we could hear hoo-rah calisthenics from the recruits in the training camp next door, and saw one jog by with a grenade launcher on his shoulder. In a sense, this Western ethic of whisking the most incapacitated children off to safety, rather than the more able-bodied souls, seemed incongruous to a subsistence tribal society, where, of course, for survival purposes the strongest adults ate first during hard times so that the clan could continue to function—but it was no more so than other strange events, like that the food sacks spewing out of the anus of an airplane five hundred feet up should take the leg off the woman who had radioed for it. Or the power locally that Ruth appeared to have despite being less competent, rational, or well-supplied than the Norwegian doctors, for example, across the river and up the road.

From spying on her, people knew about her witch's globe and spirit stick and mysterious Labyrinth. Yet these potent U.S. government agents showed up periodically, also, met with top commanders, and shortly afterward would vanish through other channels. Whereas I assumed they were using Ruth and our half-assed, amateurish organization merely because Oxfam, Doctors Without Borders, and the rest of the classy ones wouldn't allow connivances such as that, a lot of folk naturally imagined that Ruth must be linked with these guys, who, ducking in and out, were either a conduit for weapons or emissaries for deeper negotiations. Thus the favoritism we were showing to walleyed children might be explained as witchcraft, in line with Ruth's mirrored globe and Labyrinth, or else as some eccentric humanitarian impulse emanating from the luxurious nation which had allowed a quarter-million blacks here to starve to death in 1988, when it was allied with Khartoum, but now was helping feed the same tribes, because it wasn't.

Our audience—Bol's and mine—under the tamarind tree grew to include haggard parents as well as their children, plus children who had been pushed near the front row specifically to attract my attention because they were handicapped: bent over with cerebral palsy, perhaps, or a spleen that felt as hard as china from malaria, or who were blind, or scarred by yaws, or lame from rickets or a broken bone that had not been set at the time of the accident and needed to be rebroken in a hospital, or a piece of shrapnel in them that had never been removed. Even a layman could have noticed how their vitamin deficiencies had weakened them. It was pitiful, exasperating, and, to let off steam, Bol and I joked about having a drink someday in the Acropole Hotel in Khartoum, or the Fairway in Kampala, watering holes where he had hung out with—slept with—off-duty aid workers during his student days, unlike Ladoku, who'd never traveled beyond Malakal and Juba. That his government didn't care if its black population starved or fled into exile was now a given, but what had become new was the rebels' attitude, holding their own civilians as bargaining chips instead of letting them evacuate to where there was food. Bol had had an affair with a Dutch blonde who now worked in Geneva, the last he'd heard, though no one here had received mail for years. Friendships with expatriates always ended with the person who possessed a visa leaving: money and a passport relegating you to being a piquant abbreviated adventure. And since I was not a Red Cross girl, no hope of marriage, with eventual European citizenship, dangled in the offing. The fantasy involving my cooperation was for Bol to hide under my car seat and somehow get to Kampala or Kenya, where an affiliation with an NGO might provide him a foothold, teaching refugee kids where the SPLA wouldn't snatch him off the street as a traitor.

In this tumultuous landscape, spooling, ballooning complexities, with the sky cascading cloud changes overhead, I assumed that a sort of perimeter of safety surrounded my last walks. With a wink and a nod, our State Department and Western intelligence agencies determined where genocides were allowed to occur and where not. Eighteen American rangers had been killed in Mogadishu and twelve Belgian soldiers in Kigali, and Somalia and Rwanda were thereupon abandoned to the mercies of their warlords. In Zaire and Angola our interventions had been less pretty to begin with, where civil wars then killed millions and more. But Arabs were the villains here, and so first Israel, then finally the U.S., had shown up, wanting to bleed them. No one knew who I was, but even the Lord's Resistance Army didn't want to mess with white people. In fact, Ya-Ya learned she could bar the gate, not to soldiers but to ordinary people, by virtue of our flimsy theoretical authority—much in the way the roadblocks you encounter might be only a slender stick propped on a tripod of twigs that you could push over with your foot, though you might be promptly shot if you did. Ruth was going to leave herself as a decoy, a reminder that aid must be requisitioned, allotted for here. Officialdom perhaps would ask, *Is Ruth still at her place?* Like a shaman, she would exercise shadowy powers.

But I'd walk with one of these soft-spoken, educated individuals who were intimidated by their prospects—others beside Bol and

Ladoku. The tactics of the war did not delight them, or the actual killing, and they worried about the orphans they were caring for (though unable to voice their doubts) and the internecine shooting of black at black, not Arab. "They are helping me to understand your history," I explained to a camp policeman who became suspicious of our conversations.

Ladoku had Madi cousins in a forest village beyond the far side of the river that he could have run to, if he'd wanted to go back to living barefoot on sorghum beer brewed in jugs in the ground, as well as relatives trapped behind the minefields surrounding Juba, whom he hoped the Lutherans were feeding. But if there were dissident Dinkas, they lived isolated in the bush hundreds of miles away. Although the rebels did need university graduates, the ones they trusted were writing propaganda and giving interviews at the Hilton in Nairobi, or schmoozing in Dar es Salaam, where military stuff was shipped from, or finagling in Addis Ababa to reestablish supply lines that had been cut off by the change in dictators. Meanwhile, they'd ordered no paper and pencils for the new generation, and neither had we.

Bol remembered scribbling away on an exam with a roomful of other candidates for foreign scholarships in Khartoum, knowing that the winners would go to Germany, London, Minnesota, or Denmark, find a postgraduate post of some kind, perhaps, and never need to return. In retrospect, it may have been a life-or-death competition, because a Dinka suspected of apostasy was in greater danger than any mere Madi. But Bol's scores weren't high enough. He'd gone to wintry Moscow instead, where they made sure you came back.

Earlier, on the riverboat through the Sudd from Juba to El Obeide—American Catholics were teaching children in Juba, and British Anglicans in Malakal then—after he had won his berth from secondary school to the University of Khartoum, he had slept on the deck like the others who couldn't afford to fly. The war, back in 1970, still in its Anyanya, or "Snakebite," phase, was fitful, so that was how people went—hoping to strengthen their local schools with what they learned. A handful of businessmen and other students were also aboard, including three Tanzanians who were headed clear downriver for Cairo, to Islam's greatest university, along with humbler passengers, such as women and their plentiful progeny, plus a goat or chicken with its legs tied, and a lone spearman catching a ride to shorten his hike.

A Greek trader and his Armenian counterpart had rented the two cabins on the bridge deck, and three or four smaller operators, each with a half year's pile of village supplies and goods, had spread out below. A couple of soldiers were on the boat as well, which might have spooked the three Muslim boys from Tanzania on their way to Cairo if they had thought about it at all, but soldiers were a commonplace in Africa, a postcolonial sign of self-governance and independence. They'd deliberately set off to go the slow way, they told Bol when he made friends with them, from Pan-African idealism, in order to cover the length of the continent from Dar es Salaam by boat, bus, and train, firsthand and on the ground. Their famous elder statesman Julius Nyerere, the African leader most respected by the Europeans, preached a transborder egalitarian mosaic, a nonsectarian brotherhood of unity, *ujamaa,* and socialism. They spoke Swahili and English, not Arabic as yet, but had been taking lessons; and how proud their parents were that they had been accepted at Al-Azhar University, beginning their advanced education so promisingly. For Bol, too, the momentous start seemed auspicious, and the Pan-African ideal he was hearing novel and glittery—Muslim, Christian, and traditional animist to now chum along nontribally, nonracially.

The ten days or whatever it would take, after the towns of Mongalla and Bor, to bumble through the papyrus-and-water-hyacinth-clogged maze of Africa's largest swamp, the Sudd, which sometimes twisted a hundred miles or so in any direction, could be used by them in learning Arabic from new friends, such as Bol, and observing the "wading peoples," both Dinka and Nuer, along the banks. There was also an Acholi agriculturalist on board who'd been helping the U.N. inaugurate a potato-growing project up in the cool climate of the Imatong Mountains. The captain was a Lebanese, but the deckhands were Shilluk; they took frequent soundings for him, and fended the vessel off sandbars and drift logs with their long poles. All worked a twelve-hour shift, then tied up to some tree stub in an oxbow at sunset. Second only to Conrad's famous river route up the Congo as far as a tinpot boat could navigate, this was the legendary excursion, and the heart of the Cape-to-Cairo jaunt that so many British had notched on their belts when they controlled the two Rhodesias and right on up to Wadi Halfa, toward the Valley of the Kings, when most of the continent was colored red.

Herons, egrets, ibises, buzzards, guinea fowl, whale-headed storks flapped every which way over the dugouts of lanky men wielding fishing tridents. The boat stopped at hamlets of huts only a yard above the water to let people off or to leave freight, with cattle browsing in the shallows, their left horns sometimes trained a certain way by the gradual application of weights, while a herder, proudly dusted with ceremonial dung ash, poised upon one leg, the toes of the other hooking that knee so that it jutted out quite jauntily as he leaned on the point of his fighting spear, with his fishing spear dandled in his free hand. Whether Nuer or Dinka, these were people of sufficient numbers that they hadn't needed to bother learning a common language like Arabic or English to speak with other tribes, and they stared with more interest at the cargo on the deck than at the foreign or inferior strangers. The captain, although he was ethnically a Lebanese Arab, had been born to shopkeepers in Malakal and gone onto the river as a boy with his uncle, who had been a pilot during the British era, and then married a daughter of the King of the Shilluks. The Shilluks were a river tribe located just northward of the Nuer and Dinkas, sharing Malakal with the others as a hub, and, though less numerous, were knit rather tighter as warriors, if only because they had a king, so that their tough neighbors seldom fooled with them.

Bol said that although a few happy-go-lucky shots were fired at the boat near Terekeka, and later at Malek, once it entered upon the clayey tangles of the swamp, where the main-stem current became practically indecipherable and the raucous birds and rumbling hippos exercised their own hierarchal tribalism, while mama crocodiles defended their primordial nest sites along the bank with plunging roars and splashes, guns gave way to more antique, intuitive weapons. The strategy was not to rile the locals.

Bol loafed on the fantail, trading Dinka words for Swahili or Urdu and the collectivist vision of the Tanzanians. He would come visit them in Cairo, he promised, and maybe they would all do post-graduate work together in Copenhagen or Amsterdam. The war of south versus north might be sputtering elsewhere, but in this track-less morass of tricky braided still water segueing into primeval lakes and bogs—where, according to the record books, half of the Nile's water up to this point evaporated—when they dropped off a thou-sand pounds of rice and five hundred pounds of sugar and salt at Shambe, plus generator parts and gasoline, people reached for hand-fuls of mud to keep the bugs off as the bow touched shore. The water wildlife was so loud and headstrong, you'd think man hadn't been invented yet. It was glorious, interminable, splendid, appalling, but the middle-class city boys from Dar es Salaam, who were used to the servants in their families' compounds taking care of all their necessi-ties, worried because the jars of drinking water and satchels of corn-meal and other staples they'd brought to live on, apart from bananas and fresh fish, might run out. Such was the Africa of Bol's grandpar-ents, but not theirs. They prayed five times a day, kneeling toward Mecca.

And this was about when a machine gun opened up on the Juba-to-Malakal boat, from a nondescript section of the murky channel, before they reached the village of Adok, in a cryptic stretch between Lake Nuong and the Zeraf Cuts, exploding out of the papyrus rushes—as, at the first burst of fire, an otter hit the water with a slap. The guerrillas hiding there were lucky our two soldiers were standing at the bow, just lounging, without their rifles at hand and no place to dive in the extra second they had before the bullets zeroed in.

The captain immediately swung toward where the gun was, to surrender and tie up, lest it rake him on the bridge next. The problem was to locate the weapon in the featureless riot of vegetation, while his speed remained equivalent to about a walk because of driftwood and other obstacles lurking in the sea of water. His wife, who'd been dressed in jeans and a T-shirt like him, disappeared and reappeared quickly beside her husband in Shilluk robes, all African in her severity and ceremonious regalia, shouting in both Arabic and the language of the Shilluks that without the boat, these lost settlements of the endless swamp would be in deep doo-doo. To begin with, she seemed to Bol to be trying to protect the entire shebang—all of the passengers, the freight, not to mention the structure of the stubby boat, owned by her husband, which was still, two decades later, the only boat Bol had ever been on.

The guerrillas, half-naked but in fatigue pants, were armed with Kalashnikovs, a pistol, and spears as they swarmed aboard. They were Nuer, fortunately still allied with the Dinkas at this time, so that Bol was okay, once they had checked his knowledge of his birth language and were assured of the truth of his lie that his destination was not Khartoum but Malakal. However, the two government soldiers lying wounded on the rail and bitts at the bow, although they were as black in color as anyone else (they were from Darfur), were executed point-blank and thrown into the river, where no carcass would remain intact for even an hour. The Acholi man who worked for the U.N., introducing the growing of potatoes to the cooler slopes of the southern region, was cleared as well, as soon as he spoke his native tongue and named his village in the mountains, which was Gilo. And the half dozen floodplain women, both Dinka and Nuer, who were traveling locally on the deck with sheep, goats, calves, children, and family provisions, weren't robbed or molested. Neither were the pair of Shilluk deckhands in any danger. Their tribe was neutral so far in this war that was brewing, and they were set to work instead unloading the commercial shipments of varied stuff—while the captain's wife shouted, *"How stupid can you get?"* in Arabic at the raiders, with a fury not comic but rather regal.

It was hard to tell if she and her husband had a financial stake in what was being stolen off of the boat, although she certainly pointed at the bullet holes that had been shot through the hull and housing with genuine anger. The two traders, the Armenian and the Greek—who were also standing on the bridge—were more careful in objecting. Their lives were more important to them than whatever was being taken. But *she,* Bol realized, was really fighting for the captain, who was known up and down the river as a Lebanese Arab, although not a Khartoum Arab. She had draped a Catholic cross around his neck and was telling them that they would have to kill her if they took him, and that the Shilluk warriors would not be neutral anymore, but would descend upon them from Kodok and Malakal in very great numbers—the king, her father, would send them—if they dared to. Meanwhile, the Greek and the Armenian were discreetly buying personal immunity with folded bills.

This forceful princess wife hadn't reacted in particular to the killing of the government soldiers, or the checking of passengers' papers—those who had any. Bol's Dinkahood had saved him from a body search, which would have revealed his destination. But the three poor college boys from Dar es Salaam were under suspicion at first sight. Their color alone, browner than black; their inability to speak any language known to the Nuer except for English; then the admission papers they were carrying to Al-Azhar University, in Cairo, and their copies of the Koran betrayed them unmistakably as the enemy.

"Mohammedan," the fighters' officer said. He waved off an attempt at a bribe, pointing instead at the crates or sacks the deck-hands were laboriously unloading, and called the Shilluks back to leave the whole job to the Tanzanians, after the heaviest, which would have needed a crane otherwise, were done with. They'd also managed to drive off a small tractor on twin gangplanks.

Congratulating the captain for having no observably military material on board, the guerrilla officer told him that from now on he would be inspected on each and every trip. Any soldiers he carried for protection would be shot. This meant that he himself, although an Arab, was not going to be arrested now. His wife had saved his ass, and Bol could see the Shilluk lady restrain herself from yelling any further imprecations about the plain stupidity of interrupting these monthly Nile River supply trips, which several villages depended on. She also relayed in English his message to the Tanzanian kids that they'd be staying put on the bank. There was some pity in her voice, but no shrill protest. They looked to Bol, of course, for solidarity and help. He could meet their eyes, but that was all. He did hand over their mosquito nets, water jugs, and remaining bag of food—afraid, even so, of angering the guerrillas, especially because of the lie he had told about his own destination, while four of them searched the boat stem to stern and then below the deck. He'd named the church he sometimes went to in Juba, and claimed his father's second wife lived in Malakal and was going to find him work. But the commander laughed. He wasn't interested in Christians; he was interested in killing Muslims. All the Tanzanian boys' stuff he gave to the crowd of gleeful children who had collected from the nearest settlement, to taste or wear. Ropes were now tied around their necks, and their wrists fastened to these in such a way that they could balance loads on their heads and shoulders as porters. He'd already had their clothes removed, and whipped them with a switch to show how it was going to be.

"They're going to Lebanon," he told the captain sarcastically in Arabic that everybody except the boys themselves could understand. The Shilluk woman and both of the traders who had been spared capture retreated into their cabins so as not to have to witness it, and their departure made the face of the most hopeful boys change.

"I doubt they will ever drink water again," the commander said.

Bol told me, "I didn't think I wanted to live in my country anymore." That ineradicable memory was the most painful of all the pain he'd seen. But he had applied himself to his studies in Khartoum and lasted a couple of years, tiptoeing there as a Southern black, with the ticklish tests of loyalty, official and unofficial, constantly directed from the opposite camp. Even the great

Mahdi's grandson, Sadiq al-Mahdi, a hard-line Muslim but not hard-line enough, was under house arrest after being overthrown in a coup. Bol's friends needed to huddle in a safe house to endure a citywide conspiracy to beat up blacks on one particular night. Then he won his Friendship Program semester in the Soviet Union—chilly Moscow—before undertaking a return journey to the south that required him to detour through Ethiopia to reach the SPLA's lines, whereupon they were naturally suspicious of him also. Not just the fundamentalist Muslims had splintered into purist sects; so had the warlords here, enforcing a personal, not religious or even tribal, loyalty.

And the lions—as he'd found when hiking across the Boma Plateau from Ethiopia together with sundry random refugees, a collection of people who were simply trying to survive, and would abandon anybody who was a drag—had also lost their sense of propriety. They were rattled, eating human carrion like hyenas, and hauling down live individual human beings, as if there hadn't been a truce in force between the local people and the local lions for eons. Before the war, lions always knew and taught their young where they would be trespassing—what domestic beasts they shouldn't kill without anticipating retaliation—and people, as well, knew where it was asking for trouble for them to go. Deliberately spearing a big black-maned male might be a manhood ritual, but had lost all significance with a Kalashnikov. Neither species was a stranger to the other, or its customary habitat—whereas many of these poor refugees had been on their last legs, eating lizards, drinking from muddy puddles, wandering displaced hundreds of miles from their home ground, where they belonged. And so, on the one hand, young lionesses grew up stalking staggering people, and, on the other, soldiers in jeeps were shooting lions that they ran across with tommy guns, for fun. No rite of passage, no conversation or negotiation was involved: no spear thrown into the teeth, which then became a cherished necklace worn at dances. Bol regretted not sneaking south from Kapoeta into Kenya during the crush of the 1992 retreat, when people momentarily weren't being stopped from doing so.

"I was an idealist," he said.

He made me cherish my green passport, multivitamin tablets, inoculations, and money belts. I remembered driving across my own country at eighteen to experience its continental scope, like those Tanzanian boys wanting to see Lake Victoria, Lake Albert, the White Nile, Blue Nile, Nubia, Cairo, the Red Sea, Mediterranean, Indian Ocean, Atlantic, as Pan-African as Nyerere and Nkrumah and Qaddafi had preached. But a do-gooder like me was a sort of elf, in and out. If you had a cross-eyed girl, you brought her to him and he was charmed, whisked her off, fixed the eyes, fed her, and brought her back; yet not the multitude of children who were starving but not cross-eyed.

I did have such a girl waiting for me at the end of our latest walk, delivered from a Kakwa village somewhere to the west. She was small, defensively alert like the other afflicted girls had been, and Ruth had also allowed the parents of the Bari boy Ladu, with the cleft palate, to camp with a cooking fire on the perimeter close to our gate, in order to encourage me to stick him in the car as well. I realized I'd better hurry, or more children would be added. God knows what would happen to my hospice project. Without Margaret—only the inseparable Kamba houseman to help her at the clinic—how could Ruth keep juggling the balls? She knew that once Margaret reached Gulu, she would almost certainly stay there till the military situation resolved itself, and Ruth had given Margaret enough of her wages to enable her to do that. But she didn't like the juggling metaphor; she preferred to compare herself to the decoy duck who draws down other birds loaded with maize and sorghum to feed everybody their essential *posho*.

Bol wanted to try to cut cross-country for thirty miles or so and meet me beyond the bridge into Uganda, but I doubted we could synchronize our timing for such a rendezvous, or that without a mass migration to guide him, as he'd had in fleeing from Ethiopia before, he wouldn't get lost. And if he didn't, but emerged from the forest to meet me at the right moment, so we wouldn't be stalled, I wasn't convinced the Ugandan army wouldn't hand him back to the SPLA at its first roadblock, or agents grab him when he appeared in Gulu overnight. Since a friend from his hometown of Wau was a major, we went to ask him privately if it could be arranged for Bol to obtain permission to help me transport the handicapped children to Nairobi for treatment.

"How many?" the major asked, laughing sourly. "And what would happen to the hundred he's responsible for here? They don't count; you can dump them? I know Bol. He wants to be a scholar and a gentleman, and yes, we watch you guys hanging out together. Bol wants to go to London and join us again after the Arabs are defeated and it's as civilized here as London is. But we want him to help us build it up from scratch so he can be a scholar and a gentleman in it and not just inherit it from us."

He'd been examining a map on a piece of plywood that served as his desk, but laid another piece across it so I wouldn't see the map. Jerking with blunted energy, he was engrossed in the business of war in a way I didn't often observe, from the civilian side, and their boyhood memories counted for little now.

We were worse off now as plotters, having asked for clearance and been denied. I went to Ladoku's straw church, amid a huddle of mud shacks on the spacious shelf between the Imatongs and the shallow canyon of the Nile. Yes, he had letters to mail, including to "the bishopric," but betrayed no hankering to leave. "We are fasting, I told him," he said. He was curious about Ruth's plans. The Maryknolls were "hardened for solitude, even martyrdom, but how about her?"

I just said what she said about herself, which was that "Baptists are Methodists without the shoes on." And, about the Maryknolls: "At least I know what I'm missing."

She was like a tuning fork, I thought, hysteric—but registering the hunger vibrating variably outside. Once, when I'd reached to flick away a grain of rice that was stuck to her lip, she had gasped, wrenched her face away, and blurted, *"No,"* as if I'd tapped into an awful memory. Levels of frenetic anxiety and then recurring apathy surrounded her anyhow, when people recognized again that they had better save their strength because they were going to starve, even as they expected the tanks to roll down the road in another breakout from Juba, clear to the Uganda border, destroying, along the way, these temporary shelters—which the guerrillas would then rebuild after they had cut the Arabs' supply lines and forced them to retreat to Juba all over again. No baby she handled wasn't wizened.

I wondered how terrified Otim might become, while traveling to Gulu with me. His captors in the Lord's Resistance Army had drilled him to fear the tall Dinkas as monsters who would blind you and leave you to starve, Margaret had told me—which, of course, was one of their own techniques, if a village resisted them: that, or cutting off the leaders' noses. Margaret would help with him, and Ya-Ya with the harelipped boy.

Ruth had acquired a baby jackal that somebody had forgotten to eat; or maybe they'd sold it to her instead of eating it. Little Leo was jealous, watching it nurse from a bottle, but Ruth smiled at me joyfully while accomplishing this and pointed out that Otim had ventured from his corner of the kitchen. The new cross-eyed Kakwa girl and Ladu, the Bari boy with the cleft palate, were also observing.

"Just like for your trip. All squeeze in one car."

But she indicated that I should look outside by the bomb shelter. An SPLA squad had delivered another Lord's Resistance Army escapee. A sergeant, drinking tea with Margaret, told me the boy was lucky not to have been shot.

"He's old. He's like a wild man. He has no tribe."

Margaret, glancing askance at me, asked if the Land Cruiser wasn't already too full. He'd "frightened the old people," by which she meant my hospice patients; then, in fairness, she explained, "Not on purpose. Only seeing him." She had left him outside with a small helping of *posho* on a banana leaf to eat, and instructions to split a week's worth of stove wood.

I wondered why the Dinkas didn't want to keep him around for digging trenches, but the sergeant said, "He ate his parents. He wore their intestines around his neck"—showing with his hands how the child soldiers would drape them. In fairness again, Margaret said, "No, they don't know that." They had assumed it because some children, when captured, had been forced to.

She had a cough with a disturbing hack that, it occurred to me, might be TB. It hadn't before, and that might explain why Ruth kept her toddler mostly out of the kitchen, and wasn't wheedling Margaret not to leave, please. But Margaret's polite impatience to be off was persuasive, as well. She didn't like the parties to any of these civil wars—her own country's assorted Idi Amins or the spillover from Zaire's and Rwanda's atrocious conflicts. So many manifestos and commando raids, torched villages, and amputees that nobody had hated enough to kill. A bit like Ruth, in reaction to all she'd seen, she fed stray children by hand to be sure not a single grain fell to the ground.

I led Otim out to learn if *he* was frightened by the other boy. That would have clinched it; I would have kicked the new boy out of the compound. But no, although they didn't know each other, Otim spoke to him without fear. Twice as big, and burly for a starveling, the creature—who looked like the Wild Man from Borneo, of carnival fame, with muddy hair growing everywhere and a face like an avalanche waiting to happen—held his hand lower than Otim's head to show me his size when he had been stolen, his eyes pointed sideways to avoid mine. He wanted to melt into the woodwork—yes, sleep in the bomb shelter. We had no hose to clean him, so I handed him a pail, motioning for him to improve his appearance, and Otim, to my astonishment, added a few encouraging words. He had a flat reality to him, the physical collectedness of somebody who had killed: but how many?

We joined him shortly in the bomb shelter because a MiG ripped out of the sunset, deafening, to strafe the training camp and release its bombs. Looking for it, you would have been blinded, and it arrived simultaneously with its blast of sound anyway. After passing over, it banked and climbed against the profile of Mount Kinyeti, the highest of the Imatongs, with a treeline above nine thousand feet, snarly, glinty, mocking, to dart back toward Juba, more brutal and unnerving than the Antonov's slowly spiraling deliveries (like a UPS truck, we'd begun to joke). The swelling agitation in the outlying camps, where food had run out, was already hastening my departure, like how startlingly the car was filling up.

After the raid, both of us being out of breath, Ruth and I gravitated into her room, which was homier than the rest. It had a rug and a wall hanging from Iran and Pakistan, a closet improvised from curtains so her clothes could be hung, and a cradle-crib Makundi had built for Leo, when he was not sharing Ruth's bed.

"You should leave," I urged. "Al wants that. Till there's food and meds to distribute and you have a vehicle."

Curtly, she said no, as though she had put that temptation to rest.

"Makundi, no? Isn't he itching to go?"

She said his salary was paid directly to his family by Al, and since his wife was past childbearing age, what was the point of him being there? This made me laugh. Whether because of his evangelical faith or plain affection for Ruth, he had been with her for a decade or more. Once, when she had rented a place in the city but felt herself "outright suicidal," she had sent Makundi on a shopping errand on his bicycle, then started for the airport in her car to fly to the U.S. pronto. Passing him on the road, pedaling back toward what would simply be a cowardly note left in an empty house, "almost broke" her heart, she told me. But she found the States "more teetery" for her health than Africa and "after a hairy spell" bid good-bye to relatives and former friends and fled right back to Nairobi "to save my life." Miraculously her Fiat had not been stolen from the parking lot and Makundi was still holding the fort, awaiting further instructions, though he had received no wages for two months. So the house hadn't been stripped by robbers. Nor had he sold anything, or tippled her Beefeater gin.

"Come," she remarked casually. "Since you're leaving and I some-times confide in you." She took my hand and, shushing the alarm expressed at first by the baby jackal and little Leo, led me to her bed, where she sat down facing me. "We can do our own confession."

She directed my hands under her sweatshirt and to her breasts, always bra-less, as I knew from our laundry line plus, inevitably, the bounce. They were ample, as was her chest cage itself.

"Say, 'Please, miss, may I hold them?'"

"Please, miss, may I hold them?"

"Don't move an inch from where you are," she warned me while undoing my pants. "Say, 'Please, miss,' again."

"Please, miss, again."

"Smart-ass," she answered, massaging my cylinder, but now grasping my balls in her other hand so strongly that I caught my breath.

"Whose are you?"

When I gasped, she repeated her question, both gripping me and massaging me. "Whose are you? Should I stop? I will."

"No."

" 'Please, miss.' You can't have one without the other. This hand and *this* hand. And you don't dare move *your* hands."

"Please, miss," I parroted, clutching her breasts.

"Whose?" she persisted. By rubbing me and squeezing me, she kept my penis alternately stiffening and shrinking, almost to ejaculation but then wilting small and timid again. "Who's your absolute life raft?"

"You!" I groaned.

"Whose are you?"

"Yours!" I begged and grunted.

She laughed and let me remain hard awhile. "I always wanted a clarinet to play with. Will you ever jack off again?" she asked.

"No, ma'am. No, miss."

"Margaret told me you did. She saw it in your wash. She smelled it in your wash. Is that true?"

"Yes, ma'am."

" 'Yes, miss. Please, miss,' " she corrected me. "Though I was right here? Tweak my nipples, please. I like them nibbled."

I started to duck my head to obey, but those weren't her instructions yet, and so she squeezed my balls reprovingly. "I didn't say to."

"No, ma'am."

" 'No, miss.' Do you want me to let you come? Tweak me. Ask me."

"No, miss. Yes, miss, please may I come."

"I want you to suckle me first."

When I rose up for air, she let me harden and then hung a towel on my penis to see how strong it was.

"Say it," she insisted. "But keep your hands on my boobs."

"Please may I come?"

"Life raft," she said. "You're in the water. Hands on boobs. They're all you've got. Whose are you?"

"I'm yours."

" 'Pretty please?' "

"Pretty please with sugar on it."

"And who is never going to jack off again without permission?"

"I guess me."

She laughed and took the towel, milked my penis briefly, and caught what I squirted into its folds.

Exhausted and well "raped," I thanked her and fell asleep. Ruth, however, went and slept in my room of the rectory, I suppose not to feel possessed. In the morning, recovering my cocky personality, I told her she had been scared I would hear her snore.

"Life Raft!" she jeered back.

Still, there wasn't time for us to semaphore a change in our relationship because, by breakfast, and despite a panoramic rainbow in the mists above our coil of the Nile, the Antonov droned over and excreted or disgorged an end-over-end clutch of tumbling bombs, random as usual, and people ran.

"You must tell them," Makundi said, meaning not the bombing but the hunger—an anguish increasing daily—which was what the

Norwegians were gabbling about in Scandinavian on the radio, trying to reach not only their group's area officer but their nation's ambassadors elsewhere on the continent: as were the Maryknolls their mother superior in America. Even the Lutherans, weighing a series of infants in a sling in besieged Juba, and measuring the shriveling flap of flesh under their arms, sounded alarmed.

Chapter 7

• • •

IN AFRICA, WHEN YOU SAY GOOD-BYE IT MAY BE FOR KEEPS, SO THERE
is an extra squeeze in the handshake to register that. Bol had
assembled eighty kids or more in front of our cracked blackboard
with multiplications on it underneath the tamarind tree, his sad, long,
aging face carefully devoid of added expression, as they hollered,
"Saaarreee!" to me.

"Tell them!" urged Ladoku, hurrying up in a frayed, left-behind,
High Church Anglican cassock that he saved for exceptional occa-
sions. Never having been to a city with multiple streets, restaurants,
movies, clothing and magazine shops, he wasn't wistful, like Bol, or
particularly distracted by apprehension about his own safety. He led
a child who was limping badly, almost capsizing, not from an injury
but from some orthopedic problem that even a layman could perceive
might interest a surgeon.

"This isn't a bus," I told him, pointing to the fact that Margaret
was already in the passenger seat, with the paper sacks that were her
luggage and Otim in her lap, the little poleaxed Acholi boy who'd
been forced to eat strips cut from his parents' vital organs, next to the
gearshift; plus Ya-Ya and Nyoka, the two walleyed girls, at sixes and
sevens in the back; and Tongkwoit, the cross-eyed, diminutive Kakwa;
the harelipped Bari boy, Ladu; and the Wild Man from Borneo,

whose name was Oryean and whose hair we had decided to leave like a Fuzzy-Wuzzy's in order to improve his prospects at the early roadblocks, because although he claimed not to care if the soldiers shanghaied him, we didn't believe that.

"It's an ambulance," Ladoku corrected me quietly, as thin as a cormorant. He had been shrewd enough to bring along a couple of mothers, since the boy with the nightmarish hip, for instance, named Pityea, was too young to travel without a parent. The other woman thrust forward a post-toddler who had tripped horribly into a cooking fire and, somehow surviving the burns, needed skin grafts and other medical care. Resigned, I waved them toward the Land Cruiser.

The Dinka major had materialized to observe our departure and nodded at Ladoku. "We are fasting," he agreed.

I was irritated. "If you hadn't killed those four U.N. people, you wouldn't be starving." It was absurd that only children needing surgery and deportees could go, and I put my forefinger to my temple to recapitulate how gratuitously two of the U.N.'s aid experts had been executed. Ladoku looked alarmed on my behalf, but Ruth laughed because she figured that the Dinkas had finally learned that white people are tribal, too. If you killed them, the others got mad. So I was in no danger from the major's anger. And actually, he wasn't mad. He nodded, acknowledging tacitly that that action by his superiors had been a mistake.

Ruth waved, vanishing into her clinic shack. Our few fly-in Baptist doctors—who arrived intermittently, and maybe because of a midlife crisis they'd been having in somewhere such as Little Rock—knew no big wheels east of Arkansas whose strings they could pull, and neither did Ruthie or Al. So it was my ball game, as two soldiers in tiger-camouflage suits cleared me to push on the accelerator and bounce along. Ya-Ya hummed. Margaret joined in. In Nairobi, as anybody knew, there were plenty of street children with webbed fingers or crossed eyes, and nobody's taxi screeched to a halt to take them to a doctor. So how was I going to handle it? I missed Bol; he would have helped. Till the last few minutes, when the major showed up, he might have imagined that he could twist himself into the space for a spare tire in the wheel well and escape. The kids of his who weren't regarded as fighting material were already red-haired from kwashiorkor, bent-boned from rickets, or twitchy and cataleptic as they sat in our class. And me with my hospice—deserted behind me. We had no clout to feed or help anybody. Even the Catholics, with Rome in the wings, had gotten no food in.

Yes, I had my stony nuggets taped uncomfortably inside my money belt, next to my groin; but the pedestrians we passed still blanked out their expressions for fear of who might be in a motor vehicle, where there was nothing civilian money could buy, no rich, no poor, just those who were armed and those who were not. The guerrillas at Nimule, before the bridge, made me step out to show my passport and "Jane's" cardboard visa, but after peering at the forest of disordered faces inside, didn't search the Land Cruiser. Therefore we reached Uganda without incident and, to Margaret's amusement, I changed from the British to the American side of the altogether empty road. But this next stretch, being Lord's Resistance Army territory, was the most dangerous for my two escapees, not to mention Margaret herself, who, like the LRA, was Acholi and thus might hold a prurient interest for them. Because they had no history of killing whites, I was more fearful on my passengers' behalf.

After miles of silence in this nail-biting no-man's-land, we let our breath out in relief as Ugandan army sentries appeared at their forward outpost. Luganda speakers from the capital, they regarded northerners like Margaret as primitives and paid more attention to me, as I used Luganda words for "hospital," *eddwaliro,* and "eyes," *amaaso,* and told my passengers, via Margaret's Acholi, to hop around spryly so they could see nobody was sick with something horrific like Ebola fever. The children, being stiff, were glad to. And we were right to have left the Wild Man from Borneo unshorn, because once they understood that he was ex-LRA they wanted nothing to do with him.

"Gulu," I kept repeating, and "Ruth," till they signaled us through. Margaret smiled broadly. Her daughter, sons, nieces, nephews—more than ten in total, who her next-door neighbor had been feeding— were less than a hundred miles away. But we still had plenty of depopulated country to navigate, with cat-and-mouse rebels from two local groups operating: remnants of both Idi Amin's and Milton Obote's armies who hadn't dared to surrender. So you wondered whether there would be a log blocking the next bend in the road. Once they realized you were not a military vehicle and emerged with their guns to help you move it, they might toy with you. But was this scarier than traveling with Ed over the same wilderness— him two months out of flying school and come to central Africa to pray at full voice to the Lord, with his finger trailing the plane's shadow across the terrain on a map in his lap?

I'd stopped to let the kids relieve themselves. But we had no food. Their hunger nagged me. At a turnoff near Atiak I backed up and went west, instead of south, impulsively, past a concrete prison the government maintained, to another defunct stone church from colonial times, this one manned by a German who offered NGO help to refugees close by.

Felix was in. "Where else would I be?" he asked, and with calming amusement he had Margaret boil up a pot of porridge for everybody to share. A before-his-time graybeard, he let the children ride on a rocking horse that he pretended he'd made for his monkey—which indeed did ride it, but otherwise could swing in two fruit trees as far as the length of a leash clipped to a belt around its waist that slid down a wire between the trees—the first monkey any had seen that wasn't about to be eaten.

"Handy," he said; handy also in English and French. The latter he utilized with Congolese fleeing from Watsa, Aru, Adi, or Dramba who'd managed to travel on foot much farther than we had driven, chancing the buffalo and lion lands, and swimming the Albert Nile. Yet his church had no shell holes, no foxhole alongside, no starvation or training camp immediately nearby. His modesty and equanimity, annealed in Nigerian and Mozambican emergencies, were additional protection when bands of combatants passed in the night. Though sorry about what had befallen Americans like Ed, whose crash at Bunia he had happened to overhear live on his radio scanner, and the unfortunate famine specialist whose leg had been smashed off in the drop zone by a sack of sorghum intended to feed stick-armed Dinka children, he felt a bit bemused by the spectacle of a country endowed with such a surplus of do-gooders that, like grain, it could afford to ship over the disposable ones.

Ya-Ya wanted the monkey passionately now—to cherish, not eat—so Felix explained in pidgin Kakwa-Swahili-Arabic that if she was exceptionally good between here and Nairobi, I would buy her one when we got there. Since I couldn't yet talk to her, I thanked him sincerely, when he told me, for committing me to an inconvenience I didn't desire and implanting in her the idea that her first international city would possess all the charms of a jungle home. He knew me slightly from a sojourn in Malindi, where he spent his breaks, and remarked that, as jammed in as we had been, he'd thought we looked like the car in circuses that all of the clowns pile uncountably out of.

Felix served us goat's milk he bought from his neighbors. "I live on a volcano. We all do, as you know. But, oh, the vegetables I can grow!" he said. "Lava is fertilizer." Foundations sometimes sent their executives to stay with him because it seemed so peaceable in this tan, rolling, half-wooded savannah, as did he, resilient and competent, smoking his pipe like a gentleman farmer, whatever the circumstances. Thus he was able to scribble the name of a lady doctor the Rockefellers liked in Kampala who might prove to be helpful. Linguistics and herpetology were his hobbies here. "But diamonds are a man's best friend," he teased. The bush telegraph had tipped him off to the imminence of a Juba breakout, which would provoke a torrent of refugees, and his German office was responding by shipping a triple order of everything. But would that be enough? he asked, pumping me.

"Ruth, the Norwegians, the Catholics have nothing," I said.

"All the more reason for me to." He called his new housekeeper from the kitchen, or, rather, led me to her, where Margaret was bathing her scraped feet—a wordless Congolese whose life he had probably saved.

I said the closer Ugandan villages, like Larepi, Moyo, Atiak, Palabek, would catch thousands pouring south in the flood, being already known about, as he was not, and the U.N., World Vision, and similar groups who had quit dealing with the SPLA leadership in disgust would come in again, quickly, if Felix was lucky. He was a praying Christian, like a plainclothes monk, and serene in a way that stemmed from a belief that the best you can do does matter, whatever its quantity, and beyond the results.

"Why leave Africa?" he asked when I mentioned Ruth's recalcitrance, though he agreed that "repositioning to the fleshpots" might be advisable. He knew her foibles, but "Saint Peter will like her," he suggested, joking. Like Ruth, he tried not to drink until nightfall, or talk much before he did, so it was not hard to depart, except for the magnetic monkey.

At Atiak, we had to disgorge ourselves from the clown car again for inspection, while the police, who were used to a trickle of LRA escapees, confirmed that my two did speak Acholi and knew the names of hometowns no impostor would have. The chief also welcomed Margaret back with explicit irony that she should have "jumped from our frying pan into Sudan's fire, in the first place." And he wanted to confirm visually that my *eddwaliro* patients were not hemorrhaging, like Ebola victims, but only needed reparative surgery—again with an African twist.

"Why do you whites always save the least fit instead of the most fit? How can any people survive if you just 'Save the Children,' and the crippled ones at that?"

The skinny customs official, who must have been living on air for many months, was still not permitted by the chief to extract a modest bribe from me, in lieu of his unpaid salary, but I laid my hands on his gaunt old shoulders and promised to look into what was happening to it amidst Kampala's bureaucracy. Obviously somebody was pocketing it, since Uganda didn't need a customs inspector at its border with a civil war. He begged me for a ride south so that he could investigate for himself, but Margaret interrupted in Acholi to tell him to display more dignity. The car was full.

We reached Gulu at about six P.M., or twelve, Uganda time, since their twelve-hour calculations begin, logically enough, at equatorial daylight. Margaret excitedly directed me straight to her well-roofed mud hut in a dirt-street suburb. Nobody was expecting her, but she patted the bag her pay was in, so thankful we hadn't been robbed en route, because she would be able to pay the gentleman next door who'd been feeding the children all of this time, as well as their school fees. Two were playing outside. She cried out in relief, opening the door as I braked. We all needed to stretch, so there was a crowd, plus the children inside dashing out, running to fetch others and friends, plus neighbors. Indeed, everyone seemed to have survived, and Margaret briskly became Atta again, or *jjajja omukazi*, "Grand-mother," ceasing to speak English. She examined each—none lost yet to HIV or malaria—hugging them, and also the elderly neighbor who had made sure they all shared a big wooden bowl of *posho* once or twice a day, as well as some fruit, for the values that porridge didn't contain. He was a practical-looking person unfazed by so much hubbub, but pleased to be praised and paid. She was promising new clothes while weeping because of course individual children reminded her of her dead sisters, brothers, even her own two eldest, who had died of AIDS, leaving their offspring for Margaret to raise.

I was back in the world of AIDS, after not being preoccupied with it. The Sudan's war had kept most infected people out of the zone we'd been in, but within a few minutes I noticed that several youngsters clustered around were not healthy. They weren't wasted from starvation, or fascinated by a motor vehicle, like the crowds of kids where we'd come from. With the whole neighborhood gathering to welcome Margaret, I couldn't tell whether they were orphans or belonged to someone, but their stumbling, discolored emaciation reminded me of Nairobi's street children who were dying of AIDS. Inside Margaret's hut, one boy had not been able to come out. Crying, she hugged him where he was lying and gave him a piece of the candy we'd bought when entering town. The children, by creating a hierarchy to govern the place, had kept it remarkably orderly, for a home to as many as ten little personages.

It was quite mesmerizing, how in soul as well as body they had survived as a de facto family with just the food doled out daily by the guy next door, who, addressing me as "sir," told me he was a retired policeman. But early night had suddenly descended. I was nervous about where my other charges and I were going to sleep. Since Margaret's joy and worry absorbed her, the neighbor recognized the problem, slid into my passenger seat, and we drove to the reception compound of the social agency for Lord's Resistance Army escapees, while he explained in Acholi to Oryean, the Wild Man from Borneo, that the police were going to protect him, that here everybody else had been under sentence of death by those crazies, too, and therefore in this sanctuary the reign of terror was over for him. A blond Dutch therapist (I thought of Bol's lost love) was summoned by the guard at the gate for additional reassurance, the guard and the retired policeman meanwhile translating.

Thus I was able to unload the older boy—but not Otim, the frail, small one, who, devastated by Margaret's abandoning him for her own family, clung to me, raucous and horrified that retribution for all the bad he'd done must now be at hand. Luckily, the exhausted but pretty Dutchwoman, the compound guard, and even my new friend already understood approximately what graphic horrors the poor child must imagine he deserved punishment for.

"Look," she said, "keep him with you until tomorrow." When—nodding at Ya-Ya—I asked her, by the by, if there might be an eye surgeon attached to the hospital in town, she, with her hand at her sweaty collar, raised her brows like a burlesque comedian.

The retired policeman obliged me by taking Otim in his arms as we drove to the Gulu Hotel to see if one of their cottages was available for all of us to crowd into, but nothing was: just a room for me. The two women I'd brought from the war zone, with the child who'd been burned and the other child with orthopedic difficulties, hadn't visited such a large town before, or any foreign country, so they pleaded with me in sign language not to have to trust the old cop to take them off somewhere else to spend the night. Instead, he arranged through a friend among the security guards for all of them to sleep right in my Land Cruiser in a far corner of the parking lot, once they'd gotten a bite to eat. Not knowing Dinka, Arabic, or Bari, he couldn't speak to them directly, but he signaled significantly that the soldiers here might feel trigger-happy if they wandered anywhere in the dark. Somebody then gave him a lift home; and I had the room blessedly to myself for a spell—bathing, boozing, watching CNN via the satellite hookup. I did try going to the bar but found my black-and-blue sentiments too close to the surface—I turned beery and teary when a stranger asked where I'd been. I had Ruth's, Father Leo's, and the Maryknolls' letters to mail as soon as I got to Kampala, but none of my own. So the floodgate opened. I wrote my mom, and to my former wife. Then came a timid knock. It was Ya-Ya with the little LRA boy, Otim, sobbing; he could neither sleep nor abide his frightening dreams. Having no twin bed in the room, I pulled the cushions off the armchair for them to use as pillows on the floor and muted the television set, which even so was miracle enough to quiet him right away. We all fell asleep at about the same time with it flickering blue and white; or he and I did. Ya-Ya may have stayed awake in order to marvel some more.

By morning the strain caught up with me. I simply didn't want to get up; had breakfast brought to the room and sent Ya-Ya out with money for the others, while the little boy, cross-legged, safe in the corner, watched the TV and ate flatbread with mango jam. Truth to tell, my mind was fixed on that Dutch NGO girl in her twenties in the unironed work shirt and shapeless jeans, her face so tired, but so very nice! Was she lonely? After reserving my room for another night, I soaked again in the tub. Eventually, we all swung by Margaret's zinc-roofed *tukl* to see how she was doing—she had never seemed happier!—and to ask if she wouldn't take on the care of little Otim for a while, as he adjusted. But I was secretly delighted when she declined because it meant we could go on to the camp for rehabilitating child soldiers, where the Dutch lady should be on duty. I'd dreamed, indeed, that I was traveling through the channels of my own amputated leg toward a meeting with her, then reached her blond wreath of shoulder-length curls, and her kind smile, to confess that her shipment of grain had broken and spilled in crashing into me.

The guards, a grumpy pair, remembered the minor relief their supervisor had felt yesterday, when I hadn't delivered a whole carload of damaged kids but just the one Wild Man from Borneo. Now why were we back? I sat in the car till the Ugandan director was called, then got out and asked him to bring the Dutchwoman over, please. The little boy would be less fearful of her: "The LRA doesn't have any Europeans."

He laughed, and she did appear, in work boots but an expensive Indian scarf, and swiftly recognized the hunger in my eyes and face, but also the reality of little Otim's plight. We each took one of his hands, with Ya-Ya accompanying us, because of course he was used to her, and her Madi language, in any case, was linguistically close to his native Acholi. Several barracks stood about but also a special reception shack with battered toys on the tables, donated clothes in a pile, and a winking TV to watch. We led him to a corner where he could sit securely on the floor with Ya-Ya, choosing his playthings. Oryean, the Wild Man from Borneo, in a new outfit, though shorn of his locks and deloused, was fetched, so Otim could see that nothing terrifying had happened to him. They shared some USAID surplus cheese, an intriguing taste.

"My husband will come," the Dutchwoman said. "It's what you call nepotism? He's the doctor. We stay six months." Registering my disappointment, she touched my hand sympathetically. "You'll be in Nairobi soon."

He did come in—the usual brisk good guy in the early echelons of a medical career—bringing crayons and a sketchbook, and examined our child with an expert's lack of intimidation while showing Otim the colors and how freely he could use them. He glanced at Ya-Ya also, who was interested in the crayons, but she fell outside of these people's authority because she hadn't been a prisoner of the LRA, or anyone else's sex slave, either. They often got child warriors who had been traumatized by serving in Congo's surreal militias, as well.

"She'd like it," he remarked, giving her an extra coloring book. "In Amsterdam I have a friend . . ." he added wistfully, referring to Ya-Ya's strabismus.

"Anybody closer?" I said.

"No, we're new. Try Doctors Without Borders. They're in Kampala."

While Otim was engrossed in drawing, alongside his wife and Ya-Ya, the two of us walked back to the car, where he could look at the rest of the kids. "My friend could, in one morning . . ." he intoned ruefully, of the other problem eyes and the cleft palate. The burned girl and the boy with pelvic problems "should be flown to Europe," he said. We stared at each other, talking of inoculations and the Ebola outbreak in Masindi, down the road. Okay, so she had a nice husband: so I'd be watching CNN again tonight. We drank coffee as Oryean, Ya-Ya, and the Dutchwoman led Otim to a play area outdoors, fenced next to a barracks, where he could view other Lord's Resistance Army captives who had been freed in recent military operations by the Ugandans or else had escaped on their own, in case any set off a terrified reaction in him. He didn't recognize any of them, however. Neither had Oryean, the two probably having been marched farther north by their units.

"All for the best," murmured the woman, whose practice in Holland focused on childhood abuse. The morning warmed into a civilized interlude of considerate conversation; earnest although dead-end radio inquiries about Ruthie and the Norwegians, whom they vaguely knew; and some playtime for my carload of remaining kids. We settled Otim into what we hoped might become a healing phase of his young life, with minimal tears. Not that there could have been many of those. Crying had brought a death sentence in the LRA, unless perhaps it was amusing the adults.

I wasn't dealing with gross evil, like the Dutch couple and the half dozen African counselors and staff members at this center. Just walleyes and cross-eyes, thank god. And the cryptic note of worry transmitted in the Norwegian surgeon's voice was no longer a front-burner anxiety of mine. But back at the Hotel Gulu, I felt lonesome, even dilettantish, and rather sorry I'd stayed over for this spare day, though I did accomplish a swim in the pool, play handball with somebody or other with substantially cultivated biceps, then conquer my constipation, and tilt a few beers with another British bloke with the agenda, I suppose, of sounding me out—while letting my entourage enjoy the miracle of hot running water and moving pictures on the TV in my bare room. They'd need to sleep in the car again, after all, and would seldom eat as well, ever after. In the evening the same ingratiating man snapped my picture who had done so with Craig. That smile you might later see from your dungeon cell.

— ∞ —

We got safely past the bridge over the roaring Victoria Nile at Karuma Falls, and beyond the turnoffs to Atura, Lira, and Masindi, with additional roadblocks, by afternoon. Ya-Ya's errant eye pinwheeled at the spectacle, the tiers of scenery. With Margaret gone, she and the Dinka girl who had the same problem sat next to me in front, and the two mothers, with the four other children, behind. Not one of them, now, I shared a language with. Nor did the soldiers at roadblocks, once we left Acholi land. And my passengers didn't know Luganda or Swahili, the capital's lingoes, apart from English. At the green-and-red outskirts of Kampala—tilty hills, tilty shacks, gaudy billboards, kids who brandished bananas, not the poignance of a rib cage—I named our destination to the police as Mulago Hospital, the big one by the university. This was convincing but not true. Yet as we continued, I remembered that I did have Felix's friend there to look up, Betty Something, the Rockefeller Foundation's favorite, a doctor I, too, had tippled with at a hotel bar when she was with some visiting firemen one time, NGO medical people, and she had told them the hilarious, high-pitched story of being flown by the Rockefellers from the furnace of central Africa straight to their conference retreat, a most gorgeous and ancient palace overlooking Lake Como, at Bellagio, near Milan's airport, in Italy. The confab was to discuss Third World emergencies, and she had been assigned—this simmering, stocky, put-upon woman whose hands most days were emptying ambulances—a room in a Renaissance castle with a hundred-foot drop-off out her window, then hundreds more from the nearest cliff face down to the azure water, and a billion-dollar vista stretching straight toward the snow-tipped Alps, to reward her for the anguish of her ordinary job. Some passing expatriate must have noticed her here and put her name on the list, maybe somebody in this group I had fallen in with in the Fairway's lounge.

But she'd cried out in a strangled voice, that night I'd met her: "Didn't those Rockefellers know you can throw yourself out of a window, like that, when you go right cold-turkey from here to there? I was up all night shivering!"

Betty was a Batooro from Fort Portal, near the Zaire border, and dubious about all figures of authority, black or white—Amin had killed two of her brothers—with a likeably strident voice and no interest in money beyond the necessities. Consequently, she was a ward doctor, not in private practice. As we wound through the suburbs—past Makerere University's invitingly arboreal hill, with the squat, unlovely hospital at its base—I remembered that, yes, Betty had been the name she went by with whites, whatever her African persona was with other friends. So, making a U-turn, I negotiated the gate by wielding the name "Betty" with a subtle tilt of the head to indicate my passenger load. Next, parking in the staff lot as if I were an expatriate doctor, I got everybody out of the car in order to employ a full-court press. The combination of their obvious infirmities and my officious white skin afforded us entry to the huge, untidy hodgepodge of a public ward of AIDS, TB, dysentery, and malarial sufferers, and every other kind of dying person, where Betty worked.

Peremptorily she accosted me, nevertheless, but paused as I assured her that she recognized me from the Fairway Hotel, and from Protestants Against Famine, and the organization in Germany that funded Felix, near Atiak, and the Dutch twosome in Gulu, and the Maryknolls, and Father Leo, and Norwegian People's Aid, which staffed the SPLA's battlefield hospital, and Norwegian Church Aid, which cared equally much about the southern Sudanese but had pulled out in political disgust at the SPLA's leadership. Maybe, I suggested, her own foundation funders had a program for reparative surgery such as the burned Dinka girl and orthopedic boy needed. I pulled out lots of stops, to her evident amusement, but the weightiest was probably that the mothers of these two kids were next to me. Not that she didn't have to turn away dozens of desperate parents in any given week; but these moms could nurse their kids themselves— *that* was the pressing shortage—and scrounge up food for them to eat, in conjunction with my pledge to somehow produce some white funding eventually for the operations.

"I know where you stay, if I have to come after you," she told me, and instructed the two Dinka women via sign language to scrub all around and make up two adjoining cots at an extreme margin of the ward where charity patients were stashed. Ya-Ya showed them how to do that, from her experience at wrestling with sheets at my little hospice in Loa. They themselves would sleep on the floor next to their children's beds and earn their keep in the kitchen. The bubble and boil of a two-hundred-bed ward didn't overly disconcert Ya-Ya; and Betty, being a pragmatic workaholic, noticed this and gripped the girl's chin in both hands with a disarming smile to study the awry cant of her bad eye. She then examined the other girls' eyes as swiftly, too.

"If you weren't a nice guy, I wouldn't give you the time of day. You think I'm not busy?" she asked, swinging her finger across an arc encompassing a continent of beds. She pretended to kick my butt, but changed her mind as I now presented the harelipped boy.

"I know somebody who can sew him up tomorrow, if I twist his arm. We'll bill you for it," she said.

The boy being confused and scared, she stroked him. We laughed, clearing it up because the two Dinka mothers had now achieved their toehold in Kampala, and had each other for company, though no common language with Betty or anybody else around. The boy, although a Bari, knew pidgin Dinka, so we signaled that he should stick close to them. And Ya-Ya hugged him, speaking in Madi, which may be about as close to Bari as Norwegian is to Swedish, while touching his mouth, which Betty was magically going to heal. Betty herself pointed at a slot on the floor vacant enough to accommodate a half-grown person such as him—whereupon he seemed to understand that, though still scary, this might be the culmination of why he had been transported so far.

Pulling out of the hospital compound, I felt like a con man, to have cleared the back of my car so efficiently, courtesy of a hero lady, which was what she was. We had both known, however, that the Dinkas of the SPLA, just as they had the power to kidnap and murder deserters here, could prevent the pair of women I'd delivered to Betty from falling into harm's way in Kampala, if I never saw them again. Only the three barely pubescent girls with crossed or truant eyes were left. I bought them take-out suppers before we got to my hotel, so they would be content to stay in another parking lot for the night while I lived it up, as I intended to do, after tipping a security guard to watch out for them. Whereupon—reminding the bellhop that he had a cousin who knew me (like her, he was a university graduate)—I bathed, handed my laundry to the chambermaid, and went to the bar, then the dining room. As a long shot, I did ask the desk clerk whether any expatriate medical types or foundation bigwigs had registered who I ought to chat up. But we were a midprice place where Africans and front-line NGO personnel stayed, not the folks who wrote checks. A waitress slept on a mattress behind the bar during the wee hours instead of going home, in case of a room-service call, so the management wouldn't need to pay a night shift. That informality meant less gloss, lower prices, and permitted me to park my refugee children on the premises but off the books. More important, you didn't feel the reverberations imbuing some of Kampala's best hotels, which Idi Amin had used as torture chambers during his reign, when part of his insanity was that he wished foreign businessmen and diplomats visiting his country to hear the agony of his prisoners being sliced, burned, electrified, or having their fingers, toes, and teeth torn out, all night long, on the next floor down.

Remarkably soon, the bellboy's cousin appeared at my table, in time for the soup. On a previous visit I'd given her a cell phone, and now paid what her taxi had cost. Small-boned, delicately featured, from a tribe that was brown-skinned, she was wearing a maroon blouse and lavender slacks and had been fashioning ceramics for a living for the tourist stores, except that, with the latest Ebola scare and Uganda's general reputation, there weren't enough tourists. Recently, therefore, she'd begun painting logos on Toyotas, according to whomever the dealer managed to sell a vehicle to. But he hadn't enough volume, either. And rustling up a marriage was ever trickier because AIDS had heaped nieces and nephews upon every bread-winner, making them more skittish about formalizing any relation-ship, even when they were already contributing to the support of their blood offspring, and still more prone to marry in a direction where money lay. That's what the father of her own son had done, Angela said, as—fastidiously but thoroughly—she ate everything that was served. His other principal girlfriend's family had lost fewer adults to "slim," so he'd married *her,* after some dithering, because Angela was the person he loved. Angela's parents had died, leaving her just their house, to be shared with brothers and sisters, and no cash on hand or salaried prospects, and lately, although he was a white-collar junior executive, money from him to spend on their boy had dribbled to a halt.

No paper trail of paternity existed. In her lateish twenties, and while planning to have no other kids, she still needed school fees and clothes for this one, not to mention her youngest sister, not much past Ya-Ya's age. Sadly, she smiled, with an adorable crimp to her mouth that expressed intelligence. Buying a new blouse like what she'd put on to pique the jaundiced libido of an itinerant like me subtracted from *his* wardrobe. "And that pains me." I said she needn't have, squeezing her hand. She moved it under the table to rest on her knee and asked why, if clothes weren't important to me, I wasn't with the chambermaid? But prettiness was oddly irrelevant in this age of HIV. To be lucky was not whether you turned heads, but whether you had contracted the virus, and by limiting her outings to foreigners she met in the hotel gift shops that carried her pottery, she hadn't really tipped into prostitution yet. They admired her crafts, bought a piece, and entered into respectful conversation, offering the niceties of a date, under a protective roof where she had friends, in case the guy turned ugly.

I did bring her outside to meet my girls, to be sure they hadn't locked themselves out of the car, or snuck off downhill toward the dangers of the city. She was amused, yes, yet too accustomed to the doomed importunities of Kampala's myriad street children to be as charmed by Ya-Ya and company as I could have wished. I suppose if she'd been more touched—Uganda has been scalded by so many massacres that its people are cauterized—I might have been the candidate she was scouting for: the mannerly white man ten years older, of no settled residence, who in exchange for the privilege of playing with her small, comely, coffee-colored breasts and a daily hand job, would support her and her son.

I had gazed at her dimly, equivocal smile, adorable throat, and attentive eyes—her hair tempting my fingers to reach out and tangle themselves in it—over our dinner dishes, until with a widening grin she gained enough confidence to mention a kiln she needed for her business, knowing where just the right one was for sale, and also how a friend of hers had gotten an exhibition of her art financed at a gallery near the Sheraton for only a thousand dollars or so, put up by an Englishman she was living with. I was noncommittal because I wanted her in my arms as soon as possible for a lengthy bout of safe-sex frottage.

The next day, I drove to the Doctors Without Borders compound, on another hillside overlooking the town. It had an unpretentious staff of one expatriate and one in-country administrator, both female, plus a guard and driver. I led my girls straight into the office and told them Betty needed help, too, with the three other children I'd left at the hospital yesterday.

"This is a post office. Our doctors are in the field. With the Ebola, the cholera, the cataracts," the European woman said. But she did step from behind her desk to shake hands with each of my girls and called up Betty, whom she knew, to register her moral support. "I'll put on my thinking cap," she told me. A team was operating in Masindi, another at Mbale, at the moment; not a help. I wanted to start for Kenya. I was antsy. She kindly called the office there, but the knowledgeable person was out.

"We're in the field. We don't work in the capitals," she explained, rummaging through her assistant's desk for a list of orphanages in both cities that NGOs supervised, where attention might be paid to such solvable problems as an awry eye.

I wanted to unload my gold, as well. Not as dicey a commodity as diamonds, but the girls might be useful in the room to distract a dealer who was considering strong-arming me. Probably I had a pound of nuggets distributed in the money belt underneath my baggy pants, around my groin, and I double-parked outside a couple of the leading jewelry shops to tell the owners to come to my hotel room with cash to get a gander at it. They weren't smugglers but would fashion baubles, keeping the natural shape of the gold I'd secured, for the carriage trade. Meantime, I'd enlisted the chamber-maid to buy the girls changes of clothing, while they washed in the staff's bathroom. Thus they looked nice and spruce when the dealers, like two stooped usurers, showed up. I spread my nuggets, one by one, on the table. Mzei, the senior and more curious of the men, sniffed and tasted each bit of conglomerate the gold was embedded in. I hadn't tried to knock it loose because I knew from a jeweler's standpoint the geological setting might add to the aesthetics. Instead, I swayed my finger fetchingly to indicate how such a gnarly, natural artifact might hang down in some slinky young woman's cleavage. He smiled; kept a "panther" around his shop to model his wares. He knew I was an NGO freelancer who shuttled food to conflict areas, but he quizzed me as to where these placer deposits were. I only returned his smile.

Mzei weighed and bought the pieces he'd tasted for about three times what I'd paid for them, planning of course to mark them up again by a factor magnified more than that. The other dealer purchased a few, but not by bidding against him. I realized they must have arranged beforehand not to allow me to create an auction. He seemed not to have tasted as many rock formations as Mzei in his career, but understood instead that the girls should be a better clue, since I was playing my cards close to my vest. He tried some Congolese-French patois on them, such as might be spoken in the areas diamonds usually came from. No dice. Then Swahili; Luganda; Rwandan French. Nope. Then Juba Arabic. "Ah!" they both said, when the girls' faces lit up.

The tall one they now recognized as being Dinka, but Ya-Ya was more of a puzzle. "The Kit!" they agreed, when she spoke a little Madi in answer to him. That must be where the gold they bought from SPLA go-betweens also drifted in from. "You've been to the Kit, not Ituri," Mzei told me. "Good minerals and not so scary." Ituri's conflict diamonds were indeed dangerous to fetch.

Liking women, he teased Ya-Ya by showing her how the diamond on his pinkie would look on hers. He and the other guy disappointed me by not competing against each other, just nodding like bridge players at each piece I produced to indicate which of them should get first dibs. I warned them I had friends in Nairobi I could sell to, but Mzei laughed. "Same here."

"Okay. Let me ask you this." I'd been to his house once for sweet-meats after a diamond deal I'd done with some Chinese who may or may not have been connected to him. It was a secure, incognito villa with overstuffed sofas and lots of family photos on the furniture, in an unpretentious neighborhood where he told me he'd moved after the previous owners had been killed by Idi Amin—you didn't buy places then; you just moved in.

"If one of your daughters had this girl's eye problem, who would you call?"

Mzei was surprised at the question, but we were through our business, and I had cash, he had the stones, so he picked up the hotel phone and, round-faced, squat, and easygoing, spoke in the Luganda language for a couple of minutes to some physician or office assistant. "Fully booked," he announced afterward, shaking his head. "At this primitive juncture we are dependent upon you humanitarians."

We finished our coffee, as Mzei and his friend examined the eleven nuggets of gold-flecked rock I'd brought, rolling them in their fingers for the view from different angles, and I pocketed the three thousand–plus. "Double-oh-seven," he called me. It was small pota-toes, but hydraulic machinery could soon be extracting three million, or thirty, or three hundred million dollars a year for investors when the war wound up, and since foreigners would be needed to invest in that machinery, for the first time it occurred to me, through Mzei's appraising gaze, that I might be employable to bird-dog for a mining company, despite my zero geological training. In Zaire, with diamonds, it was different: huge open pits of mud where prisoners of war labored like slaves, digging their lives away, whose location mili-tias fought over. I'd met white men willing to stomach witnessing such scenes of horrific servitude in order to buy gems in bulk, but I couldn't have. Mine were just stray stones a villager might have stum-bled across, alone in a bog in the forest, or that had been acquired by a shopkeeper from some dollar-a-day free miner who had swallowed it as soon as he saw it in the dirt, then vomited or shit it out when he got home.

Somebody would come for me on a motorbike, over a jungle range, to where my trucks had been delivering beans or lentils, and I'd perch on the back, cling to this stranger, and be bumped over two or three dozen miles of ridgeline on trails no car could have traversed, to see this storekeeper and haggle awhile and get dysentery from his hospitality, then be brought back to my starting point, wondering if I'm going to be shot off the motorcycle en route, and board my NGO truck with my intestines bursting, for Kampala, if I can bluff through immigration at Katwe or Fort Portal without being stripped.

So, that's diamond smuggling, if you're not one of the creeps who fly in and out of Kisangani in a Lear or a Buffalo. Mzei and his friend bought me an early beer on the Fairway's terrace, while they tapped me for information about the siege of Juba, the politics of hunger in the camps, and gossip from Nairobi, which for them, too, was a hub. Gems trickled into Kampala from disaster zones the way the gem had been formed anyhow: under great pressure, underground. Generals in the Ugandan army brought them in, or Rwandan generals, Zambian generals, Zairean generals, tribal officers, and ragged crooks and fugitives. The crucible of dictatorship had smelted out the straight arrows. However, Mzei didn't do much export; for Interpol stuff you went to a different hotel terrace.

I tried a few more phone calls, but Kampala is not my town, and cripples lie splayed on the hot sidewalk all day to attract coins as a result of several simple problems that surgery done long ago could have solved. My mood had lightened after the night's rest, and I let the girls enjoy the novelties of my room—TV, shower bath—not relegating them to the parking lot. Ya-Ya even wanted to continue with our arithmetic and spelling lessons. Instead, I led them downtown to observe the traffic, so Nairobi would seem less intimidating. I was dreading a phone call from Betty at the hospital saying, *Pick these folks up,* but my phone didn't ring. Al was ebullating about his daughter starting private school, when we talked. He was in Africa for keeps, but losing interest in our agency, it seemed to me: whether because he was angling for an upgrade to a better NGO or wanted to go into business. He'd told me he was already doing some cold-calling, because there were offshore investment funds looking for money—which wouldn't be riskier, he pointed out, than leaving your nest egg in Kenya. On his advice I'd wired what I considered a wager to the Channel Islands. After you'd sounded out all of your friends, he said, you merely looked in the daily papers for who might be scoring somehow somewhere and gave them a jingle. It was hairy in Africa. He'd arrived as a "water expert," traveled all over, till he'd tired of sewage. You didn't sit still. If Nairobi bored you, you could try Lagos, or real anarchy in Sierra Leone. Africa will best you, if that's what you want, but it helps being a white man, and especially a Harlem landlord's son, as Al was, whose father for years had brought him along on rent-collection days.

Al faxed me official instructions to bring Ya-Ya, Nyoka, and Tongkwoit into Kenya for necessary ophthalmological surgery, on Protestants Against Famine stationery, for the purpose of showing at the border checkpoint tomorrow. But I wondered what I would do if the officials said no. That hungry, teasing waitress who was nursing a baby at home, who I'd given a chicken dinner to on the trip in, joined us and the chambermaid with a room-service supper for everybody before the girls went back to the parking lot to sleep in the Toyota. I visited the bar, talking to a Zimbabwean in town on business. When Angela showed up to see if I was feeling horny again, I shook off her cocked eyebrow like a pitcher rejecting a catcher's sign. Chastened, she sat alone in a booth while I planned for an early bedtime, then winced when the Zimbabwean bought her a drink, since I'd warned her avuncularly against having sex with African strangers the night before. I was rehearsing my speech for the immigration station tomorrow. A condescending leniency was generally displayed to white "missionaries," as regards their quirky, quixotic gambits, by all concerned: which I hoped was going to apply to these paperless girls. If smart Ya-Ya had been the only one, she could have wriggled past the controls among the fat market women who strolled back and forth through the boundary slot with bundles balanced on their heads, and just the occasional whack by an officer's cane on a particularly, temptingly waggly, overripe rump. For a thousand shillings one of these ladies might have sworn Ya-Ya was her daughter and given her part of a load to tote.

―――⊶⊷⊷⊶―――

In the morning I checked out rather crabbily because nobody at the desk could translate into these girls' tribal languages what I needed to tell them in order to prepare for what lay ahead. They seemed to expect more larking, although apprehensive at the same time at being carried ever farther from home. Their errant eyes, flicking away in habitual embarrassment whenever you looked at them, were not transparent windows, as many children's are, but trouble spots, and to glance at all three faces at once was a bit like watching a billiards game. But they leaned against and bumped each other, twined their arms and hugged as the car swayed, chatting in a mix of Madi, Dinka, and Juba's dialect of Arabic.

At Jinja, we stopped to look at Owen Falls, where Lake Victoria's weight at its lip powers Uganda's turbines, and where fish plants were drying loads of protein, copper was being smelted, and tobacco, plywood, beer, and sugar processed: quite wonderful, if you've never seen a factory before. They were riveted, when I got them out of the car for a practice inspection—yet not actually knowing what I would have told them if I had been able to communicate. Tall Nyoka acted like a leader, perhaps because Dinkas always do, feeling superior to the more sedentary, agricultural tribes but not rubbing it in. Ya-Ya, whose name Margaret had said meant "floating," "free spirit," or "flighty" in Madi, was interested in independence, not leadership, whereas Tongkwoit accepted the fate of the handicapped to be downtrodden.

We drove another seventy miles, to Bumulimba and Busia, where the trucks and buses were lined up in the heat, and ate a front-seat lunch of passion fruit, baked corn, and shish kebabs bought through the window from vendors whose whole livelihood was the slow-moving queue. I made the children wipe their faces carefully so they looked neat in their new clothes, as if securely under the care of an international agency: perhaps even in transit to America—who would quibble with that? I peered through the dusty clamor for an official who might recognize me, but I was not enough of a regular, and my greenhorn notion of having the Land Cruiser washed in the hotel garage last evening so that its white paint and PAF logo stood out bright and clear appeared less authentic than the battered exteriors of the leatherier expatriates' vehicles: real missionaries and "old Africa hands" who could have gone through the barrier with a passportless albino, though they themselves looked hardly white anymore.

Many lorries were empty, returning from Rwanda, Congo, or Uganda to Nairobi and Mombasa after a delivery, and didn't require intensive inspection. Just the paperwork and double-checking that a peek in the back provided, and they were waved on. But every bus or van disembarked its passengers laboriously, with boxes, bags, then everybody lining up patiently, while the market women sashayed past, anticipating an approving whack.

A fixer in civvies approached, for speedy facilitation, and I gave him my sundowner grin. But when he saw I just had my own credentials and car registration and Al's letter for documentation, he wished us good luck and moved to the car behind me. The uniformed young man who followed, eventually, had a sense of humor. My "harem" did not possess papers? he asked. No passports or travel clearance? He looked at each girl carefully, while I thought to bring out my SPLA "visa," validated by "Jane," permitting me in rebel-held areas, to prove where I'd been. No, I was not transporting them into Kenya for purposes of prostitution ("Black olives?" he said), but medical care, clearly; and, as a recent language major at the University of Nairobi, he happened to be intrigued to hear the relation of Nyoka's Dinka words to Kenya's Samburu or Masai languages, plus Ya-Ya's ignorance of Swahili yet responsiveness to Arabic in rudimentary form. He confirmed with a flashlight, poking under the car and under the dirty seats, that I'd been bouncing about the bush a good deal, despite the incongruous washing I'd paid for.

"They're like birds, aren't they?" he observed, after discovering the girls didn't know English, and referring to their eyes' swiveling. "What are your plans for them?"

"My plans are to fix them up properly and bring them back on my next trip."

"To build the new South Sudan on their slender shoulders! But I'm going to assume you're an honorable man. An honest Protestant Against Famine!" he exclaimed with a laugh, and stamped my reentry back into Kenya, waving us through. We'd been lucky in our inspector. A trim college graduate with a family doubtless positioned to pull strings and land him this job.

Sweating, we enjoyed sodas and chocolate in Busia, alongside the hustlers and market women whom I'd wanted to secret Ya-Ya among to attempt the crossing. But I noticed their tribal differences were quite marked, in color, physiognomy, and build; and her wandlike eyeball gyrations would have drawn extra attention to these. The officers would have questioned her, found her incomprehensible, and we'd be in trouble now, not Nairobi-bound.

Smugglers were offering me watches and stuff, whichever direction I might be headed, figuring that no undercover cop would be embroidered with the company I had. The girls habitually looked upward a lot—I suppose to avoid meeting the snicker in other people's eyes—but this was catching, and the sensation of casting your gaze up, watching the sky even in daylight outside a roadside café, was like leaning back in a planetarium. You saw too much, in other words, in a way, as if, disoriented, you took in all of the stars at once because, in concert with them, your eyes or consciousness had become unhitched.

We hit the road and, ignoring hitchhikers, reached Nairobi past nightfall. I aimed for the storefront shelter for street children, not knowing where else to go, though no beds were available there, either. The girls slept in the car yet again but, not being used to softer conditions, regarded this as a continuation of their adventure. I slept head to foot in my sleeping bag in half of the director's bed, since his wife was on hardship leave in the States.

Chapter 8

• • •

I SLEPT LATE, WAKING TO PLAYGROUND SHOUTS AND BALL-ON-THE-
wall impacts. My girls had already picked out new outfits for
themselves from a bale of church-shipped clothing from Dallas or
someplace. I was so tired I made Al come to debrief me at the church
office down the street, where cots had been found for Ya-Ya and
company, and to pick up the Land Cruiser, which needed a lube job,
oil change, springs replaced.

Al's wife was the sort of spectacularly beautiful Somali woman
who could have been posing for leggy accessories ads in front of the
Carlyle Hotel on Madison Avenue if she had married another kind
of American, instead of cuddling AIDS orphans on her lap in the
Kibera slums of Nairobi. But any man who would have taken her to
Madison Avenue wouldn't have discovered and rescued her from
death in Mogadishu, in the first place. When other whites ogled her
and suggested a modeling career, she remembered that. She had
appeared in shoots done for East African publications, or hotels in the
Seychelles, displaying the unflappability of a woman rescued from a
warlord's concubinage (boosted surreptitiously into an NGO's chartered plane at a bare airstrip), who knew she never need worry where
her next luncheon yogurt was going to come from. Nonetheless, she

wouldn't have been so unflappable with our street children, as well, if she hadn't once been in Mogadishu herself.

I groaned, though, when we were alone, telling Al and her that I was beginning to find discouraging the task of teaching the alphabet to kids thinner than hunger, who might be dead of AIDS before they had occasion to use it.

"Well, Ruth enjoyed your company," he answered dryly, as if to pose an alternative, and handed me my check. "I'll send you back when her ship comes in. Or you can do a balloon safari for some Japs." He said she sounded unchanged on the radio, "except in survival mode"—which, of course, was how you would be when you had neither food nor medicines to dispense and a hundred thousand refugees around who needed them.

My girls were learning the rules of hopscotch and soccer from others in the courtyard. But who knew such a surgeon? – Al muttered to himself. Triage ward doctors, yes, that you carried a child to who'd been hit in traffic. The phones were out in much of the city, so even a brainstorm today wouldn't have solved the puzzle. The hangdog middle-aged Oklahoman who ran this shelter and soup kitchen for street kids, with the Swarthmore interns, didn't know an eye surgeon any more than we did (and, it turned out, his wife had told him she was going to stay in America if the interns didn't leave). But Al was smarter than me. He remembered Beryl: "That San Francisco divorcée you were shtupping in Karen. Why don't you take them over there? She might pay for it."

I yawned because, although it was a pretty smart idea, I didn't have the energy right now for the winsome type of phoning that would be required, and to clean the girls up to look adorable, and myself enough to remind Beryl why she had once accepted me as a housemate. In the meantime I wanted to get back to my rooftop swimming pool at the New Stanley, after mailing everybody's missives and stopping at the bank, and then to my hideaway across the street at the Arab's pocket hotel, where I could lie like a lizard on the balcony in dishabille and give myself a Tusker headache. Tension had wrung me out.

First, beside the pool, Alitalia and Swissair crews were rusticating with margaritas, the pilots inevitably outnumbered by the stewardesses, who looked immaculate even in their bathing suits and cover-up: invulnerable, too, against anything Africa might throw at them because, of course, no matter what happened *they* would make the plane. At an airport besieged by frightened and stranded expatriates trying to escape a city afire with mutiny and riots, *they'd* be on their way to Fiumicino, along with the luckiest few. I remembered, on the Nile, watching with Ruth as the Antonov circled our area for a target to bomb, while, three times as high, tiny but potent, like a platinum cross, the daily British airways flight from Heathrow crossed the sky.

Like me, each stewardess was a sizer-up, yet quite often lonely travelers themselves, maybe wanting a human touch, someone else's hand to rub the sun cream on, before they went down in the elevator alone again. That sun cream—that creamy internationalism, to Paris tomorrow. I was asking a petitely energetic Italian in the deck chair next to mine if she couldn't smuggle my Ya-Ya through passport control in Milan, describing the reasons why.

"Half the continent!" she replied. "But how cute. I wish." She laughed and touched my arm, presuming my appeal to have been a fruitless form of flirtation. Yet I realized after her departure that it really wasn't: rather, more like a preoccupation. Back at the Arab's, not having expected to see Beryl again, I couldn't find her number in the duffel bag of miscellany I'd stored in the closet behind the bar. I thought she would have found a jodhpured gent with a sufficient checkbook for her to carry on the *Out of Africa* game, but when I called a Westlands linens store the next day, where I knew she liked to schmooze and shop, and they had her contact me, her voice did make me want to reconnect.

"Still truckin'? Sure, come over if you want." She told me that financial considerations had tied her up. I didn't mention Ya-Ya, who should be scrubbed, pigtailed, and outfitted appealingly in a Dallas dress by the Swarthmore interns from our churchy piles. Meanwhile, I obliged Al by sharing soup and sandwiches at the Thorn Tree Café with him and the Maryknolls' regional supervisor for a debriefing. She was a plain-mannered, beige-faced, self-contained woman in civilian clothes, unbending yet somehow limber, wanting to hear about the particularities of the station Nancy and Elizabeth were serving at. The risk and nutritional situation, the personalities of the SPLA commanders who were in charge, and of the Norwegians, the danger posed by other militias and figures, the reliability of certain truckers and suppliers. I could vouch for how well-grounded everybody thought the nuns were, with Father Leo an ideal adviser and backup on the scene.

She picked my brain as to conditions in Aswa, Amei, Loa, Opari, Juba and jotted down my number in case she needed to use me later for a transport, though I doubted from her demeanor that I would be her first choice. On the other hand, she smothered an abrupt, playful, startling smile as she collected her floppy briefcase before half an hour was up, to move on to another appointment: emergencies in Somalia, Ethiopia, Rwanda, and other countries were within her responsibility; you talked to her as to someone at a different level of commitment and expertise.

"When are you going back to Ruth?" she asked, winking at Al. And yes, she agreed, Leo was a wonder—his bravery, his experiences, and how he could communicate information over the radio by implications that eavesdroppers couldn't pick up on. Her attentiveness seemed momentarily encompassing in the way that can render confession a plausible ritual: this sallow fifty-year-old I might have been able to tell about my embezzlement in Alexandria, or silly quarrels with school boards in America that had been self-defeating and my marriage's breakup. "Thank you." When she waved a finger goodbye at Al and me, he murmured that she had been in the furnace of Central America when the CIA and the Maryknolls had been operating at cross-purposes and four of them had been murdered.

Later that afternoon, when Ya-Ya and I presented ourselves at Beryl's place, she was effusive, kind, and welcoming, despite being unprepared for the girl tagging along. She led us upstairs to her dressing room so Ya-Ya could pick through a tray of costume jewelry and choose what she wanted to wear. Watching her examine a coral necklace, then another of gold-framed, pink-tinted blue beads, "Never had a daughter!" Beryl exclaimed. She pretended to ignore the awry tilt at which Ya-Ya was required to hold her head in order to see. The news of her own son at prep school in Massachusetts was cheery.

"Lovely hair. Do you like ponies more than pigs? Sit you down at the mirror. Why not let's us do you a ponytail?" And she proceeded to convert the little-girl pigtails into a more grown-up style. "Lovely. You should be proud. Oh, I ought to have a girl!" she repeated, primping delightedly.

Beryl was having periodontal problems—"Not advisable here in Africa"—and papers needed signing. "Too much capital tied up." Which explained her delay in leaving. Her phone bill to California was becoming astronomical, and she was staying overnight at the Jacaranda Hotel in Westlands frequently. I glimpsed no traces of a man in residence, but a maid, well-trained, whose previous employer, Beryl said, had "scrammed," fixed us vichyssoise and aspic salad with anchovies and cups of sorbet. She asked where Ya-Ya and I had met— "Obviously not in Nairobi"—since we could not communicate except wordlessly. "Her hearing's good."

I went to an antique map displayed on the parlor wall. "On the Nile." I pointed to Fashoda, the site, now abandoned, of a famous British-French confrontation in 1898, during their competitive scramble for territory to rule in Africa. "Her village is close to there."

Although Ya-Ya had never seen a proper map before, she recognized the general shape of the continent from the outline I'd chalked at Ruth's and traced the river's wiggles with her finger. Then we moved to Beryl's globe to show her where *we* lived, on North America's coasts, with oceans about—oceans amazingly bigger than the quantities of land. Clearly, she'd heard of their existence (whatever the Arabic word was) but not their extent, and that the water tasted funny, so you didn't drink it. Beryl shook some salt into a glass for her to taste the difference, and because not only Khartoum but Juba and Kampala were marked on the globe, I could show her how minuscule our long car trip to Nairobi appeared, compared with the dimensions of the earth. England's location interested her, too, because everybody on the White Nile knew about those British Airways flights. And "Russia" she'd heard of, and China, Tanzania, Israel, Addis Ababa, Egypt.

The roundness of the planet fascinated Ya-Ya—though it was hard to fathom whether she knew about planets, or if the sun went around us, or vice versa, to produce night and day, or the nature and role of the moon. Was she aware men had already walked on it? Had she even been told before that the world was round? Or was her amusement, excitement, simply aroused by how graphic and curious this representation was, with all its graceful scribbles, complexities, and coloring? We burst into giggles, including the Kikuyu maid, at the difficulty of conveying important information, interrupting each other, rotating our hands. How much easier to have Ya-Ya think the sun revolved around the earth, as it seemed to do, just like the moon (if she did), so long as she knew that day, in Beryl's California, was night here. Knowledge of *that* preempted all of the other stuff we wanted to say—about the stars, about South America, Antarctica, ships, whales. Elephants were not as big as whales, but the Nile exceeded the Amazon in length. I pointed to the Mississippi, the Yangtze, the Amazon, which "is wider," I insisted on saying.

We did several tours of the house, up, down: the sofas, the rugs, wall hangings woven symmetrically of brown and white Ethiopian wool, and massive shields fabricated for war from buffalo hide by the Masai—who "could beat the Dinkas," we agreed—plus the icy white fridge, the French kitchen range, chests of silverware, cupboards of china in the pantry for the formal dinner table. In the bathrooms, the medicine cabinets, and mysterious bidet, versus the toilet, and faucets that turned on and off, hot or cold—not to mention the Jacuzzi, of all things, terry-cloth towels as tall as Ya-Ya herself, and closets ranked with extraordinary, unimaginable clothing; and bureaus the same. An architect earlier had inserted stained-glass windows along the elbowed, spacious staircase, with a wide banister, and these colors darkened yet enriched the damask-covered walls, the wide-boarded floor. Then there was the dishwasher, clothes washer and dryer, a tumult of ornamentation and revelation. We were astonished ourselves, and Beryl canceled a yoga appointment to enjoy the experience—held Ya-Ya's hand, hugged her, showed her agate gewgaws and ivory treasures but never mentioned the outlandish contortions of her head Ya-Ya needed to engage in to peer at everything we pointed out. Leaning like a pool player calculating a given shot, she employed either her left eye or else the errant other.

"What intriguing work you do," Beryl told me, making no reference to our leaving, so we didn't. "Not just wars." With a swelling, gleeful confidence, Ya-Ya began exploring on her own, leading us, decked out in scarves and lace and rings. "I'd like to keep her forever."

The fax machine slowly spat out a three-page document, but not the one Beryl wanted. "What I've been doing since you left is paint that screen." She indicated a divider, freshly floraled, that separated the living from the dining area. "You'd be surprised how long it takes. And you can probably guess where I was sober and where I wasn't. Just being creative till I leave. How much do you pay the maid for severance, by the way?" The house not being rented or sold, it would be crazy to leave it vacant. Meanwhile, the candy bowl was full, the liquor cabinet needed emptying. I had a feeling we could move in for a week or whatever, till her paperwork had gotten untangled. She was having panic attacks—"maybe not clinically, but it's like Cinderella at midnight. You know, here I've been, for months, and I've never slept with an African!" she mused. "Is that *me*?" Then she reminded herself that Ya-Ya couldn't understand what she said. At the dressing table, Beryl was letting Ya-Ya style her hair, examine the tools of the beautician's trade, and mug in the trio of mirrors. "My father wouldn't have wanted all this for me," she added, laughing mournfully. "He was so protective. Always the best in tennis lessons, dancing lessons. Mills College."

To be helpful, I suggested that her real estate agency could hire guards to protect the property as a stopgap. She was glancing across the bookshelves for anything she wanted to ship. And she owned Lobi and Bambara figurines and Congolese masks, like those I had trucked in wholesale sometimes for the tourist shops. I smelled them for authenticity for her, although dealers will often smoke replicas in burning palm oil to make you think a fake has spent a lifetime scented of jungle cooking fires. Upstairs, we could hear faucets tested, squeaky drawers, creaky beds.

"The Three Bears," I said. "Or the Magic Kingdom. But I have six eyes to fix. Not only hers. Two other girls."

"I shoulda hadda daughter," she repeated, after taking us to the Jacaranda club and explaining to the bartender what a Shirley Temple was. Having enjoyed watching her trying on earrings, plus jewelry to decorate her neck and wrists, luscious scarves, shawls, and turbans, in a paroxysm of dressing up the way white women liked to, and getting Beryl to paint her fingernails, we'd inevitably wanted to show off Ya-Ya, at thirteen going on seventeen, to the general public, "like a Bollywood star in an Indian motion picture," Beryl chuckled throatily. "You know, if you're driving anywhere in the city, you'll glimpse these homeless children by the dozens, and you'll wish, for a moment, you could stop and collect a particular one and improve her life forever and ever. But you don't know which it would work with, and, like going to the Casino Club, it could be very, very expensive, either way. Do you pre-select, at your center? How do you do it? If they have TB, you segregate them, but in a different room from the AIDS kids, because TB would kill the AIDS kids?"

I agreed we should have separate rooms, yet we didn't. "But Ya-Ya has parents who love her. She's not up for adoption, at least if they survive."

Beryl, complaining about the lack of liquidity in her checkbook, seemed relieved, and decided, on the strength of my company and a newly acquired pistol she showed me, not to sleep in the hotel tonight. So we watched Ginger Rogers and Fred

Astaire in her rumpus room and tucked Ya-Ya into a four-poster bed, with canopy. Sharing Beryl's, I shared, as well, her jitters when the garbage lid clattered. Was it just the leopard again or, finally, bandits?

Next morning, we discovered Ya-Ya long since up and practicing frying eggs for us on the Lacanche stove, while the maid, Wacuba, hovered diplomatically in the background. (Wacuba *had* worked for diplomats, she wanted us to know, sensing a bout of unemployment in the offing.) Then we went to the National Museum to observe Ya-Ya's pride and surprise at certain ethnographic "Nilo-Saharan" displays that held reverberations for her, and various beasts, from the hippo to some frogs, and the sunbirds, whose taped songs we heard. We also swung by a small upscale shopping center where Beryl's real estate broker, a New Zealander, had his "one-girl" office, with a decor in antelope hues that complemented the sunlight falling through slatted awnings to create zebra striping on the flagstones outside, as you approached.

While he showed Beryl an ad he'd written to circulate throughout the NGO community, his Kikuyu in the anteroom spoke rapidly to a couple of phone numbers in her own language and in Swahili about Ya-Ya's infirmity, until, shifting to BBC English, she informed me that the wait for an operation would be two or three months at a minimum, and the fee a thousand British pounds, negotiable down to possibly the same number of dollars. "If it was my daughter," said the Kiwi, overhearing us. "I'd take her to Europe."

Next door, an optometrist in a white coat sidled away as if we were street people when our little girl first presented herself. He turned unctuous in the face of Beryl's Bay Area élan, which pretended that there would be no smirking plainclothes immigration officer barring the head of the debarkation ramp at San Francisco's airport to prevent Ya-Ya from swimming in Beryl's lap pool every morning, before the school bus arrived. Did we want glasses?

Wacuba fed us a lunch of pink chunks of melon and roast beef, with lemony iced tea, and I napped on the divan while Beryl fingered communications she didn't want to read. Her ex had been a developer—his, a mentality she'd hoped to evade but now was mired in. My money belts, "under and over" my underwear, amused her, when she got a gander at them. "Maybe I should go that route!" she wailed.

I was so poleaxed, now that those weeks in the Sudan had caught up with me, that I loafed passively while she fielded phone calls from the pal in Sausalito who paid her credit-card bills and other Statesside stuff, from appraisers, a bank officer, a California real estate guy, and a therapist there returning her calls to check that she was staying off the sauce. She had a brother in Dallas, too, eager for this phase in her life to end.

Click-click Ya-Ya's spike heels sounded overhead, till she appeared downstairs in rakish headgear in this castle of wonders, her fantasies mushrooming, and propped a rug into a tent. In shirtsleeve heat, we were cool indoors because the eccentric placement of the small windows cleverly ventilated yet wittily lit the darkened rooms. Beryl was describing, across eleven time zones, how "at the roundabouts, where you have to slow down, a car full of thugs will circle with you, if they see a white face in the window, right alongside, to try to herd you off at their exit instead of yours."

"Beryl, come home! Come home, Beryl!" I'd hear the hollers from the phone. She wanted that, encouraged it, and what she said was true: could happen to anyone. Al dealt with similar dangers, first, by having married somebody he wanted to stay at home with and, second, by buying a house next to a police station. Her wee-hour dreams had become so vivid, however, that I was sorry she'd bought the pistol. On the other hand, if she dreamt about her husband, not a robber, it stained her attitude toward any man she was in bed with, even a man "off the books," like myself, whose income was mostly cash. And she didn't dignify me with a name on the phone; just said she had "somebody" staying with her "for protection." I'd catch her glancing covertly at me when we ate as if I might be chewing with my mouth open or my dentistry was not shipshape. How far below her echelon was I—the schoolteacher you wouldn't quite ask to the house but paid attention to in his limited sphere?

"We've got to fix those eyes!" I whispered to her as we watched Ya-Ya, with Wacuba, who was holding her hand, imitate the spinning cycle of the washing machine by moving her head round and round. Wacuba had five or six children of her own, whom she walked a bunch of miles one day a week to see. But Beryl glanced quizzically at me, as if to ask whether by taking us in she had committed herself to fulfilling my responsibilities.

"On Nob Hill there's a doctor who might do it for free," she mentioned, leaving the matter at that. I told her about a loony millionaire from Long Island I'd done a little work for, a trust funder who flew his own Beechcraft to Africa to do good works—the happiest weeks of his life, he used to say—lifting crateloads of condoms to cities that needed them, or wildlife biologists to potent locations off the regular map. I'd been his low-rent fixer in Nairobi occasionally, and *he* might have smuggled Ya-Ya to America on a return flight sometime, if he hadn't had a heart attack during a takeoff, back on Long Island, at fifty-something, and crashed and burned. She smiled with the wince of somebody who knew trust funders.

I was as jumpy as she when the phone rang, because it might be Al. "I mean, I *would* want to go back," I explained when she expressed a certain startlement, her vanity perhaps miffed. "You've got a hundred thousand starving, just where I was. But I also *wouldn't.*" However, it wasn't Al at first. An importer called me because a hundred gross of batik cloth had been misappropriated in a bankruptcy and fire-sale proceeding. I helped find it in the maze of warehousing near Kibera's slums. Even Nairobi's *Nation* newspaper would have headlined a start to Khartoum's offensive against the southern Sudanese, so I knew Al must be receiving no news from Ruthie except for the worsening starvation. Beryl said, "having burned my tongue," she would never come back to Africa, whereas I'd "keep sipping the soup."

With Ya-Ya, we swung by the melee at Nairobi's general hospital's waiting room, to be finally told "all surgeons are fully booked." Her bad eye scrabbled crabwise at the nurse's shake of the head, while Beryl's grim frown indicated that the magnitude of poignancy at the hospital was distancing her from it. We stopped at the street shelter, too (Ya-Ya suddenly afraid we might "trade" her for another girl), and the smaller orphans housed there lifted both arms to be picked up, having been told somewhere that this was the way to get adopted and taken to somebody's home. STREETWISE, ADVOCATES FOR CHILDREN IN EAST AFRICA, announced a new sign over the door.

On her voice mail when we returned, Beryl heard a message of real estate import that teared her up. "I'm being dumped on. You can almost hear them laugh." She drank too much at supper and began to burp, a telltale sign with her, then fart, and talk of her home tennis club, where hedge-fund managers scouted for a second marriage. We irritated each other—me cracking my big toe in bed, and baring my feet and scratching at the fungus patches on the soles—"strewing spores all through the house," she said—which had annoyed my former wife as well. I claimed it was too hot for flip-flops. She tightly bunned her hair, not caring that I preferred it long and loose. Her experiment on this raffish continent was over, and our swan song— Ya-Ya's and mine—was already playing, but speeded up discordantly when we all glimpsed a sticklike figure, as thin as a silhouette, vaulting over Beryl's eight-foot front fence at sunset and, racing as though for his life toward the rear, scramble over that one as well. No chance to confront him, even had we dared to, or guess who was chasing him without opening the gate, which we were definitely not of a mind to do.

"Oh, *okay,*" she decided after a minute, not explaining what she meant; but I knew that it was to take her medicine, cut her losses. A shell company had offered to buy the villa and doubtless turn it over for a profit after she left. In a few days, money materialized in her San Francisco account, besides what was going to remain awhile tied up in Kenyan red tape. She snagged an Air France seat, as the shippers were crating her impedimenta for seagoing transport, and sold her Land Rover to a tile-shop owner she'd been friendly with, for cash, which she laughingly took my advice on and folded into a belly belt, while bemoaning "another failure, another wild goose chase, another *bath*."

We drove Beryl to the airport, Wacuba, Ya-Ya, and me. She'd sequestered herself from people of her own class, I think, to cut her regrets. So we stayed a couple of held-over hours to keep her company at a lonely time, as well as for Ya-Ya to watch the huge passenger plane, first on the ground, then taking off. Especially in a Third World country where flights are late and last-minute bribes may be demanded, you feel better with a witness. It's a sweeter, more solid departure, being seen to the gate. In fact, her British newsman, dropping by against her instructions, told the story of a tycoon he knew whose chauffeur had standing orders never to leave till the plane was out of sight; and sure enough, in Joburg one time, at the end of the runway it bloody crashed, and his limo sped straight onto the tarmac, beat every other vehicle to the flames, and his bloke pulled him out of the wreckage and got him to the hospital long before any ambulance would have.

Ya-Ya, watching the silvery Airbuses and Boeings, five miles up, arrowing down the course of the Nile, had been told they were "for white people," she said. So it was exciting for her to notice that half the passengers boarding the airliner alongside Beryl were not white. Then the lumbering, accelerating, breakneck, deafening, utterly amazing magic-carpet tilt, lift, and climb. Her life had not been such as to teach her to miss people unduly who vanished as though into the sky, or to complain at returning from Disneyland to her gritty cot at the shelter, with honking traffic outside. I did feel a pang for poor Beryl, knowing she would carry her problems back with her, just as she'd brought them to Africa from California in the first place. The roar at the airport had reminded me of Ruthie, too, waiting in her shell-shot church compound under the drone of the Antonov searching for a target to bomb or, conversely, for the rumble of twenty

Bedford lorries carrying sorghum and corn to stanch the hemor-
rhage of deaths all around her.

My hole-in-the-wall at the Arab's was so much safer than what
Al reported about Ruthie. She was eating Meals Ready to Eat, her
last-ditch military rations, and my hospice patients had quietly
coughed themselves to death. The checkerboarded patch of soil
where, twice a day, kindergarten-aged children sat cross-legged in
sixty or eighty squares chalked on the ground to have mush spooned
into them was empty because there was no food. Every family fended
for itself and carried a club, so that a hungry person watching others
nibble a bit of nourishment had the choice of starving with a broken
leg, if they tried to grab some, or just watching. Ruth, on the radio,
didn't spell out what she knew we could visualize because the Arab
side, listening in, would want to hear that the Dinka civilians, behind
the SPLA lines, were falling into chaos. Her curt phrases, "Ready to
Eat," "beds empty," "quiet at the clinic," "the Norwegians have had
no deliveries either, but the Antonov is up near them," sketched the
tale. Most ominous was her word that Father Leo had stopped by:
"Brought me stuff." One could interpret that as meaning he and the
Maryknolls were anticipating clearing out.

When Al asked, "Want us?" she told him, "No, no." "Because
we'll come with bells on," he promised her, thereby committing me
without asking me, though I was in the office, listening by the radio.

"You mean you'd spring for a plane?" I asked, once we were off
the airwaves. I sure didn't want to drive again.

"We'll see."

Maybe if I could get behind a Ugandan army truck, with a squad
of soldiers bouncing on the balls of their feet in back, it would feel
safe—then sleep in a fenced compound in Atiak, with drinks with a
colonel—or as part of a relief convoy, the drivers paid by the trip, not
the day, pushing to get it over with. In the middle of the thing, I
thought selfishly, a mine wouldn't pluck me out.

Al had aid projects near Addis Ababa and Dar es Salaam, and I
accompanied him on the latter as a minder for two VIPs, decent,

twinkly folks of Baptist good intentions, not like the Bechtel construction guys we drank with one evening. Though brutal them- selves, they couldn't hold a candle to the local Big Men in Nairobi, who, for instance, had been confining political prisoners in under- ground cells half full of water, so that they had to sleep sitting up and were perpetually wizened, with their feces floating all around them. The Bechtel and Halliburton engineers didn't visit refugees, but my church wardens did, and I managed to introduce them to our three girls who needed strabismus surgery, after they had been to Kakuma camp and witnessed how Ya-Ya and the others would have been interned if their legal status were known. Kakuma is in the northern desert, and tens of thousands of Sudanese and Somalis were fenced in there: doubly so, because fenced apart from one another as well, with virtually no activities to occupy them, and the sand so hot at midday it burned their feet if they had no shoes. We saw two girls of a similar age hopping, screeching, toward a food distribution point—shrieking in both pain and fun because they had only a pair of sandals to share and, rather than take turns, found it less excruciating to each leap along with one leg held up. Surrounding Kakuma were even hungrier children, who weren't fenced in and being fed by the U.N., belonging to the local Turkana tribe, whom we drove by without stopping to let them beg from us.

So my church board chairmen, before they caught their plane, arranged through other contacts for an Asian doctor to schedule eye exams and surgery in a month or so for Ya-Ya, Tongkwoit, and Nyoka. What I was reminded of in the give-and-take of accomplishing this harked back to how tightly wound I must have been in negotiating in the States with vice principals, school board committees, and the like, either clamming up or getting myself fired for not shutting up on petty issues. Yet here, where sorcery as much as small talk was the gristle of so many neighborhoods, I could chat with visiting firemen and not break a sweat.

I was never to hear from Beryl again, but Wacuba, the house- maid, walked clear downtown from Karen, carrying a plastic sack with her belongings in it, having been fired by the new owners, who wanted Luos instead of Kikuyus around, she said they'd said. The doorman at the New Stanley tipped her off to where I lived, when she showed up. I was closeted across the street at the Arab's with a university student, a science major, who, for once, I wasn't exploiting but infatuated with. I'd already bought her father a hearing aid and now she wanted school uniforms for her brothers and sisters, lying on one elbow with her mane of ebony hair half-covering her breasts, studying my face as if calculating how hard I had fallen for her. Wacuba's knocking broke up the power play. I phoned the few of Beryl's acquaintances I had met; but no dice. Beryl had given her a hundred-dollar bill, more than a month's pay, as severance, which I changed for her. She'd been afraid to take it to a bank for fear the police would be called to ask how she'd gotten it, or to a street hustler, who might simply snatch it.

Josephine, my latest heartthrob, was amused, Wacuba being no threat and so far removed from her league. I'd given Josephine a cell phone the previous day, and she tapped this significantly, tucking it into her purse, as, seeing that I was going to remain engaged, she took her leave. I sat down to commiserate with Wacuba, who was crying while she folded Beryl's payment into her socks, the last place muggers would look, for the trip home. The sunlight, on my balcony, shone white on her face.

"Don't walk," I said. She shrugged. Already fond of her because of her kindness to Ya-Ya during our week at Beryl's place, I pressed her not to, offering *matatu* money, plus some time now to talk, which was what she really wanted. We ordered tea; I explained aspects of Beryl's position that more knowledge of America would have helped her understand. Then, to my surprise, she teased me about this Josephine—being "wound around her little finger. What is it that does that?" Not flirting, she invited me home to meet her five kids. Her brother-in-law had a car, so it would not be dangerous afterward to come back. She let slip, however, that her husband had died, not merely left her, as she'd always told Beryl, and thus she was more

vulnerable than I'd realized, living with in-laws now that she had lost
her job, with no absent husband in the family's politics to stand up
for those kids. And for expatriate employers like Beryl or me, death
brings to mind HIV and AIDS. Had he? Does she? I asked, but she
shook her head noncommittally.

"What is this love at first sight?" she teased me again in the
matatu. With so many hungry girls on the street, when and why did
it start and stop? A particularly enticing nose and mouth, provocative
hands and eyes. A man like me who had had his spells of going to
strippers' clubs couldn't put into words why he begins to tip one
performer and not the others. Twenty dollars in her G-string? It's not
her "measurements" or sympathetic heart.

Wacuba's brother-in-law lived out at the city's eastward edge of
the veldt but within sight of its sewage pools, glittering blue in the
distance. He and his wife had built a bamboo-spike palisade
completely around the little stucco house and patch of ground they
rented, and densely planted every foot of soil available with corn,
sharecropping a bit more for the landlord outside the fence. It was
intricately, obsessively irrigated for thick productivity as insurance
against such a disaster as this: Wacuba returning jobless, unannounced.
Her husband's sister and sister-in-law didn't work except at caring
for the collection of children they had, and cultivating the corn,
though the sister was educated enough for a pink-collar typing job
downtown, if it wasn't a two-hour walk every day to hunt for one.
She, like Wacuba, was bereft of a husband for unmentioned reasons,
and the breadwinner left was Wacuba's dead husband's brother. He
had a rickety Subaru whose door handles had fallen off, so that he
had to climb out and use a screwdriver to let out the passengers he
had picked up on the roadside, who had tired of waiting for a bus at
rush hour. His gas tank was never full; he'd pay for a couple of gallons
at a time as the shillings trickled in. Rather than give his sister or
Wacuba a lift to hunt for jobs, Kariuki preferred to sell seats in the car
as a sure income till the engine failed and have them weed, water, and
hoe the corn in the meantime. It was frenetic—all of those young

mouths to feed, and a sense of doom impending, common to so many Kenyan households, though a truce occurred in the mood, to offer hospitality in Wacuba's name to me—and I would never have survived a walk with my possessions intact back to Moi Avenue in Nairobi. They even kept a watchdog—an obsequious but hypertense mutt loose at night, in a box during the day—which was unusual among a citizenry worried about where next month's meals would come from. I filled the Subaru's tank in exchange for a ride to the shelter that evening to look in on Ya-Ya.

I was tutoring the accumulation of orphans who had settled in at STREETWISE, ADVOCATES FOR CHILDREN, beginning with the ABC's. "How are you, Mr. Hickey?" they knew, but not how to spell it. The jowly, tan-faced eye doctor the Baptists had enlisted, who'd been kicked out of Uganda along with all the other "Asians" and therefore was habituated to a wildly fluctuating patient pool and ad hoc proto-cols, "far from London," as he put it, having done a residency in Britain two decades ago, fit my three girls into a cancellation. ("The ayes have it!" he said.) And Al's Somali wife, who in stockings and heels, as somebody's executive assistant in a high-rise, earned nearly as much as he did, had taken such a shine to Ya-Ya's karma since meeting her that she invited her to recuperate postoperatively in their house, where the chance of infection would be reduced, and where her daughters were fast-tracked for American or European schooling already. One even had a blue passport, having cleverly been born on a trip to Tulsa. Ya-Ya would never see the Nile again, Norah predicted: any more than she had revisited Mogadishu.

Ya-Ya had divined that the brown man in a white coat with eye diagrams on his walls was the magician who was going to transform her future into a golden one, and her confidence was peeling off its timid mask. She was less apprehensive about hearing a snicker, although she still needed to screw her head around to discover a workable angle to look at anything. The doctor said that, though born in Africa, he expected himself and his family to be kicked out of Kenya eventually, too.

"Idi Amin never lost the support of his people for doing that. You Americans like underdogs, but you are very choosy on who is an underdog and because you are never the underdog, it's your amusement. Now that godless communism is over, you will try to convert even the Hind*oo*!" He smiled, waggling his head slightly in the Indian manner that signifies yes but appears to a Westerner like no.

My Arab landlord also mocked me a little about how Israeli helicopter gunships are always, to Americans, supposedly the underdogs. But now he had heard from my new girlfriend, Josephine, that I was experiencing bombing myself for a change, and not enjoying it, waking her with nightmares. He told another guest, a northern Sudanese, how I was earning my living, and the guy, a Khartoum businessman, burst rudely into laughter.

"You lengthen the war! You feed people who otherwise would leave and let us negotiate a peace. And so they will die instead. And then we punish you by arming the war in Uganda because Uganda is in your pocket now, after Idi Amin, and we are just 'ragheads,' 'sand niggers,' to you." He stared at me as though at a freak.

Annoyed, I asked if it was true, as I'd heard, that Khartoum traded a Kalashnikov for every Ugandan child the Lord's Resistance Army turned over to them at the airstrip near Torit where the LRA was resupplied, to be flown north and become slaves to rich families in the capital.

"You've been watching too much *Uncle Tom's Cabin* and *Gone with the Wind,*" my landlord interrupted humorously. He had ventures that took him abroad, even to Canada once, he'd told me. But the other businessman was not amused.

"Your nuns, they don't treat blacks who are naked, I have heard. Men who are naked in the bush: they reject them, send them away to die without medicines. What kind of a 'missionary' is that?"

Having heard similar stories about the Catholics from Ruth, I didn't argue with him with a cheap shot like what, anyway, are Muslim women permitted to do, out in the world, but said the lady I worked with was continually giving SPLA soldiers hernia exams, when she had a chance to. This shocked both of them so much they refrained from laughing. When I took advantage of their silence to mention starving children, however, they again seized what they considered the high ground by pointing out that America gives Israel its helicopter gunships to shoot rockets from the sky and kill the children of Gaza. I began to worry that I might lose my comfortable berth in this hotel, but my landlord only smiled, seeing I was stumped.

The radio preoccupied Al and me. Our attention to other responsibilities, and even my sexual poker game with Josephine, stalled with dread about events on the Nile far away. The Maryknolls sounded as enigmatic as the Vatican concerning their plans, and Ruth as stubborn as a clam. "Mammoth," she said, about her needs. The Norwegian trio chattered in their own language to their one-man base office in Nairobi, which for security purposes was as good as a code. But the pitch of their voices was not reassuring, and they didn't bother to close in English, as ordinarily, in order to greet everybody else.

I did promise, against my better judgment, to return if a food delivery was organized. Lone autos did seem to trigger the killer instinct in guerrillas, who might let a convoy of huge mufflerless lorries go by—not knowing which would be the last, to shoot its tires out. Though sincere, my pledge was not likely to be called because everybody knew that in the face of an impending offensive, no deliveries would occur. When not exhausting my infatuation with Josephine, I was showing a toothpaste marketer around the bureaucracy, which involved leaving bribes in envelopes in various desks, after putting up with the officeholder's officious jollying that the best dentifrice was a twig tweaked off a toothbrush tree; every Kenyan boy would surely tell you that. The guy from Cincinnati talked about a level playing field—his Indian competitors shipping into Mombasa were underpricing him—but meanwhile had contracted an intestinal complaint. I had his hired driver take him beyond the metastasizing slums to the veldt, where we gazed at wide-open skies stretching over wildebeests and gazelles scattered toward the horizon, then to our street shelter, in hopes that he might spring for a substantial contribution to Streetwise. But he only bought soccer balls and basketballs, borrowing a ladder to nail up the hoop himself, and showing the kids how you dribble and shoot, before his Cairo plane.

Al was dickering with a pilot we knew who flew rented two-seat propeller Cessnas into hairy airstrips in Zaire, where Uganda, Rwanda, Burundi, or Sudan bled into it, usually with some Serb or Slav along who bought and sold items he shouldn't have—thugs who'd participated in more brutality than most other Europeans lately have, or fought as mercenaries for apartheid in Rhodesia and shot a lot of blacks. Our pilot was the type you needed to deal with to extract a person such as Ruth from a place like Loa, in the absence of an Ed. He looked like Mickey Rooney, so answered to "Mickey," and had learned to love war in Vietnam, then stayed in the Pacific doing contract flying for an oil company, with Australia as much a home as America. He was a gambler who didn't gamble much on the ground, although you'd watch him circulate at the Casino with dancing eyes, as if craps, blackjack, and roulette weren't quite real enough.

These people liked you or loathed you but didn't make a lot of distinctions, and didn't want any "tell" in their face to let you know where the chips fell. On a bush airstrip, you would probably have to shoot them while they were grinning and greeting you, because that's when they would be likely to think it opportune to shoot you. And on an outlaw militia's airstrip in the Congo, there are no police or consular officials or coroners: just vultures to do the autopsy and record the fingerprints and dentistry. You'd be recycled into wings.

Despite their terseness on the radio, the Catholic and Norwegian offices in Nairobi were frank with Al when he phoned. Father Leo, Nancy, and Elizabeth were going to sneak away toward Chukudum, if the coast was clear for half a moment. Once they were in the Imatongs, they should be safe with the mountain tribes, Acholi and Latuka, whom Leo had been ministering to for years. But the strafing had gotten so bad that they would need to hit the road when Khartoum's two MiGs were on the runway in Juba being refueled, then calculate when to hide underneath the trees somewhere en route during their dash (since night travel was out) when the MiGs jumped airborne again and came back. During daylight hours, however, patients and parishioners still lined up in front of their clinic or chapel for counsel or care, even though their last supply truck had hit a mine in Uganda and they had nothing to give out except affection. "So it's difficult to leave," as the two nuns' supervisor we'd lunched with explained.

The Norwegians were not out of medical stuff. Since they were furnishing the SPLA's only surgeon in this theater of the war, minimal night deliveries were somehow reaching them. But the surgeon, his wife, who was the surgical nurse, and the anesthetist were all a wreck, the guy at their Nairobi office said.

"Can you imagine how he feels, seeing every night young men brought in, howling on a stretcher, whose lives he could save—they need to be sewn up at least to stop the bleeding—if he hadn't already been operating for twelve or fourteen hours and can't lift his arms or squint his eyes to focus on the scalpel and the needle, and him dehydrated from diarrhea, himself. His scrub suit is soiled, his hands filthy, and the new ones die on their gurneys while he tries to sleep. But in the morning ten more are carried in before he grabs his breakfast. And his scrub suit hasn't been boiled because his wife needed to try to sleep, too."

In other words, they could neither function nor conscientiously leave, and their transmissions to Nairobi were no doubt being monitored from several directions, not just ours—perhaps recorded for translation by someone who knew Scandinavian. I'd gotten a gander at them—him tense, with thinning hair, already astonished, appalled, pale, and girding himself, as if shedding pounds, after what he had seen along the road, like a drumbeat of preliminary disaster, and his wife edgy, game, but alarmed—only as they'd passed Ruth's place in their jeep, arriving for their first tour in a war zone. The anesthetist was a younger man than the surgeon, sitting up straight, expecting to be surprised, wearing his idealism on his sleeve. And even the unflappable Felix, across the border, sounded perturbed, because the mine that had exploded under the Maryknolls' resupply truck in LRA territory near him, mangling but not killing the driver, had caused his usual middleman to radio saying there was a work stoppage. For the first time since he had left Ethiopia, he was running out of food and medicines. "And bandits are all over. They know if the Arabs come, they will get the leavings." "Emperors," he called them because of their life-and-death power, point-blank executions, and he was tempted to take a vacation he was owed by his NGO to Capetown for a rest, yet knew he couldn't, with the landslide of refugees that would be tumbling his way, building. "I need reinforcements," he told his boss, but using English, not German, for the rest of his radio audience.

Mickey, the pilot Al and I had a drink with to explore the possibility of a rescue flight, was a short, prickly guy, all pep but a little tone-deaf, like Rooney in the movies; I don't know his legal name. He'd just enjoyed some R&R in Dubrovnik with a Croatian pal, plus a "wife-for-a-month," apparently a Romanian illegal he'd found on the scene: "Until the joystick called. The other joystick!" He mimicked how the yoke in his rental plane jutted up between his legs. "But I might retire there if I ever clear my chips off the table." The charge for Sudan ought to be higher than for going into Zaire, he added, because there were no MiGs or Stingers when you flew into Zaire, just what was scary on the ground. Any MiG in Sudan's airspace knew you were flying for groups that were helping the rebels, and the rebels had a few dozen Stingers some out-of-sync kid might pick up and point at you "to see what happens."

I liked Mickey, though, because the rush for him was in the landings, not the diamonds his Serb or Slav or Croat smugglers grabbed—landing in a clearing and then finding out if it was the right one; and if not, if he could possibly take off again. In New Guinea, while flying for the oil company, Mickey freelanced for an anthropologist who sought to be lowered, naked, on the end of a rope into openings in the jungle canopy in the territories of tribes that had never experienced contact with Europeans before. Being naked, he claimed, frightened them less, since they were the same, and the natives could see he had no hidden arms. For Mickey, to share the first part of the experience had been like when he surfed, riding a wave.

The Catholics had vanished off the radar. No transmissions as of yesterday. Overland was smarter, Al and Mickey agreed. People would think it was bad luck to hurt them, and there were Christian Dinkas who could have helped; whereas Ruthie was a solo operator, without Rome behind her. Mickey liked Ruthie and could hear the Kamba's worried voice behind her when she was on the radio. "But no space closer than the Norwegians' to land."

Ya-Ya and her friends awaited their surgical appointments by the gigantic adventure of exploring Nairobi on foot, hand in hand. Parliament, Government House, the Hilton, the Anglican and Catholic cathedrals, the U.S. embassy, glassy skyscrapers, the zebra-striped newspaper building. They crossed the gridwork of avenues as red lights turned to green, traffic-dodging, window-shopping, running in the parks, locating the railroad station. I felt bad about spending more for Josephine's brothers and sisters—who needed those school outfits and uniforms—than on them and, separately, buying an adorable chemise for Josie herself, who was "testing" my "chemistry" or "wiring" by having me comb and brush her hair and dress as well as undress her in my room. But she made me search her out in student hangouts, as the taxi waited, instead of obliging me by coming to the Arab's on her own. She wanted to be a pharmacist, which lent her a pragmatic take on sex. Although she knew an American was almost certainly free of AIDS, after teasing me with her mouth, she expertly pushed my dick aside as it began to ejaculate so it squirted harmlessly into the air; then waggled its limpness, smiling wryly as I fluffed and buried my hands in her hair, and gazed at me judiciously, as if to gauge how to move from tantalizing to managing me. My voice was too husky to use, but I asked whether she respected what we aid workers were doing.

"Of course. But you're so lonely! Maybe I should go over to teach algebra for your country in Harlem. Lick me," she added, and pointed a red fingernail at a crumb of coffee cake that had fallen onto her stomach, somewhat south of her navel. I really was speechless, so, smiling into my pleading eyes, she dabbed a drop of honey on each nipple and spilled another crumb or two. "Hurry. I have class." Finally she straddled and tickled me until my writhing wriggling underneath her vulva completed the trick of causing her to come. Then: "Hurry. Dress me, so I can go to class."

I had to get over to Al's, myself, to meet Attlee's widow, who wanted a monthly pension, in addition to the lump-sum compensation paid. We didn't have pensions, being a temporary, if not to say fly-by-night, NGO. But I ought to have met with her in these past couple of weeks to praise the loyalty and courage of the man.

She handled the heads and shoulders of two gangly, discombobulated boys she'd brought with her to make her case—Attlee's, although he hadn't had the chance to teach them English yet—as well as a brother, whether hers or his, for further moral support, who lived with her for her protection, she said, though he was slightly drunk on home-brewed *kumi kumi*. He worked irregular hours on a loading dock.

"Do you want them to do that?" she asked, meaning the boys. "No education?" She squeezed their necks—a gaunt woman, not underfed on the African scale but like a Depression photograph from the Dust Bowl era in the United States. And when I mentioned Ruth's high opinion of Attlee, she snorted.

"Ruth! She was a funny one," she said.

"She *is* a funny one," I agreed. "But doing good."

"And now he's dead."

"Yes."

I shook hands with the two young boys, feeling calluses they already had. Al gave them each the equivalent of twenty dollars, as well as their mother: about two months' worth of bare-bones living. Al had outbid another agency for nine truckloads of beans and cooking oil, and was distracted by phone calls relating to this, and by his diversion of them to a less hard-pressed camp than Ruthie's, not in a war zone. We were listening for her to turn on her radio and check in, so she could say a few words to Attlee's widow and end our saddening spate of guilty bickering.

Instead, Father Leo's welcome brogue broke in. "Brendan here. We're in Dublin. Nancy and Elizabeth, too. So, not to worry."

Then the Maryknolls' supervisor we'd lunched with answered: "Okay! Super news! I read you. Ten-four. We won't! Thank God."

Saint Brendan, the sixth-century Celtic explorer was Leo's nom de plume when he preferred to use one, and of course "Dublin" meant safety, wherever in the mountains he and the two sisters had holed up, eating bushbuck meat and drinking millet beer with a tribal clan. Nancy must have knitting with her, for nieces and nephews in the States, and Elizabeth her dog-eared copy of *The Oxford Book of English Verse,* which she dipped into nearly as often as the Bible.

Thereupon, Ruth burst on-air chuckling, transmitting from what she called "Dodge City," and pretending to try to goad Leo into revealing his location. "I bet it's Gilo. That's where the British used to fish and hunt. There's a golden-skinned woman who lives up in Gilo on the mountainside whose father was a Brit. Are you friends?"

"Brendan" laughed. "You'd have to ask Liz and Nancy."

"I can hear the rats in your thatch. That telltale rustle."

He didn't answer because the Acholis who most likely were sheltering them would indeed have lent them thatch-roofed mud huts.

"They'd sure be eaten here!" Ruth remarked. "But not much is moving due to our Russian friends."

Ruth meant the MiGs; and my memory immediately regurgitated their bass banshee scream, which you didn't hear until after they'd gone by and the warning was too late. Attlee's widow left with her boys, quietly, bitterly, hearing no reference to her loss, as I was asking about little Leo and the jackal puppy, in between Al's more probing questions to Makundi, the Kamba, in Kikuyu and Swahili, languages the average Dinka listener or Arab eavesdropper would not be fluent in. The gist of his replies was that the war of nerves was getting them and everybody down. That sense of emergency caused us to neglect her.

"You can't shoot a Stinger at the sunset," Ruth said, which was where the planes came from. But Al cut her off, lest Khartoum's monitor be offended.

"We need to extract you," he volunteered again.

"Before the crunch?" No guerrillas were detailed to guard her nowadays, she indicated; and Bol's schoolboys were at the front. "When somebody dies, one of them gets the gun." Ladoku, the Madi Anglican minister, was still around—"as thin as Christ in frescoes," she told me. That she remained so sharp made her rescue seem all the more pressing. Yet thirty miles or so as the crow flies separated Ruth from the Norwegians—if they were ever going to evacuate—as well as the now bridgeless Nile. And they did have a separate road on their own side of the river that wound clear into Uganda at Moyo, toward Felix's refuge. "There would be a price in added risk for them to detour to fetch me. Besides, I don't think they're leaving," she insisted. And her tone stiffened. "They have a patient load you wouldn't believe. Witnesses are needed, too, you know? They're trying to panic us."

Loopy as she was, Ruth's forceful voice made me miss her. Such energy to bend to a task, if she had food to dole out, meds to apply. Was she tramping her Labyrinth obsessively, while an inferno whipped up outside and thousands crowded into her compound to sleep, on the theory that the Muslims wouldn't shell or bomb it— that the tanks and the MiGs would go by?

"Is she paralyzed? Can't say she was wrong?" Al wanted to know after our chat. And had he mismanaged Ruth? In business you didn't hire screwballs, but people looking out for number one. Yet odd ducks gravitated to the front lines of charity work, and sometimes those right on the rim of being screwballs served Christ best. Al suggested I drive up at least as far as Atiak and pre-position myself with the vehicle and supplies.

"Mr. Expendable. No kids, no insurance policy. Write him off," I joked. I was wistful, though, watching a child clasp a bouquet of bananas in her arms in our kitchen—wishing I could whisk that sumptuousness to Ruthie's churchyard.

But the splendidly various sky, from the New Stanley's rooftop, full of clouds scudding, and kites and swallows, exhilarated me—even ignited a sort of continental patriotism, *Africa über alles*. When I heard several ignorant tourists topping each other's dictator tales, Malawi's having kept a special crocodile pool for dissidents, etc., I said to them, "That's actually not the point. Get out of town for a while. Open your eyes. Womb of the world." The climate felt that way that day.

The trouble was, the Arab's phone rang for me the next midmorning. The Juba breakout had begun, and a bombing accidentally (as Khartoum claimed) hit the Norwegians' compound along their road, killing all three of them at the dispensary, plus dozens of patients, Al told me. And the Norwegian embassy was organizing a twin-engine Cessna flight with Mickey to their little grass airstrip to retrieve the bodies. That fiercely partisan Irish girl who thought the SPLA was like her country's IRA and had served as the doctor's gofer had survived because she was bunking elsewhere with a Dinka officer when the offensive began. But she wanted to clear out now, with the coffins, and head straight home, she confessed through sobs. It was "a charnel house, horrible," the gore of revolution, and yet since the Norwegians' jeep had been with her, it was intact, so Al's reason for calling me as soon as they got off the radio was to point out that she could give me the key if I went in on the plane during the cease-fire the embassy had arranged and go and round up Ruthie.

"The plane'll wait?"

"No, no. It's a five-hour truce, including the time in their airspace."

"So?" I said.

"That would get you there safe and sound and give you their jeep. Safer than the hassles of driving in our vehicle all the way from here." To my silence on the phone, he added, "You can't beat that logo on the door, and tie white on the antenna. Their logo will get you anywhere unless you're going toward Khartoum."

I laughed, but could picture all of the forensic washing and lifting I would need to help with or witness, not even to think of the hospital's patients strewn around, dead or alive, in agony but not being airlifted anywhere.

"A sort of head start," I said ironically, because the tanks would be following me down to Ruthie's.

"They're loading the coffins. An embassy guy's flying in, too, with Mickey. Double protection. I'll meet you there with what I've got."

For a minute I supposed he was coming along, but no, he had children, he said; he meant he'd meet me at the airfield with a trunk of rations and medicines. I could hear in my memory the MiG pilots' voices, two or three hirelings from the former Soviet bloc who flew the planes Khartoum had acquired, gabbling incomprehensibly to one another in abbreviated Russian, or whatever Slavic language it was, from their cockpits. Once an SPLA officer told Bol their wavelength and Bol tipped us off, we tuned in whenever the jets screamed over Loa like bass banshees, hearing snatches from "behind the Iron Curtain," as we said. I doubted that they personally cared about having plugged the poor Norwegians—and Khartoum's had been crocodile tears, since the Norwegians had been aiding the enemy— or, after the truce, would hesitate to zero in on my little jeep scuttling south toward Ruth's place, with no diplomatic instructions to spare me: unlike Mickey's little Cessna gliding through the Imatongs with a consul aboard.

Al understood my mental processes. Without explaining or deciding, I asked if Ruth was willing to be retrieved.

"Yes. I think the news sobered her, if that's the term. In fact, she apologized." When I was quiet, he added, "There's a window." Didn't refer to loading the coffins again but employed comfort-zone phrases like "I'll meet you" and "The jeep will be yours." Knowing Al, I wasn't swayed by these: rather, by Ruthie's plight. That she had "apologized" was extraordinary. I'd guessed, feeling foolish, she would never let on. Like me, I sensed, she believed she had made something of a hash of her life and, without admitting that, was trying to compensate.

In one of those snap decisions, a one-eighty, a flip-around you come to, I said yes instead of no, and so for the umpteenth time found myself packing my battered kit bag, tossing the extras into another duffel to store in the Arab's behind-the-bar closet, and crossing the street to the New Stanley's taxi stand.

Chapter 9

• • •

A T THE AIRPORT, THE COFFINS, AN ELOQUENT PINE THREESOME, AS advertised, had been delivered and loaded. The junior Norwegian diplomat was on hand, and even a pathologist from the city morgue with a camera. Al met me with his hundred-pound, leather-bound, mercy-flight trunk full of necessities, and other medical or nutritional cartons, plus a jerrican of extra gas for the jeep and two fifty-kilo sacks of cornmeal. Because this was so squeaky clean, aboveboard a gambit, with clearance in advance from Khartoum, and reporters on the tarmac to record the takeoff, we didn't have to stoop to any scuzzy subterfuge in the paperwork, like you'd do in a diamond flight.

Promptly then, Mickey had us barreling down the runway, tilting brusquely into the air, with all Africa and the heavens themselves laid out in front—me in the copilot's seat. Mickey, sporting a shoulder holster and boodle belt, a coffee-can spittoon wedged next to him, looked raffish. He loved takeoffs like a NASCAR event, and grasping the yoke, he gobbled that great vista of the Rift Valley, precipitously cut in the gargantuan veldt, with Lilliputian umbrella trees stippled about. We flew over the Aberdares and the Mau Escarpment and the pastoral plains between Mounts Kenya and Elgon—both higher than us—and Lakes Hannington and Baringo and the Laikipia Plateau.

Then the parched lands east of the Cherangani Hills; the twisty blue of Lake Turkana. Sitting behind me, the man from the morgue was suitably callow, "a convert to atheism," he informed me, although he had sought a posting to India instead of to Africa, in order to steep himself in the Eastern religions, he said. "Here it seems to be the Crusades all over again. Minarets versus nuns."

Landing at the U.N.'s relief-operations outpost at Lokichoggio, we tanked up for the Sudan leg, while Khartoum confirmed again that its two MiGs at Juba's airport would be grounded, expecting us. A chartered Antonov sat on the runway nearby, used by the U.N. for food deliveries to designated famine areas in the southern Sudan, with permission from Khartoum. A mission-of-mercy Antonov, but it was startling to be parked next to the familiar shape of a type of plane I'd watched in other hands on bombing runs over the Nile. The crew, too, gabbing in Russian with each other at the coffee machine in the office, gave me the creeps because they sounded like the hireling Slavs we eavesdropped on from Ruth's place when a MiG or an Antonov went over, mercenaries bombing the blacks for Khartoum. These guys dropped sorghum instead.

The U.N. operates a delicious cafeteria and pleasant dormitory facilities at Lokichoggio for staff who deserve some coddling after arduous weeks in the field. But with the unrefrigerated bodies of the Norwegians decomposing, and our consular officer and Zanzabari coroner consequently turning antsy, Mickey and I couldn't hobnob and sample the menu as we would have liked to. Wobbling into the air again, we swung between the drier Karamoja Range and more verdant Dongotona Mountains, with the comely Didinga Hills and Boya Hills off our tail, as we turned west, lifting like a puppet swaying on a string into the serious altitude of the Imatongs. Lotuke, Chukudum, Ikoto, Isoke, and Kapoeta were visible if you knew where to look, but mostly a roller coaster of seething, thrumming, roadless green, an anarchy never logged, underneath us as we surmounted one of Kinyeti's shoulders.

"Leo!" Mickey called out his window, while we were joggled like a loose balloon in Kinyeti's private turbulence of winds. Although the peak was turbaned in clouds, we could see the heath above timberline on top. Elizabeth, Nancy, and Leo might have holed up anywhere below, perhaps peering up at our cicada buzz, our minuscule glint in the sun.

"They're okay," he told me, as if I didn't know. "I'll get the call to fetch them at Chukudum. The Acholis will have passed them off to the Latukas, and the Latukas to the Didingas and the nuns at Chukudum." He imitated a quarterback doing something of the kind with a football. The Arabs controlled Kapoeta, the district capital but, as in Juba, were under siege, and outlying hamlets like Chukudum, where the Maryknolls had their clinic, were garrisoned by the SPLA. He pointed toward a few huts in a mite of a clearing in the forests three-quarters down Kinyeti's north massif, where the golden-skinned woman was said to live, left behind among the Acholis in Gilo by an itinerant English officer half a century ago as a baby and a mark of brief and nominal European occupation. He never came back, so she spoke no English and had survived on the shamanistic powers ascribed to her locally, and midwifing and so on. Mickey, though a collector of arcana, had never been to see her; even Leo never had—"Unless now!" he said.

He could point at Katire and Torit, Obb and Parjok, Magwe and Palotaka, Karpeto and Kerripi—settlements like pimples in the heaving ocean of vitality, tracklessly green and stretching twenty-eight hundred miles to Liberia and Sierra Leone, sufficient to sap the bravado of any bush pilot except the likes of Mickey, who was beating a rhythm on his knee with his fist, or eating hummus from a can with a forefinger, and drinking thermos coffee. It didn't seem a particularly funereal or hairy flight to him because he often flew into rebel-held enclaves in the Congo, Somalia, or Sudan without any protective clearance or diplomats aboard for a guarantee. The Allied Democratic Forces, fighting Uganda from Zaire; or a rump Nuer faction fighting the Dinkas from the swampy village of Lafon, north of Torit; or the

Equatoria Defence Force, of Mandaris, Baris, and others the Dinkas had persecuted; or the homicidal lunatics of the Lord's Resistance Army, who cut people's ears off in the name of the Christian God: all might be operating somewhere underneath us, not to mention the SPLA's militias, or their Arab enemies. That's why Leo and the nuns, during the walk from Opari to Chukudum, if the car broke down or had become dangerous to use, would need the protection of people who loved him from his years of pastoral care. Just one jughead with a Kalashnikov could splat them as anonymously as some small band of Somali *shiftas* searching below a ridgeline for gold or ivory, and themselves fair game for anybody.

Mickey hadn't known these Norwegians, because they came to Africa on limited stints and left. "But Ruthie's a good old bag," he said. "One time I had hepatitis and she could tell by looking at my eyes and told me to lie down and get treated. Otherwise I'd have kept right on flying and collapsed someplace you wouldn't ever want to be."

He pointed to the collection of hills surrounding her church at Loa, when we reached the river, and down to the Catholics' chapel and mission, twenty miles north of Ruth's. We could also see Juba—my first glimpse: a scattered locality including an airport with a tower and runways expanded for the military, and a dock on the Nile where a defunct ferryboat was moored, two or three blocks of cement stores, a paved street with several squat brick administrative buildings, some bungalows or villas for the honchos in charge, barracks for the soldiers, a down-at-heels, one-story stucco hospital, and an awful sprawl of slum neighborhoods of thatch in disrepair and mud, oily with stagnant sewage, hodge-podged by the three-year siege and housing a couple hundred thousand wretched souls who hadn't managed to tiptoe through the rings of scrubby minefields both sides had laid irregularly around the city and get safely out. It was ugly. There were vultures on unburied bodies, both goats and humans, in this huge circle, and jackals that glanced up at us with flesh hanging from their mouths. Yet people who made it through encountered famously rough treatment from a Dinka cadre suspicious of why they had remained in Juba for so long in the first place.

Besides the ring of mines—where two goats that hadn't finished dying, apparently panicked by the birds, were staggering, trying to stand—the city's spraddled slums had been partly appropriated for military use, and mortar-blasted by the SPLA. Other mortar shells had strayed into the pathetically jammed-together hovels where women, children, and the elderly had been trying to survive the siege, fed by the Lutherans' weekly flights into Juba from Kenya, balancing the Catholics' feeding on "our" side. In Nairobi, the aid facilitators joked mordantly about how they might have unintentionally prolonged the war—Lutherans feeding Muslims, Catholics the animists—which was not what they wanted, regardless of the egging on they might be getting from the diplomats. To look down for the first time at the squalor and privation our side's siege was inflicting upon tens of thousands of trapped civilians was breathtaking—"enemy territory." And there *was* the Antonov that bombed us, and two MiGs, on the airfield waiting for us to do our business and the truce to end. But when Mickey chuckled and reminded me of how I'd demonized those hired Slavs, "you with your CIA guys," I had to admit that I might be flying against the Dinkas, too, if I were living inside the siege lines.

We saw muzzle flashes, burning huts, and a blackish tank askew on a roadway as we banked. Inside that broken circle of machine-gun sniping and mortar explosions nobody was moving as in a normal provincial city, just scurrying for bare essentials, even though the breakout had loosened the guerrillas' grip. My sorrow spread so far beyond the three Norwegians who had died for their idealism that I wished I were back in New Hampshire teaching American schoolkids about our own Civil War, instead of watching this one. From the air, you could spot the positions that were crumbling and who, hunkered there, was doomed. The disintegrating siege line reminded me of burning my bridges in Alexandria, after watching my company's ships being destroyed in the Umm Qasr harbor on CNN during the Gulf War, and how I'd emptied its Egyptian bank accounts and stuffed the cash into my girlfriend's leotard before we flew to Heathrow. On the flight itself, joking with Amy about the corporate "coffers," I'd realized I had committed an irreversibly stupid act. She later changed her name by marrying someone else, and she wasn't a signatory anyhow, bless her, so I was more a target. And here I was, slanting steeply toward the Norwegians' hand-mown, stone-picked airstrip, a dozen miles south of Juba, wishing I wasn't, especially when Mickey muttered, "*Holy shit.*"

The MiGs had vaulted into the sky behind us but, instead of plugging us, were bulleting away toward one of the other government towns under siege: Wau or Kapoeta, Torit or Malakal. Our location being known, every other battleground in Equatoria was open to them. We could see the Maryknolls' stubby steeple up the curly, gorge-gouged Nile, which boasted a slick stretch near where the Norwegians had built their infirmary, and where the Irish girl and several others were waving frantically. Mickey's prematurely gray hair shone silver in the sunlight, to match his wicked grin at how bumpily we were going to hit the runway, the crescendo of a trip for him. But the blitzed hospital building wiped us clean of our preoccupations.

The bodies, black and white, were mangled, discolored, concussively dispersed, and not yet in bags, as we had anticipated. The surgeon still registered his amazement, but his wife, the nurse, in her green scrub suit, looked agonized, with ghastly shards of glass and stone and wood embedded in her, punctures that had bled profusely. The second Norwegian man, the anesthetist, appeared to have lived awhile, crawling aimlessly, hemorrhaging from his gashes. Four or five times as many Africans had died, patients and helpers strewn like after an eruption. The wounded had been lying for all these hours untended in the jumble of the crushed building, with any means of helping them also smashed. The Irish girl was not a nurse, had no bandaging or morphine, and felt constrained not to move the corpses until they had been photographed. So, except for a few starvelings who had been scavenging for survival items like dented containers, stained tarpaulins and gurneys, fly-covered scraps of bloody cloth, it was unmitigated horror.

She had assembled a pitiful pile of belongings to go with them. But in the meantime, the injured Africans were begging for water, painkillers, a tourniquet, a situation to recline in without stones poking their backs. We unloaded the coffins. The coroner and the diplomat indeed took pictures. We then washed, adjusted or painstakingly tended to, and wrapped the three eloquently white bodies, which spoke volumes in the din of war, though not so poignantly as the living who pleaded for care. They and the unburied dead had no relatives or buddies around to minister to them. Nobody was digging either graves or foxholes, and it became unutterably sad when a bloodstained English speaker upbraided us, then wilted to the ground.

"We kept our hopes up because we thought a doctor would come," he said. That is, a replacement on the plane, not merely a burial party. Mickey and I were loading Al's trunkful of front-line medications into the back of the jeep, along with the hundred kilos of cornmeal he had sent. Moira, the Irish girl, had handed me the key, kissed her Dinka officer good-bye, and vanished onto the plane to keep the coffins company. He radioed permission for me to cross the Nile to Ruth's side on a certain secret ferry the SPLA maintained now that the bridges had been bombed out, then jogged off to rejoin his unit. The antenna still sported a Norwegian flag, to which I added a square of white sheeting, and topped up the gas tank from my jerrican, in case that got grabbed at the first roadblock. The hospital's fuel drums had exploded in the raid. Only masculine pride kept me from sneaking back onto the plane.

The moaning of the dying asking for family, for shelter, for water had been a counterpoint to our hasty undertaking arrangements— the folding of amputated arms, closing jellied eyes, capping the doctor's half-scalped skull. The temporary coffins, one-size-fits-all, seemed uncomforting. No respectful proprieties were possible when we were all in such a hurry, and yet the Zanzabari suggested in passing that it was a much more compact scene than a militia massacre, where the dead and dismembered have run in all directions to escape the machetes: "So you take it in only gradually and forget it more slowly when you are home."

I nodded. I was digging out ampules of morphine, intending to leave along with the plane in order not to be swarmed by rubber-neckers who needed something to eat, if left alone here. But I wanted to give some relief.

"It was not so human." He pointed upward, at the air. "That you can forget easier than what the machetes do."

One person was herself a nurse and instructed me as to how much to shoot her with. A Dinka, she thanked me when she saw she wasn't going to be evacuated, her humor intact. "Tell Ruthie I had a hysterectomy," she said, pointing at her gory wound. She had managed to crawl into the brush for some shade. Ambulatory patients with shrapnel in them thronged around as I administered a couple of other lethal doses to those worse off; and Mickey yelled.

Under my driver's seat I'd felt a few days' worth of Norwegian army rations and a first-aid kit. Mickey started his engines and yelled again, so I walked over, noticing Moira in the copilot's seat and really no room for me, though I'd half-hoped he was telling me there was. Instead, he surprised me by throwing out his emergency fanny pack containing a compass, duct tape, water purifier, Cipro, hardtack, kippered herring, and the like.

"God luv ya, man! See you in Juba if they catch you—or Khartoum! Al will pay me back." He laughed, being used to dropping daredevils off in goose-bump situations, and pointed me toward the jeep, so we could leave at the same time. Gripping the yoke, he taxied to the leeward end of the strip. "The doctor, the doctor!" people were shouting, as they recognized for sure that they were being abandoned with no assistance, no food, unless the Arabs brought some. White-man-style, I scrammed, slipping my motor into gear to reach the spindly road just as he mounted over the trees and could no longer radio the SPLA to rescue me from the crowd. And now, when Juba's control tower confirmed his departure, the offensive would no doubt resume.

Once clear of the disaster zone, I drove slowly, with my pennants fluttering from the aerial and the good-guy logo on the door, hoping not to tempt any hair-trigger bozos at either side. Roadblocks might be my least risk, compared to ordnance hidden at free-fire angles to kill an APC or tank with infantry advancing south that you'd never see till you were safely past. And the road was fitfully mobbed by civilians burdened with bundles on their heads and tired, undernourished, disoriented children frightened by the crump and thump of shelling behind us—which, although the people parted for me without catcalls, sometimes startled them right back into the middle of the lane I had. I drove with one foot on the clutch, the other on the brake, wasting precious gas, as I suppose you must when bugging out of a civil war.

I wasn't forcibly stopped. Nobody set a baby down in front of my wheels or banged on my fender with a club. But lame, wraithlike people cried out to me in Bari, Arabic, Dinka, or English for a lift, with that edge of hysteria when norms are breached and breaking down. They had self-hacked canes and blistered sores and a mango or a wad of cassava in hand and were bent into the shape of question marks. But the huts along the way had not been torched, the trees not stripped of their leaves for soup, and kids who weren't clinging to their mothers, piggyback, might hop for fun with a stick like a vaulting pole. The casualties lay behind, where the noise was, and the grief of leaving them. People were in survival mode, dazed, yet trekking by the thousands through the rolling, tawny, still luxuriant landscape in the direction of Uganda. If they were footsore now, they'd be reeling soon.

I'd kept excusing myself for not picking any riders up because I was going to turn off, and finally a wooden crosspiece on a post did finger me left to the ferry landing at a fat stretch of the Nile where islets could conceal the rope and an acacia forest the pulleys on either bank. The Dinka soldier who was preventing civilians from boarding nodded at the sight of me, and the Bari ferryman chocked my wheels on the raft, as he and his son began to pull us toward the opposite side. The currents, greeny brown, revolved like supple cylinders or parallel crocodiles, though I noticed an actual crocodile swimming crosswise to them, like us. The ferryman worked mostly at night, when the MiGs didn't fly, and said this had been his grandfather's livelihood, paid for at first by the English and the Italian White Father missionaries.

"No oil here. Why this war?" he asked. The oil was beyond Juba and Malakal downriver; he hadn't been that far north. When I tapped his biceps, he showed me trotlines he had strung from an island into the river that kept his family well supplied with protein. When I asked what he would do when the Arabs arrived, he waggled his thumb at a dugout pirogue hidden next to the slip he was pulling toward.

"They don't swim. I know them! Not watermen. No camels here." He pointed at a mountain torrent joining the river beyond where we were. "Scared," he said, as if shivering; then pointed at a black-and-white fish eagle soaring to dive on the fish bewildered by the water's change in flow, and gave me a piece of white crocodile tail meat to chew.

A Dinka guard helped him, me, and his son to push the jeep up the landing to the dirt road on this east bank, where an equivalent crowd, inflamed by rumors that the guerrillas were no longer able to hold their positions surrounding Juba, was fleeing south. Mostly Dinkas, not from these local river tribes, they weren't afraid to step right up and berate the Dinka soldiery: *If you have already lost your cattle herds and homelands, do you want to lose your children and old people, as well?* They couldn't melt into the forest on ancient footpaths and shelter with relatives who may have never made either army aware that they existed. It was their fight, not mine, but being on Ruth's side of the river, I could fill my empty seats with a handful of the thousands of souls who needed a ride. Fearfully raucous, shedding the discipline the SPLA had imposed on its refugee camps, the retreat was not yet a free-for-all, and neither deferential nor hostile to my NGO logo. I wanted to find Bol, but the name is a common one and nobody responded to my inquiries except with puzzlement.

I let a broken-legged old man with a spear lie on top of the grain sacks and medical gear, on the understanding, conveyed by sign language, that he would defend them if necessary. Next to me in front, I allowed an exhausted, bulgingly pregnant woman to sit; her stained toga indicated that her sac had burst. It was a crazy notion, but could you have turned her down? Ruth might help; she had no one else. And children climbed in and out, over the back bumper, because I drove with stymied intensity, seldom above five or ten miles an hour in the crush. Crones and geezers were attempting to evacuate, and women of all ages with or without toddlers in tow—long-legged savannah folk but limping from the downed timber hereabouts, with shins barked, knees knobbed from weeks on a meal or less a day. Some figures leaned or lay a few yards off the line of march, awaiting their fate or for the pain to let up, or their marrow to release more calories. If they were already dead, nobody knew.

I met no vehicles. The guerrillas had thrown their stake-side trucks and pickups into carrying troops, not acting as ambulances, and mounted machine guns in the latter. So I was afraid that a cruising MiG might spot me, only a minute's flying time south of the fighting, and assume I must be a commander. I didn't want to go slower than I could help, yet couldn't drive fast. Whole families were walking in front of me, their ears hearing echoes of the crackle of battle, not attuned to a minor motor nudging their heels. Gamins and gravid ladies strode like marathoners, carrying whichever members of the newest generation who had endured. All turned in vague alarm at the snout of my jeep, expecting a hollering commandant. SPLA politics were so lethal, their expressions showed relief mixed with chagrin that a last NGO was leaving.

I thought of Herbert and Craig, who always cleared out before the shit hit the fan. Herbert, after his three passports spilled out of his bag in my presence, had opened up a little, not to speak of his work but saying he had "a cocoon" at home (wherever that was) where his wife raised dogs and he had a "den" with all of Bach and Mozart at his fingertips and the finest technology to render it. "Soothing," he said.

Passing a man stumbling in gait, his hip bones, almost fleshless, wagging as laboriously as a sick fish's tail, needing both food and first aid, I realized I would have picked him up at any other time. Too many blackish birds were spiraling in the sky, as if congregating off the mountainsides to head toward the civilian conclaves where Ruth's clinic was. Her fence had been knocked down. Her compound was filling, Makundi, her Kamba assistant, had told Al, sounding uncommonly worried on the radio, with a babble of squatters as background noise behind him, not because they imagined she still had rations to feed them but in the belief that the Arabs might not bomb her church for fear of "angering America." When the exodus reached them, a panic would block our route.

I was still wondering whether Ruth's baby jackal had gone into one of Makundi's stews and whether Bol was at the front or if I might meet him again when suddenly, on a hunch, I spun the car to the right into the tall grass, a dip in the ground practically flipping it, simultaneously with my ears registering the bass banshee hurricane scream of a jet cannoning the road where we'd just been. I lost my back-seat passengers, wrenched my shoulder, bloodied my nose, and the lady beside me began to shriek. I was gasping in simpleton's shock, spitting nettles and spiderwebs out of my mouth, till the pain in my shoulder, almost out of its socket, became nothing compared to hers. The baby must have been crushed: it would have to be extracted. I dragged her out of the jeep.

The tangly turf of the jungle, such as it was, had cushioned the falls of the old spearman and the two or three small orphans who had been riding with him. He reassembled his dignity and his three good limbs, scrambled to the road, and began badgering passersby to help. The trouble, of course, was that things were worse. I had never assisted in a birth, aborted or not, but wiggled the inert fetus out of the canal—the mother's hands like trapped birds beside mine—along with a horrendous flow of blood. Easing her into a peaceably woozy position in which to lose consciousness, with the inert child beside her was the saddest moment so far, but a wider devastation had been inflicted on the stream of pedestrians next to the shell craters and strafing pattern scribbled on the road. They were now in louder agony, and nobody could minister to them, either. In the chaos and congestion we did enlist enough bystanders to right the car, and I found another vial of morphine, good for ten quick shots, and some absorbent compresses.

A stillbirth in the midst of a famine, a bombing, an auto accident, and triaging. I tied tourniquets onto stumps; these, alone, were not going to save anybody's life, but the anguish of the surviving family was diminished. We bounced on, another very pregnant woman in the passenger seat and the broken-legged man, with a retaped splint, lying on the bags and trunks, yelling imprecations in Dinka when necessary at the new arrivals, unmaimed, who surged around, walking south but begging for a ride.

She was a Kakwa, with relatives in Atiak, she said in storekeeper English, watching the MiG perform more important errands on the horizon than coming back for us, its afterburners banging as it climbed away from any Stinger that might be fired in retaliation. I believe in premonitions, or a sixth sense that can save your life, but the plane had probably not been supersonic so close to the ground on its strafing run at us: so I might have heard it, as an assist to my hunch. The Kakwa had seen our escape but lost a sister in the attack and thus was betting on me, split between hope and grief. The Dinka had a herder's voice, sharp and loud, rattling his spear, but she could negotiate us through a crowd better, using Juba's Arabic argot or Kakwa, which is close to Bari. She was also soft-hearted. We soon had kids perching on both front fenders and the spare tire bolted to the rear, which disarmed the walking wounded who otherwise might have yelled at us. Another woman, stick-armed yet pouch-bellied, tall yet bent, with pain creasing her face, and too timid to look at me, swung herself aboard in the back-seat area at the invitation of my friend with the spear—he explained the reason in Dinka, and she yammered to him in her distress like, perhaps, a fellow villager.

People stepped around the more outlandish dead, depersonalized by ghoulish wounds or grotesque postures, when a sort of all-fours, slaughterhouse animalization had occurred in the throes. But where I couldn't drive around, I needed to drag them, with the kids' help, out of the road. I might stop anyway, visualizing how the tank treads would chew them up if they were left where they must have collapsed. Sensible individuals would have availed themselves of the woods to die; but who's so sensible, or not afraid of hyenas, at that tipping point? Better the company of the living before the vultures land. We hauled them underneath the nearest tree, as well as people in convulsions, not finished with the process yet—braying in misery at the departure point. There is no dignity to dying of dysentery along the roadside among the myriad feet of a retreat. The tanks would suspect an ambush and grind right over them.

Waifs and walking wounded I steered around, as if becoming acclimated. The spearman growled half-sympathetically at how I trembled: our close call catching up with me. New crowds swallowed us, oldsters wagging their bones like a carp's tail, laboring south on the shoulders of the road. The adrenaline still had me panting. I ached. My wrists and fists remembered how hard they'd wrenched us off into the ditch. A granny holding hands with four children blocked our way, but I didn't honk, or even regret leaving Nairobi. I was in the flow, Uganda incongruously the safest haven. Incidents were blurring together because people held their youngsters up for me to see—whether to take them or inoculate them or feed them—and I didn't stop, except finally in the case of one woman who appeared to be dying. Afflicted as though by a stroke caused by some shrapnel, she could use only half of her face, which worked to express her urgency.

She was besmeared and encrusted, with another girl, who was shattered likewise. I'd spread my hands to indicate my inability to take them anywhere that would have mattered, even if I'd had the space, and pointed at a shady tree where they might sit. My motor stalled in the milling crowd. Then the jeep felt jostled, but before I could get irritated, the detonations of the Antonov carpeting a refugee camp followed. More panic and congestion would ensue.

What good would it do? I signaled. They were supporting each other at my window. Bandages, penicillin, if I stopped and rooted them out to administer, and wasn't swamped by other petitioners, would be of no real use now. What the mother with aphasia or semiparalysis wanted, however, was to pass, with the help of her friend, a boy of kindergarten age, catatonic with fright, from their slippery arms into my lap. Whatever might happen to him was better than watching her die. The mortuary immobility of her face told me that; and he didn't begin to grab for my ears and eyeglasses until I drove away. The kid on the rear fender yelled at him in Dinka to quit doing that.

I needed a sling to ease my shoulder's ache, but would see a person losing blood at a catastrophic rate. Even though I didn't stop, the armor behind me would be less merciful. It would be a rout by then. My spearman's bad leg looked badly set, lucky perhaps that it didn't smell of gangrene yet, and his spear mostly functioned as a cane. But he groaned at the anxious scenarios we squeezed through, the dramas of families split by who could continue to walk and who could not, believing, I think, that needier people ought to have his space in the car and he should be facing the Arabs with his spear: take one with him. I hadn't stopped, for him to catch the chance to slide out, but at the Maryknolls' former post, now teeming with refugees, I felt duty-bound to check in, as if Father Leo's voice were prompting me. A few parishioners and a Tanzanian X-ray technician left behind, whose machine had broken long ago, were preserving order inside the shell of each building, and my presence bolstered them, especially when I said that the NGOs were all coming back, regardless of who won the war. Who could survive for a month or so, was the question. Those whose starvation had progressed to the monkey-cheeked, eye-socket stage had been provided with a dimly illuminated concrete room to lie in; malarial patients, another. The latrines had flooded.

My car was claustrophobically surrounded, and I was surprised to find the Tanzanian stranded, but, raising his eyebrows, he indicated the thronging children, the veneer of civility still masking desperate circumstances, so how could he desert? Leo and the nuns were "precious, God's instruments." It was crucial they not be killed by mistake, like the Scandinavians. I hugged him and gave him one of the fifty-kilo bags of maize I'd brought (Leo's brogue prompting again), which was immediately set boiling in the fifty-five-gallon steel drum they cooked mush in. My spearman lay down on guard in the weeds, and we lost our collection of urchins to the prospect of a palmful of cornmeal apiece.

I took the opportunity to skedaddle, but my remaining passengers, the heavily pregnant Kakwa and the other woman, were so dismayed I gave them energy bars from Meals Ready To Eat packages and snacked on one myself. Around a couple of bends we met more waifs in the middle of the road, who mounted the fenders and the spare tire fastened upright in back. I picked up a third ailing woman, to fill the back seat—the eye is hardwired for triage, I think—and peeled a tangerine for the child in my lap. Unfortunately he was wetting it from more than one orifice, but I had resisted the awful impulse to leave him at the Catholics' place, to be smothered in terror. A railroad train could not have collected all of the women and children in need of rescue. The listlessness of true famine was spreading, people eking out their last calories by as little exertion as possible, and I had no radio to start the aid groups in Gulu moving north to receive them.

We slowed to a crawl again when a soldier with a Kalashnikov, although nodding in recognition at my logo, squeezed off a warning shot and peered at my passport, then asked for a candy bar. Imagining

the furor in the European press about the Norwegians' deaths, I
wondered what the rumor mill in Nairobi's NGO community was
doing with Ruthie's holdout status. Selfless or neurotic and pigheaded?
She and our piffling organization, Protestants Against Famine, were
minor players on the overall scene, but this disaster would train a
spotlight on her. She was probably going to apologize for endan-
gering me, but would she even be considered employable out on the
edge again? Combined with what was already some gossip about her
Labyrinth and witch's globe and spirit stick (maybe the truck drivers
had snitched), would this seem a stunt signifying unreliability? People
knew of her sudden return to Ohio a year or two before, but not that
she'd come back to Africa precipitously because she'd felt suicidal
there. Burning out was okay; anybody might do that. The code
involved how you handled it.

"I don't believe in tragic sacrifices," I muttered to myself, as if
rehearsing my first comments to Ruth. My shoulder hurt as I
eased the tires over the bumps, praying that none would go flat,
and blaming her was easy. On the other hand, I'd begun to anticipate seeing Bol. Now, in the anarchy of the rebels' defeat, I might
be able to rescue him, help him fulfill his dream of reaching the
cities of the West. The river in its purring gorge was lit by curva-
ceous intensities of tawny light, the hills like combers over it,
overenthusiastically endowed with flora. But in my lap the little
kindergartener who had been thrust upon me, and was clinging
to my sore ribs and interfering with my driving, had also vomited
up the pieces of an energy bar he had eaten and further dehydrated himself by releasing more of his diarrhea onto my pants, as
though to remind me that this was an ambulance I was driving,
and I was probably going to dump the patients out in Ruth's
churchyard to await the tanks. The pregnant woman next to me,
in tribal dress, with necklaces, amulets, earrings, a hair band but
bone-thin, offered the scrawny boy the bits he had thrown up in
her tweezer fingers. When he shook his head, she popped them
into her own mouth. Good god, was I kidding myself that I could

save her and him as well as the carload of people I had undertaken to pick up?

"God luv ya!" Mickey had called from the cockpit, when he'd tossed me his crash rations and kit with flashlight and so on. And I was thinking how accidental it was, who you "saved." Makundi instead of this famished Kakwa; or *her* instead of another of the women in their seventh or eighth month I had noticed struggling along but passed? A stooped fellow clutching a few cassava roots by the roadside (and relieved I wasn't stopping to steal them) indicated by gesturing that Bol might still be around, when I said the name. I thought of my legendary Hickey ancestor, however, who as a child had starved with his family through the Great Potato Famine in Ireland a hundred and fifty years ago. When they sent him out to search the fields one last time, after nobody else had strength enough to go, he walked back, like this man, with three in his hands and knowledge of an undiscovered pocket, to save their lives. A sumptuous sunset had begun, as large as the sky. Would we get away by dawn? I didn't dare leave Ruth's till daylight or we might face mob rule.

"God bless you!" She grinned wearily when I drove through the ruined gate.

The courtyard was like ten gypsy encampments piled together, with hunger the theme song. Her hair had whitened, so she looked sixtyish instead of fiftyish; and even Makundi, who had been skinny before, was thinner still.

"You find us in reduced circumstances," she added self-mockingly, while grimacing at the arrival of yet more weakened women, swelling toward deliveries that were sure to be wretched and sad, and also the small boy curled fetally, with his snot bubbling into my lap. Two Dinka clan chieftains' wives, Nyadoul and Nyajal, one in a red toga, the other in blue—"They are heroes," Ruth said—took charge of my last fifty kilos of cornmeal, though it would need to multiply like Christ's five loaves and two fishes in order to nourish the multitude who gathered around the steel fuel drum to smell the aroma as sticks were lit.

"This way they're dying by inches," she said; and, turning, asked me, since I had remained almost silent, "Should I apologize?" In fact, according to Al, she had, over the radio. Yet on the scene I was uncertain. Maybe you really ought to stay as long as you could, if only as a witness.

I cleared my throat. "I don't know." Because that sounded a bit stupid, I added, "Truthfully."

Ruth was sleepwalking by now, compared to when I'd left, but still cherishing young Leo, who continued to hug her right hip in addled confusion, and therefore she was none too pleased by my introducing an obviously sickly, faintly weeping new waif right into the household, so to speak, who might be fatally contagious. I wasn't, either—he'd been handed to me as a stranger by a stranger a couple of hours ago and had been dribbling on me from both ends ever since. But his mother's anguished expression from the side of her face that still worked was potent, imperative, as Ruth, without asking, could see. Not touching him, she examined him sympathetically.

"No measles," she said. "They have measles in Kajo Kaji. Can you picture what will happen if those two armies come tearing through here and all get the measles and everybody on their feet keeps running?"

The drone of the Antonov, never grounded as early in the evening as the MiGs, moved us indoors, to "the priory," as she called her quarters jokingly, to collapse into chairs for a pot of tea. Not that the roof made it safer than the dinky ditch she'd had dug for a bomb shelter—and which stank now of feces—but you could ignore more. She was in a diminished mood. There was no protocol. She wolfed down a Meals Ready To Eat from my stash, chewing pieces Leo could swallow to finger into his mouth. I gave my boy soup. The generator had run out of fuel, so we used a candle. The radio's battery was dwindling. The baby jackal had indeed gone into one of Makundi's stews.

"It's so random it's bedlam," she said. "You have to believe in heaven, and I don't know if I do."

We did reach Felix, nearby in Uganda, who ran the closest NGO station and could relay the news to Al the next morning that I'd arrived at Ruth's. His radio was on because he was attempting to reach the German embassy in Kampala, in case they could pressure an army general to organize a convoy of food north along his road from Gulu. Another mine probably planted by a rump group of rebels called the Allied Democratic Forces had blown up under a routine delivery, killing the truck driver, and set off another drivers' boycott. Knowing that an avalanche of refugees was tumbling his way, he sounded frantic to get resupplied. "I can feed a hundred at most for one day," he said. Ruthie groaned. We were watching a line of our own souls, supervised by Nyadoul and Nyajal, each receive a handful of mush to last them indefinitely. These Ugandan rebels weren't crazies, like the Lord's Resistance Army, but a collection of leftover military folks who had served previous dictators, so their mines were meant to disable not aid groups but Museveni's army. The LRA's evil genius wished to punish the world for its sins.

I wanted Ruth to massage my sick shoulder, but she was too tired for me to ask. She showed me a knapsack she'd packed for tomorrow's vamoose. Makundi, meanwhile, was guarding the jeep. She also pawed through the meds that remained in my trunk for what to distribute to patients she recognized before we left—irritated now that Al hadn't remembered to put in powdered milk and eggs for Leo.

"But he's never met Leo. And we had about ten minutes," I pointed out, though afraid then of being blamed myself.

The complaint was shelved when the Antonov pooped a crap-load of explosives onto a temporary settlement down the road a bit, where it might impact the exodus the most. The route must be choked with the injured, the panicky, throttling possibilities of either resupply for the front or an orderly guerrilla retreat. Flames flashed up like blood briefly, and I pictured the airplane's crew, Soviets cashiered at the end of the Cold War without ever having had the chance to bomb American targets; this could be their apotheosis. We continued doling out germicides, rehydrating salts, malaria pills, so nothing would be left to fall into less deserving hands, a random, surreptitious process nonetheless, because everyone needed stuff. The chairs, beds, blinds, bins would disappear as soon as we were gone, and after I emptied the rest of my jerrican into the gas tank, I rinsed it obsessively to carry our water, since the jugs had been stolen already. The other jeep's tires, up on blocks, which I'd hoped to cannibalize for the Norwegians' vehicle, had been cut up for rubber sandals.

Makundi wore a pair—and so did Bol, when he showed up, looking skeletal. I hugged him, gave him an energy bar. No, no firing squads; nothing for him to fear if, like us, he made a dash for it. The big bright rising moon tempted us—if it might not tempt the Antonov into trying another bombing run—instead of the alternative, succumbing to a nap. But, coughing badly, swallowing an aspirin, he advised us not to.

"At night people have less conscience, you know? No witness. In daylight they know you did good, so they wouldn't hurt you."

He didn't want to discuss what had befallen his various schoolboys, except to say that the unaccompanied minors program had been scrapped by the SPLA even before the offensive. No food for those not drafted, and so those twelve years old and under had scattered, chasing bush squirrels and grasshoppers. He grabbed at the air, as you'd do to catch the latter and crunch them in your mouth. I fell asleep on my cot while we caught up, but Ruth, being worried that his cough was tubercular, did not act welcoming, and Makundi, no fan of the Sudanese, had always been cool toward Bol. He liked to say that the Brits had given the Sudan its independence on a silver platter well before Kenya's and without anything like the fight Kenya's Mau Mau had had to wage. So here they were, fighting each other instead: Arabs versus Dinkas; Nuer and Zandes against the Dinkas. Bol would scowl defensively. "Do you think we've made no plans?" But in their arguments, Makundi evoked the chaos everywhere within a hundred miles by waving circles in the air.

This wasn't in contention now. And Ruth was preoccupied with preserving the poor toddler, Leo, still marked with the monkey eye sockets and cheeks from the starvation he had endured before Father Leo had happened to scoop him up. Like Bol's, her attention had narrowed, but she still had a child to focus upon. She had no soap left to scrub with after touching her patients, which bothered her visibly when Leo was standing by, wanting to be touched, too. No food to give them, either—the cornmeal I had brought vanished even before the end of the line reached the cooking barrel—but a gargantuan scale of privation within a stone's throw of the church itself. People may have congregated in the churchyard in hopes that it would be spared in order not to anger the Christian powers, but flickering on the hillsides all around were campfires anchoring individual families against the atavism of the sky.

I slept for what resembled half an hour of nonstop vigorous dreaming, with this emergency transposed to other settings (or me trying to prevent the pews from being burnt as firewood), until Makundi woke me. The sky was pink tentatively whitening toward blue: "Like America," he said ironically. Logy, I had three adult passengers ready, plus Leo permanently hitched on Ruth's jutting thigh or knee or hip. We could have identified a thousand people in need of the services of an ambulance, but the point was to dull or mask one's compassion and briskly clear out, as everybody watched. I was able to play that role except for the sticking point of my little dribbling, whimpering, feverish, dysenteric, dying boy. I think Ruth was ready to come to blows, if I had laid him in the car alongside Leo: "It's not just malaria. They would isolate him in a hospital." He was as hot as soup, doubled over with cramps, too scared to sleep. She was afraid of cholera, which was stretching it, but she was right that sticking him in the jeep to bounce like a jumping bean until he died would be simply cruel. With his mother's haggard, aphasic face in my mind's eye, I remade my bed, sheets and all, then laid his head on the pillow, with a chocolate in his mouth and water at the side. Leaving him incongruously ensconced like that in luxury on an expatriate's cot for the short remainder of his life, he had made me feel better. Yet it is as regretful a memory as any I have.

Otherwise our departure was anticlimactic. Nyajal and Nyadoul thanked Ruth in a mixture of English and Dinka, via Bol, with the gravity of women about to flee themselves, in separate clans, and far from the first time, having already walked from the Nile to Ethiopia and back, losing crippled kinsfolk at every stage. We could see the smattering of Dinkas, lying or sitting, and raising their hands to us, who would get no farther than here.

Makundi, Ruth's onetime houseman in Nairobi, had a coil of snaring wire under his shirt and Attlee's sheath knife on his belt. This was not his war, and he was prepared to walk home across a fourth of Africa, if it came to that, using the woodcraft of his youth, but he was coming with us. Bol, having a minor civil administration position, however, was pained. He told the crowds that in Uganda the United Nations would find and feed them, and if they were stalled where they were to remember that the Arabs had lived alongside their ancestors for a thousand years and were not bogeymen. Most of their soldiers were not Arabs anyhow, but blacks from the region of Darfur who the Arabs hired to fight for them. "We all went to school together before and we will go to school together again," he translated himself for me. I was dunked into a chilly memory from Keene, New Hampshire: the school board quizzing me about why I'd taken an hour of class in Beginning History to make a point of getting fourteen-year-olds to understand the difference between Norman Thomas and communism.

Our Slavic friends droned overhead to choose another target. Fires scattered on the horizon included thatch huts burning, whether set ablaze by other guerrillas attacking our guerrillas or people destroying their own homes as they fled. Then the geysering explosions of the Antonov's pass caused the mob on the road in front of us, already arena-sized, to quail. Oldsters, and Dinka mothers of child-bearing age bolstering one another, cicatrixed Mandaris, Nuer scarified on their foreheads, Acholis, Baris, and other minority tribes mixed in this mass that surged like a stadium emptying through a tunnel. Bol's diplomacy helped part a path, and although people I vaguely recognized made thumbing motions for a ride, it was good-humored, as if granting that, all right, our service was up and we were entitled to board one of those British Airways flights that once a day followed the course of the Nile at three or four times the height of the Antonov, clear north, entirely out of Africa to Heathrow, leaving only its contrail behind. I was teary from the tension nevertheless, · and because my lap felt empty, though it and the seat were still stained and smelly from that little boy's bloody flux. And now when he woke from his daze, as hot as a teapot and desperately thirsty, the sheets gooey, his innards on fire, and looters tipping him onto the floor, wouldn't he have been better off if his mother had never pushed him into my arms in the first place?

Ruth's face was pursed from a migraine, and indrawn from the calamity. The Zandes, Bol said, were drifting to the west toward Zande land, and the Kakwas toward Yei. Ladoku, our Anglican minister, had set his sights on reaching Palabek, a Ugandan village, by a network of trails that one of his Acholi parishioners knew about, with such of his flock who could attempt the trek, after kneeling down publicly to beg forgiveness from the rest. The enormity of the relocation permitted us to bob along as noncombatants, with Bol assuring any soldier of our bona fides. People hollered for help occa-sionally, pointing to a wound or somebody who'd collapsed, yet we had turned stony. None of us was inclined to stop. Ruth even muttered, "Donor fatigue" to a supplicant who trotted beside her window, without asking what his problem was. We did acquire a tiny entourage of boys who hadn't been dragooned for combat but had no favors to ask. They just recognized Bol or me from those classes under the tamarind tree and, not being too lame, started to follow, like a Secret Service cordon, as Ruthie joked, when they perched on each front fender or jogged by the tailpipe, holding on to the spare wheel bolted upright in back. I didn't adjust my speed to accommo-date them, but couldn't go faster anyway.

Unaccompanied minors to begin with, they'd been left to comb the debris of ruined villages for scraps of protein or boil grass and leaves. The wedge of space behind the car as we nosed through the throngs provided a collecting point for more, only stymied by the aerobatics of a MiG that dived in an ear-damaging pendulum over us—I nearly squirted off the road again—suddenly throttling the flow. Red and black detonations miles ahead of us announced the blowup of the bridge over the Aswa, as we later learned. Not a river as formidable as the Nile, but neither drivable nor wadeable, and guys were going to have to spear the crocs and snakes in the belt of swampland before a horde of people swam. We'd stopped seeing weapons— a bazooka, a Stinger, a Kalashnikov—everything being at the front, and some of the sad sacks slumped pitifully at the shoulder of the road were never getting up.

The jam was such that Makundi made it plain that he would rather have struck off on foot for himself if it weren't for Ruth. He had his pay. "Alone is best." But Bol was flogging the case that the SPLA's commanders had delegated him to get us through so the international community could hear the news. Although not true, this might have worked if it were possible to slip us past the people who hadn't been able to hear his voice. The noise was bedlam; the crush, fearful. When we did move, the impetus was everybody's need to continue south, bridge or not. Khartoum had broken the siege on all sides and was shuttling in more troops on another Antonov for the push, a man with a squawk box at a roadblock said, and these Dinkas, being in foreign tribal territory anyway, couldn't skitter off the road to hide in the mountains like the locals and find food without their soldiers to protect them. The Acholis and others had scores to settle. And yet, beyond the Aswa, the LRA was lying in wait with a machine gun to pick the refugees clean, once they got into Uganda, he said. "They listen to the radio, too," Bol translated.

Grannies and aunties signaled us in dismal urgency when a feebly blubbering child with wrist bones larger than her arms collapsed, or an older person not beyond rescuing. My fingers twitched on the steering wheel, wanting to help, at the same time as I groped for my canteen beside my seat to make sure it was out of reach of the witches' brew of germs inhabiting the mouth or hands of any child we might relent and try to save. Ruth's face was like when you're scurrying through a rainstorm with no covering for your head, flinching, bent—mumbling, though, that Ethiopia had been worse.

We weren't in the middle of an Ethiopian or Somali desert but in central Africa, the very scenery of prehistory, as pristine as it gets, if you left the road blocked by these uprooted thousands for a matter of days. "It's shattering," I suggested. "Not like glass," she told me. "More like mercury—it'll get back together." She held Leo up occasionally, for people to know we had a child in the car. Then Bol, when he was spotted by an eight- or nine-year-old we recognized as having taught together, hauled him through the rear window to sit between himself and Makundi, which made two. Not dumbfounded by his good luck, the boy began to recite half the English alphabet for us. Makundi, less touched, lectured Bol on how the Dinkas should have budgeted some troops for border control. His composure was equal to the task of slapping people's hands away when they reached inside to beg for food, as if they were pickpockets in Nairobi. Exasperated as he was by our late start—the blame was not mine, but he didn't hide his belief that a CIA spook like Craig would have been of more use—he didn't rate schoolteacherly niceties, educated gentilities, like Bol's all that highly, either. With his languages, Luo and Kikuyu, Arabic and Swahili, English and Dinka, plus, intact from childhood, his woods wisdom, he might be illiterate but could slide out of his door and strike off southeasterly for home pronto, if his loyalty to Ruth didn't say no. Ruth reached back to feel the forehead of the new little boy, then nodded her approval because the fires of vitality but not a fever burned there. As stringy as a sparrow, he chattered to Bol about subsisting with cousins' families on their meager leavings after his parents died, till they sloughed him off and he "lived like an antbear," Bol said, keeping himself alive by tweaking dead bark off windfalls in the woods, eating termites or whatnot.

Either we were obstructed in the crowd or burning too much gas in fits and starts, with our hopes flagging alongside the footsore souls surrounding us. They seemed to think a helicopter might soon arrive to hoist us to safety, an intervention they wouldn't resent if the notice helped them. But no, unlike my last exit, with Ya-Ya and company, this was not to be easy. And, again, a plane's horrific shadow and racket swept over us, the Doppler effect dropping its original scream into a blast furnace snarl. We were as terrified as everybody else, but so hemmed in that to have swerved would have killed half a dozen people. I was yelling, and in front of us one woman among a bunch broke her ankle, twisting to escape the shadow. Malnutrition makes your bones fragile. Her friends pulled her out of the way—and the MiG had apparently expended its ordnance—but in the fright and hectic scramble I wound up with a youngster clambering into my lap. I hardly glanced at him at first, I was so distracted, or remembered which woman, the injured lady or another, had been carrying him, or whose arms had almost immediately deposited him through my window. They didn't want me to know—have the opportunity to object—and so pretended that it hadn't happened, lest he be thrust out.

His heft was reassuring, at least. Not a starveling with reddish, kwashiorkor hair. And instead of crying and peering outside for his mother, to provide me a clue in the confusion as to who she was, he lifted his hands straightforwardly onto the wheel, imitating mine. Every woman looked about as worn out as if she'd been toting him on her back or in her arms for twenty miles, and nobody betrayed whose he was. He kept mimicking my motions of steering.

"Maybe the MiG brought him," I said. A fait accompli! I wondered idly how I would be able to describe his mother to him someday. Ruth offered him a morsel from a ration packet, evidently a new taste, to settle him; and Makundi chimed in acceptingly in a backhanded sort of way: "Anyhow, he's not a Dinka." Mig, as I began to call him, did look Bari-ish.

"Bravo," said Bol, whose own adoptee was gangly like him.

I was watching for a Bari or an Acholi, in fact, to lead us off this hysterically demoralized passage to a pulverized bridge. We wanted untankable terrain, no planes, and a back entrance into Uganda, which may sound logical until you are in the trackless wilds, which of course are a maze of tracks.

Ruth asked Bol whether during his studies at the University of Khartoum he had "known any generals?"

"You mean who are generals today?" He laughed. "Well, Dinkas like me went to Moscow afterward to be trained because, if you remember, the U.S. of A. was an ally of Khartoum then, against Libya, and you didn't care if we black men all starved to death down here. So you invited Khartoum to send its military prospects to Fort Benning, in Georgia, for training—and we in the SPLA went to Moscow. And that's why the Arabs are so kind in these wars, because they were taught by your army at Fort Benning how to be."

"True," she said. "And I'm Old Mother Hubbard," she added, describing herself. The Antonov groaned over, perhaps on reconnaissance. Makundi was fiddling with our radio; we'd forgotten to bring the frequencies list. With a weak signal and the battery failing, the point was to alert one of the NGOs to where we were, not to mention the looming catastrophe when this cataract of savannah refugees fetched up at the Aswa with Uganda's forests to starve in on the other side. Sure, the crocodiles and child soldiers of the LRA could be disposed of shortly, when a hundred thousand evacuees crossed the river, but what would they live on then? Meanwhile I was squandering fuel to travel at scarcely above walking speed toward a humanitarian disaster, where we would arrive without resources ourselves.

My new lapmate, though clinging to my midriff like a baby primate a bit past the Swee'Pea stage, was still not crying—"A child of the woods," Bol concluded, after trying both Arabic and Dinka on him—so I wondered if he hadn't already been an orphan when he was handed to me. The motor's hum, our magic locomotion, and the theater of cloud shapes and windy treetops against the backdrop of the sky, as he lay on his back gazing upward out the window, kept him entertained or spellbound, as the case might be, but how could we feed him?

"They will find slim pickings, your generals!" Bol told Ruth and me, teasing about the Arab officers who would soon be rolling over this territory, after having been trained at Fort Benning. "No pretty girls wringing their hands for mercy and begging for a banana! Mobutu, Haile Selassie—your government likes brutes. You would have liked Hitler if he had been in Africa."

Startled, I nodded even so because there was some truth to that; we had let a quarter million blacks starve to death in Sudan in 1988 to hold on to our alliance with Khartoum. And long-haired, limber-limbed, olive-lovely Nyajal would not be hanging around to be toyed with by the conquerors. Slavery was no historic abstraction to these tribes; the Arabs' name for them remained synonymous with "slave." Nobody who could walk wasn't doing so.

We heard a snatch of military Arabic on the radio, and playfully daredevil-sounding Russian from a circling plane in answer, shifting to an undertow of thrill, and shuddering explosions miles away. But we did reach a nun at Chukudum. "You're weak, Ruth," she said. "Leo and Liz and Nancy are in Lokichoggio. Going on leave, I think. They came through Dodoth country. A trader helped them." She couldn't hear our transmission clearly but said she'd contact her Nairobi office on our behalf and they could call the bishop. "But armies don't move because of bishops. I'll call Al. The agency could do more than us."

After we lost her voice I realized she was probably referring to the CIA, not Protestants Against Famine. But when I'd started describing the mob, slick with sweat and foundering, surging around us at the checkpoints, she said, "Been there," soothing me.

Our small phalanx of twelve-year-olds, two girls among them, in torn tribal togas or church-basement cutoffs tied tight with a scrap of string, moved ahead to clear an aisle for our wheels. A blind man waved his staff, having been deserted by whoever was leading him, while people paddled by in the disorderly mass. "Shouldn't we all maybe walk?" Ruth suggested. But Bol and Makundi were intent on turning off. For me, I was transported dreamlike into the World War II *Life* photographs of a book I'd had, captioned "Ahead of the tanks" or "After the bombs," when not engrossed in braking, etc. The kids' enthusiasm, however, seemed less fearful, nor animated by the novelty of helping whites out. Instead, it was the presence of Bol, known to be a schoolteacher—"Two times two!" they chanted. "Three times two!"—as if by preserving Bol they were protecting their chances to go to school again. "New Cush," the SPLA sometimes called the infant Nilotic nation they intended to build in the southern Sudan, using a biblical term for "Upper Egypt." Thus New Cush would have schools! It made tears come; yet how would we feed them?

"Ever been trapped in an elevator? I want outa here," Ruth said, pointing at a trio of vultures wheeling gaily to contemplate us. There were already corpses for them that wouldn't get buried because people were hurrying too fast, a jumble of souls nearing gridlock. Bol, out his window, comforted those who couldn't walk any farther by advising them to wait where they were. Help would be sent when the strongest alerted the rest of the world.

"And the Tooth Fairy," Ruth said, when he translated. We had all turtled into ourselves, as a MiG banked sharply over us to stay out of Uganda's airspace after one of its lethal runs. Ear-whacked and unstrung by its bass banshee hurricane scream, I felt like the jeep was a dinghy, the ship sinking around us, and watched a dead man robbed. We couldn't move. Then Makundi spotted some Baris sneaking eastward on a twin-rut spur, and, without arguing, I swung left to follow them, although they scowled their displeasure and shook us off as soon as the forest permitted so we couldn't tail them to a source of food. Father Leo might have known what lay ahead of us in the way of settlements or river crossings, access to Uganda, or maybe that rogue airstrip the Israelis had supplied the guerrillas from before the U.S. took over. If it hadn't yet grown knee-high, Mickey might land there for Ruthie and me.

Streams flowing off Mount Kinyeti's foothills, some requiring a push from our posse of kids to ford, and the guesswork of trails made this unconscionable but tempting scenario unlikely—that is, climbing into a Cessna, abandoning practically everybody else. More plausible was that we'd break down and starve in a cul-de-sac. The choppy terrain of thorny woods and elephant grass offered few clues as to what we were going to encounter in the next mile or so. It was dicey, sliding down into a muddy cut, our options zero if we got stuck. The war wouldn't stop while a hunt was mounted for us, like the diplomatic imbroglio of the Norwegians being killed by an Antonov's bomb. In the glove compartment was the Norwegians' map, but even if you could figure out where you were and mustered the strength to walk to a village your finger was on, it might long since have been leveled and burned.

An ibis flapped out of a froggy marsh, to Mig's delight. Knobby-boned, he was struggling in my lap, eating raisins from a box Ruth had flavored her oatmeal with.

"Thank you," she said—at first I thought ironically, because she must have intended them for Leo.

"Oh, you mean for coming back?"

"Of course."

"You're welcome." The peaceful moments of this precarious excursion were precious. There were songbirds and lizards that hadn't been slingshotted and eaten—indeed, red meat on the hoof, in the shape of a warthog trotting off, tail high, that, to our painful regret, we had no means to kill—and paths that hadn't been matted by strangers floundering around. The kids scouted in front with our one machete for traces of where our road in its heyday had gone, slashing at the brush and sticking poles in the mudholes. Bugs that fluttered up, they grabbed. What an emaciated crew they really were, and watching for the fat, fingery rosettes, in the wild and woolly moil of natural vegetation, that could signify a banana tree. A family's *shamba* would be designed to be hidden behind a hump of ground so bandits might pass unsuspectingly—the garden of

peanuts and yams, plantains and sesame. Hunger made me preda-
tory, too.

We had serious altitude to avoid toward the north. I tried a dry
creekbed south, and ultimately a boy did spot a yellowing patch
in a plantation of extravagantly elliptical foliage in a distant hollow
tangled with vivid green. Five trees—thank god—but we approached
cautiously in case anybody had a gun. Being an ordinary slash-and-
burn Acholi farm family, they did not, and feared us, hearing our
approach. Two white faces changed the complexion of the encounter
but were almost as hard to deny fruit to as men with a firearm
would have been, and our kids were soon munching industriously.
Fortunately, I was able to pay for everything we consumed, and in
Ugandan currency. Sudanese money could have gotten them shot as
spies by the SPLA, or American cause the Arabs to suspect them.
This they could spend, about a day's hike away through the forests,
the man conceded, although protesting, and wouldn't show us the
trail. His women had already fled, with his parents and children, at
the sound of the car, but in Arabic with Bol, he volunteered no
more.

Each of us began with a couple of bananas, while the okra and
cassava boiled, some plantains fried, and Makundi wrung the rooster's
neck to barbecue him for Ruth and me. Who knew when we'd feast
again? From comfy daylight, the sky grew rosy, then a cleansing
yellowy silver, and silvery yellow, as the moon lit the tumid canopy of
trees. We'd let the poor gentleman keep his three hens, but a civet or
a genet or mongoose or wildcat was after them, to judge by the
squawking, so we ate them, too, paying another three thousand
Ugandan shillings toward his fresh start in Acholi territory in that
country. Both Idi Amin and Yoweri Museveni had treated the Acholis
harshly, as had the loonies of the LRA—themselves Acholi—and so,
squatting on makeshift plots like this, they trundled back and forth
between persecution there and the mercies of Arab or SPLA rule in
Sudan. Embittered, he slipped away from us for good on an indecipherable path in the balmy dark.

We had bats twittering, amphibians trilling, a jackal yapping, an owl, world-weary, hooting. Even a lion grunted, which was a fine omen to hear because people with guns shot lions and elephants first thing. We had outrun the battle zone, but a wind shift combined with Kinyeti's contours above us to deliver faintly concussive reverberations from what must be going on.

"I love this work," Ruth muttered mirthlessly, though hugging Leo. My own charge, Mig, equally stuffed with food, scarcely knew me as a person yet and restricted his reactions to watching the eight-year-old Dinka boy for tips, who in turn was cued by Bol. The moonlight bathing a swaying stand of equatorial trees let me anticipate unwinding under the palms at a hotel I knew in Mwabungu, on the Indian Ocean, and taking stock, angling for a stationary, safer job, teaching again. But my mind insinuated a premonition: *Your number is up.* Too many chances taken and tragedies witnessed unscathed.

"No mines so far," I said. But we were going to need to drive back up our creekbed to the track we'd been on; for a vehicle it had dead-ended. Ruth's view seemed to be that, like her recurrent symptoms of malaria, which she'd had for a decade or more, Africa got chills and fevers off and on wherever you were. I thought of the young bodies, including the three small ones who rode with us, processing almost as in a physiology diagram the mammoth meal consumed. Like the gas in our tank, how long would it last?

In the morning we finished the rest of the yams and millet mush, plus some porridgey home brew Makundi found buried and ripening under a hut. It was tempting to close one's eyes, sink back down, and procrastinate in the shimmering sun, except he was concerned that the Acholi farmer might have "put bad words out." More pressingly, numbers of fugitives from the war had followed our route of flight by now and collected nearby overnight. Bol and Makundi were jittery that the politesse accorded Ruth would break and instead of the begging they were hearing, we'd be rushed. Okay: I roused my aching shoulder to drive again, refusing Makundi's offer because I doubted he would nurse the pedal and our mileage as well. I wished the farmer whose crops we'd eaten could see that they would have been devoured today anyway, and no money given in exchange. We missed Margaret's presence, too: an Acholi translator when we needed one to find the road to Kitgum. Kitgum was a junior version of Gulu, Atiak-sized, but none of us had been there.

Cool drafts snaked down from Kinyeti's massif to this lovely, various country of pretty brakes and bluffs, elephant-grass parkland and gallery forests. We were still driving east, into the sun's glare, but wanting to go south. In the region's forty-year history of war, our ruts must have sometimes accommodated military lorries; we did pass a blunt, same-age strip of bush where planes may have landed to load them, but it was now grown to head-high scrub even a helicopter couldn't have managed, if we'd had the coordinates to report on the radio. Mickey had been in Vietnam when the Israelis were flying in arms; he wouldn't know where.

We saw a baboon scampering round a windfall and a waterbuck leap from a lope into a gallop, signs of leaving our famine far behind; then an elephant's platter-prints next to a spring. When we met a spearman he sprinted to escape, until Bol yelled in Juba Arabic that we had no guns. "Boom, boom," he enunciated, grinning at our white faces, Norwegian logo, and pennants. As we grinned back, wondering whether he was an Acholi or Latuka, the next tribe in this tier of territory alongside the Imatongs, it occurred to Makundi that he might be joking about the gamble of mines in the road, not referring to guns. No army, not Khartoum's or Uganda's or the SPLA's, controlled this border strip, and Bol, using Juba's pidgin dialect of Arabic, confirmed that he did mean mines. Flourishing his hands in dough-kneading motions, he represented how one would explode under our chassis, and, taking our eight-year-old's hands, showed how the Lord's Resistance Army utilized their kidnapped children to set the trap because of their small fingers and footprints at the site.

Then the thugs emerged from hiding to cut throats and loot the wreckage afterward. He plucked at my shirt to indicate how it would be valuable to outlaws who never went to a town.

He also demonstrated how to throw a spear, and rubbed his forefinger and thumb, in case I wanted to pay him for a lesson in how to do that. But oh, no, he laughed again when Bol spelled out our proposal in the Juba patois. Being hired to guide us was not what he had in mind.

"He's telling you you people have the atom bomb, so what do you need him for?" And, further, Bol followed his narrative by pointing far up the mountainside. "And he's telling you somewhere there's a sacred ancestor cave no white man or Arab has ever visited, where the wind growls and bats whirl like swallows and a magic leopard eats them if they fall, and he dedicates his soul and spearpoint every year." The spearman vanished down a footpath bright with light and succulent scenery—fingers of forestland broken by rolling openings—leaving us lonely and to our own devices. We knew where south was, but how to get to Kitgum?

Mig, my four-year-old, as if hardened into his orphanhood, was perky but untroublesome, sensitive to the rules of the road without a common language between himself and his meal ticket. His history thus far would remain a blank until we reached someplace like Gulu, where Margaret could translate, but already I felt guilty for having half-wished we could palm him off somewhere along the line, if we'd bumped into a party of his own people, most likely the Baris: which, except for the first, scurrying bunch, we hadn't. He was experimenting with the wonders of a jacket zipper.

Being perhaps midway between the nuns in Chukudum and Felix's feeding station, west from Atiak toward the Congo, Makundi was trying to raise either one on our faltering radio. But the nuns couldn't read us anymore; we just heard a faint salutation, "God bless you," from their frequency. Felix said, "I envy you. I've got ten thousand people in the yard—and there will be ten thousand more tomorrow. And no food!"

"So nice to be envied," Ruth murmured. I thought of Ya–Ya's monkey, probably in a pot. Gazing up at Kinyeti's complex lower slopes, the most massive in Sudan, she looked wistful more than intimidated—to know where your sacred places were. Her own beliefs, pantheism dappled with Christianity, were "like the back side of a cow," she liked to say, triangulated between the Labyrinth and Bible-thumping. Like me, she believed heaven was nowhere if it wasn't on earth, but for me a double negative wasn't necessarily a positive. She believed there *was* a heaven.

What worried me right now, ahead of suppertime (one meal a day was fine for these kids, more than they were used to) was watching the most energetic of them still jogging ahead of the jeep, trouble-shooting—looking for axle-bending boulders, mudholes, and the like—instead of behind. They were snake-smart and wary of other savannah dangers, but how could I justify the zanily criminal idea of employing twelve-year-old kids as mine sweepers? "Boom, boom!" I warned them, with Bol helping to translate: whereupon they would stoop more closely to scrutinize the surface of the ground.

Just as in that old creekbed, we took a blind-alley turn, wasting gas and time in avoiding sand traps at about walking speed. But then we did reach a three-corner junction—maybe the auspicious thoroughfare leading north to Ikoto and Dongotona, or south toward Kitgum, where we wanted to go. It seemed a luminously leafy location, like the right-angled right turn we'd been praying for, and somewhat more traveled. Months ago, the SPLA might have run guns up this way from Uganda to Ikoto for the siege at Torit, Bol said. No recent tire tracks, but a passable lane. The only not-so-propitious sight, as we stopped to congratulate ourselves, was the low-slung figure of a happy hyena galumphing away from the scene. Not a big deal: something was dead; vultures flapped sidewise, too—till we saw a ransacked *tukl,* and another hyena swinging a fleshy scrap in its jaws, then its jumbo tongue licking its chops, a leisurely departure that indicated firearms weren't a regular feature here. *That* was good, and we needed to scavenge the *shamba* for edibles, but I wanted to shield our kids, shy away from any terrible little massacre. They saw jackfruit, plantains, papayas, a melon garden, peanut flowers, sweet potatoes, and darted in, skirting the bodies, whatever their number and condition was. I didn't investigate, either. The less you knew, the less guilt you felt about not holding up our escape to become a burial party. We had been exceedingly lucky to spend last night short of this point. A white chicken was hanging in a tree, and sometimes families were slaughtered by the LRA for owning a white chicken. But it could have been any reason. They had accomplished the job with machetes, including gratuitously slashing the trees, hacking at garden produce they couldn't carry away, as if to deprive later travelers of nourishment. A dog had been butchered and eaten, but a few goats, whose pellets we saw, driven north daintily: that is, their prints were dainty, and thank god, headed north.

Out of sight of the murdered bodies—I never entered the hut— none of us was too fastidious to consume a split melon, a fallen banana. Outlines remained in the grass where the marauders had slept, a party around our own size, and the area still smelled of spilled millet beer and sex, Makundi said, with women who "I think were not having fun." The imprints, so fresh the grass had not begun to recover, were creepy. Nevertheless, the kids scoured the area for mouthfuls of food, and we encouraged them despite the scent of scorched thatch, the notion that the same pangas chopping the yams we now salvaged had chopped arms and necks.

Borrowed time, my mind kept intoning. *Borrowed time.* In the Congo, bordering Sudan, Mai-Mai guerrillas—their name translates from Congolese Swahili to "Water, Water"; because they believed bullets shot at them would turn to water—committed atrocities as random as these, and when pursuing diamonds, you might hear about similar havoc but avoid the bloodier scenes yourself.

"It's too much. Let's go. We can't sleep here," I said, rotating my throbbing shoulder before gripping the wheel again. There was nothing ghoulish about our kids scavenging some calories from a massacre scene. Certainly the victims wouldn't have objected; and they had survived by doing the same before. I was antsy, crabby, cowardly, picturing the eerie LRA band half a dozen miles north of us, moving on toward Ikoto, Dongotona, Torit, killing folks they caught unawares and outnumbered, kidnapping the kids who didn't resist to draft as porters, but circling the towns or other armed groups. At Torit's airstrip, if the Arabs had broken the Dinkas' siege, they could be resupplied with arms—one child per Kalashnikov—because Khartoum helped them bedevil Museveni tit-for-tat for Uganda's allowing its territory to be used as a pipeline by the SPLA.

Although this high-bush Africa, with clotted gullies, ridgebacks curving like a sickle, and leopardy trees overhanging the road, favored guerrillas, I acquiesced in Bol's allowing the older boys to continue trotting in front of us as scouts. He or Makundi sometimes walked with them, ready to shout ahead to a roadblock that we were *mzungus,* white, not to be casually shot. Also, even if another LRA gang wasn't following the first in order to plunder refugees and maybe rearm at Torit's airfield, now that Khartoum's victory around Juba had become a rout, the soldiers we had been lucky enough to miss might have laid mines behind them in the road in order to hamper pursuit. And if so, they would have tied signals for themselves, like a feather on a branch, to beware of when they returned.

Makundi and Bol were watching for these, Bol much preoccupied now, too, with the fate of the bloody town of Torit, which had changed hands repeatedly since the south's revolution against the Arabs had begun there, way back in 1955. If Arab garrisons besieged in Torit and Kapoeta broke out, the SPLA might lose Dongotona, Ikoto, Chukudum, and other villages: pushed into oblivion.

My damsel in distress was not groveling in gratitude to me for coming back. Nor did I want her to; she was right that a few expatriate witnesses had been needed here—I just regretted being one of them.

"You want to go home?" she remarked, reading my thoughts, but remembering my tales of school board fracases: "That guy in Keene, New Hampshire, that garage owner who didn't vote for the new school building to have enough windows put in because he said it might increase the furnace bills, and since his garage had no windows, why on earth should the children?"

I laughed, as I had in New Hampshire. You might as well laugh as cry.

We met two civilian families, who were terrified of us, however. Specifically, our children frolicking on the road in front of us panicked them because the Lord's Resistance Army utilized children tactically to trigger an enemy's ambush and draw its fire; then, later, to bind, blind, and mangle prisoners. These individuals simply fell on their knees, surrendering, till the jeep appeared, when—greatly relieved, and armored from us and our questions and curiosity by their nakedness—they professed to understand no language except Acholi, which prevented us from obtaining any information. Once they were sure we had no weapons, they slid into the forest like fish wriggling into a reef.

We'd communicated the danger ahead of them, and they the fact that they couldn't vouch for the road being safe in front of us, either. Yet now I got us stuck in a washout, squandering fuel, tire tread, and a lot of noise, which in Makundi's view was the worst because it could draw guerrillas to intercept us who weren't traveling or camped nearby. His snappish fear seemed out of character and thus alarmed me, whereas Bol's more abstracted attitude reflected not different assumptions but what I realized were twinges of guilt that he wasn't at a proper post, among his defenseless countrywomen, directing foot traffic in the chokepoint back at Nimule, instead of dodging that crisis.

This was enough of a crisis. "Its muchness," as Ruth agreed when I kept pacing, chewing my fingers or nails, and groaning, "Too much!"—if not helping to lay sticks under the wheels and gunning the engine to spin them free.

"So, are you going to stay in Nairobi?" I asked her, meaning long-term. But she replied that she was thinking of Crete. This took me a moment to process.

"Have you ever been to Crete?"

I laughed. "To Rhodes, not Crete. But what I meant was, after your vacation."

"The problem is, with no papers, Leo can't go to Crete. I can't leave him with strangers, even responsible strangers, after what he's been through."

I sighed in agreement, but also because by ignoring my question she sounded undismayed to be Nairobi-bound.

"Bound to Nairobi," I said, playing on the words. Both of us knew I'd been asking partly about myself. Where should I land? "Well, not necessarily for life."

The children were chanting their tables of numbers. "Two plus two"; "Four plus four." And just so, Leo was two, Mig was four, Bol's little nameless boy—actually, he called him Chol—was eight. In an hour we were moving; then, at a smoking hut, we saw a scrounging pye-dog and a frantic hen that evidently had escaped a massacre. Again I tried to discourage the kids from poking about for any remnants of food, but they turned up no bodies and little to eat. By now we must have crossed into Ugandan territory, a lemony, tawny, undulant, lightly broken forest full of secretive, abbreviated vistas radiating all about, implying the hundred miles or so stretching intricately eastward toward the mountains at Kaabong and the next scraggly dirt road that might parallel this one. It was the original Africa, the riot of life seen by Speke, Stanley, Burton, and Bruce, with primeval bluffs and cuts and turbulence, giant trees, buffalo thickets, black and silver creeks tunneling through to elephant pasturage, grass half the height of a giraffe.

The trees' tentative shadows pushed me to hurry. Kitgum, a town of several thousand, had a military post, a hotel, and a bus schedule, although I'd just glimpsed it once out of Ed's cockpit window. "Gracious," I said, "is it lovely or scary?" Mig, maybe sensing my tension, had climbed over the seat into Bol's lap, but Bol got out to coach the several youngsters who were jogging slowly as scouts in front of the car. Ruth, who hadn't yet ever visited Crete, kept speaking of dipping her toes in the Mediterranean there: "More character" than the lesser islands. I was touched. Fractionated was what we were, like riding two horses, one foot on each, standing up—half not in Acholi land at all, but with the Eurotrash in Rhodes or Alexandria or wherever. Meanwhile, the airwaves being full of the SPLA's catastrophe, these Lord's Resistance Army units must have heard the word on the radios Khartoum provided them, and would naturally leave off their God-given task of purging Acholi land and the rest of northern Uganda and adjoining regions of what they considered forbidden behavior, on behalf of a grisly Jehovah, and infiltrate the conflict zone—every commander an emperor, with life-and-death whimsy and a mission to breed a new populace from the loins of captured girls.

Common calculation, as well as telepathy and the unfortunate hour of extra racket our motor had made, prepared me a little for the dreadful conclusion. I heard my tire burst with a *crack*. The rear sagged at a tilt. I also heard Bol yelling and saw that a child had been hurled into the air—another sideways!—by an explosion in the roadway in front, which immensely augmented the crack. Bol was pointing, I was yelling, Ruth cursing. Makundi hopped out of the back seat, but then buckled like a puppet jackknifing.

"Stay," I said to Ruth.

Makundi had been shot through the abdomen and was trying to hold himself together. Bol, in front of the bumper, also fell, hit through the back, with a shriek of surprise. Fathoming that it would be better from the gunman's standpoint to capture the jeep intact, just with one wheel bent, I thought we should sit frozenly, waiting for instructions—except that Ruth now reached under her seat for the first-aid kit because of the cries of our friends.

There came an incomprehensible shout from somebody hidden. But we put our hands up, even the eight-year-old—Bol's skinny Chol—and finally Mig and Leo, imitating me and Ruth. Three teenagers carrying machetes and looking like the Wild Man from Borneo on a larger scale approached from the bushes and motioned us to step out, which we clumsily did.

Bol was gushing blood from his midsection, both front and back, into the dirt, lacking breath enough to flop about or scream. Or possibly his spine had been split. His voice box had no certain pitch but, like an accordion closing for good, exhaled all the last sounds a groan can contain.

Makundi's agony was louder, high, low, more blasphemous, and he thrashed weakly while trying to close the holes in his intestines with his fingers, or at least squeeze them inside the rip in his skin. He lay on the gray road, pitifully close to a green thicket that would have at least afforded him more privacy in which to suffer and die. Ruth and I, our hands awkwardly raised, had to watch his face contort, its energies alternately spent on panting groans or opening and closing his eyes. The boy who had been blown into the air, torn partly in two, by stepping on the mine, seemed half-conscious but stiffening horribly, like some kind of roadkill, in a weird curl. The other child, thrown sidewise, lay twitching in shock, whimpering or mute, red next to white, all tissue and bone.

More youngsters clutching pangas emerged, as fast on their feet as our own kids were—in fact caught one who was making a break for the woods and promptly hamstrung both his legs in the space of a moment, throwing him as a fifth casualty sprawled on the road. The surviving children whom we'd brought, aged twelve or thirteen, were being forced to kneel in front of the car, near Bol, while their hands were tied, according to the directions shouted in Acholi by an adult who still remained concealed. Then they murmured to each other, hearing the anger of our captors, that they had grabbed only six. Two Dinkas must have gotten a jump on the LRA kids during the turmoil and outrun their pursuit.

"Oh, Mac!" Ruth exclaimed to Makundi. Bol coughed painfully, trying not to strangle. I remembered how easily I had expected we could cure his TB with the facilities in Nairobi. The "Fuzzy-Wuzzies," as I dubbed them, being reminded by their unkempt hair of old films of Australian bushmen, though their robotic manner was more like science fiction, soon outnumbered our pinioned children. They emptied the car of its leftover medical stuff and food as well as spare trophies like sneakers, socks, and pants. When they pointed at us, waggling a finger to tell us to strip, we didn't, however, because they appeared so young. And probably because we were white they refrained from chopping our hands off, although flourishing a fire axe they'd discovered under the back seat that I hadn't suspected was there. Neither Leo nor Mig intrigued them, but Chol, Bol's eight-year-old, was clutched, weeping, by the ear and made to kneel in the row with the others in front of the bumper, with his elbows tied together behind him.

So Ruth and I spontaneously submitted. Wordless except for a grunt—I don't even know whose reflexes flicked first—we knelt between Chol and Bol, who was still alive, on his side, unable to move, as if his cord might indeed have been severed. The Lord's Resistance Army children surrounded us in puzzlement, less meek or sadistic than astonished, perhaps never having captured a white person before, due to the deep bush they operated in, and wondering about *our* rule book.

A rawboned, ragged man in dingy fatigues with a battered Kalashnikov, the stock cracked and splinted, and a face like a bowling ball, revealed himself as our shooter. He checked the condition of Bol and Makundi, each dying in the dirt like a stepped-on spider, in excruciating pain. The hamstrung boy was scrabbling along on his elbows toward the weeds to hide, but the two children who had triggered the mine looked mercifully inert, in their separate comas, or dead. With a lopsided, feast-or-famine grin, the man examined his booty, picking up my spare shirt, which might fit him.

Semaphoring with his rifle muzzle, he signaled us to stand again. Yes, little Chol could, too, who'd understood our gestures; we were all to strip quickly. My money belt pleased him, and he let a frenetic lad with cactus hair try it on like a bandolier, before wearing it that way himself. The girls in his party picked up Ruth's blouse, purse, and skirt—in that case a mismatch, except for the purse, which the commander again appropriated for himself. The process had a berserk but practiced efficiency, and robberly laughter. Then he walked down the kneeling line of Dinka children and pumped each one's face against the crotch of his pants by yanking their ears. A couple of girls had kept up with us all this way, and as their clothes were given away, he wet his finger and poked it up their vaginas to see if they were virgins.

"NGO!" he said to me, as if that were my name, and signaled "naughty, naughty" with his finger.

Ruth and I, hands covering our nakedness turned our attention toward the possibility of comforting our dying friends. Ruth called out Makundi's wife's name, but the commander interrupted. "NGO!" he warned: again, the "naughty, naughty" signal. Speaking in Acholi to the nearest child soldier, he had him fetch our radio, which he dialed to the wavelength he wanted, but it produced only static. "NGO!" he repeated, when he found no key in the jeep's ignition. The child retrieved it from my pants pocket for him; but he was next startled when the car, being in gear, jumped and stalled, fortunately before hitting the children kneeling in front of it. He ordered them moved, but then sounded as though he were stripping the gears, before throwing the key away.

Another grown-up appeared. His face, not as round as the first commander's, was about as affectless, and he was carrying a single-shot, King's African Rifles–type World War I or II gun. He, too, insisted that each newly captured child kiss his crotch, jerking the muzzle like the tip of a fishing rod under the captive's chin to produce the desired buzz. Ruth was shielding Leo's eyes, so I covered Mig's, then pointed to our medical kit on the ground, remembering a few morphine shots that might be left. The first guy, jagged, peremptory, not used to contradiction, divined my meaning and rolled up his sleeve. It occurred to me that if I popped air into his vein I could kill him—if I wanted to die very slowly, roasted alive with my friends in retaliation. But he wasn't serious, either. Instead of asking for a vaccination, he beckoned to an angular late-teens boy whose pride in sharpening and brandishing his machete blade seemed like a fencing master's.

"NGO!" our adversary announced again. He waved at Bol, spidered belly-up, whom I especially hoped to help, and the boy strode to. If you had one howl left in you, one allotted final shriek, this was the scream Bol, who knew all about the LRA, emitted now. The boy inserting the point of his panga into Bol's bullet exit hole, sliced him from gonads to breastbone, crosscutting afterward to lay him open for autopsy. Using the flat of his blade like a spatula, he brought out the long intestines for display and draped sections around a couple of other boys' shoulders like two dripping shawls.

Makundi was trying to hold in his innards by closing the hole in his groin, while the commander who had shot him examined the jeep's blasted wheel rim, as if he had forgotten he'd already stripped the gears and thrown the key away. His exasperation swelled until he had the car tipped over to salvage wiring from the underside and so his people could cut the tires up for sandals. Our shoes didn't fit anybody, though they had occasioned a Cinderella scene. The second-in-command, holding the single-shot rifle, was pumping a Dinka girl's nose against his crotch while staring at Ruth's nude boobs, as if to demean them both. But the guy with the Kalashnikov was cleverer. Observing that our attention didn't stray from our surviving friend, he whirled his index finger again and pointed at the boy in the badly fitting army tunic, obviously pulled off a corpse, whose finesse with the machete had just been proved, and then to Makundi, cradling himself on the ground.

With our voices constricted in horror, Ruth and I were squeaking in protest, swinging away to limp toward Kitgum without waiting to witness the last. "Mister!" the poor hamstrung boy screeched, realizing he was going to be abandoned. The uninjured children, hands behind their backs, had knives at their throats, as grinning child soldiers taught them how to grin as well. Though whimpering for help, they were learning that in the discipline of the LRA they were required to smile or be put to death. Ruth in her anguish kept sidling in Makundi's direction, which left her vulnerable to further pain and humiliation. He was swiftly eviscerated and his intestines hung around the necks of nearby kids in uniform.

"NGO, go," suggested the round-headed man, emotionless as a bowling ball. I almost sprained my ankle in wrenching around; then panicked momentarily, feeling two hands grasp my leg, until I noticed it was only Mig, knee-high, who I had originally set down when forced to strip, and picked up and set down again in the dismal confusion, but who knew enough not to attract attention by bawling out loud—his face spoke it all.

We stumbled off, carrying Mig and Leo; I held Chol by the hand. Yet the commander had one more outrage in store. A boy scarfed with Makundi's intestines brought Ruth his cock and balls as well. Numbly, in bewilderment, she turned, accepting them in her hand—then, bleating like a lamb, dropped them in the dirt and muffled her mouth. When the goo, the bloody smear, began to register, she spat and scrubbed at her face, retching in grief and disgust. Soon, though, we were out of sight of our tormentors, but in a cloud of mosquitoes drawn to our bare skin. I put an arm around her, till it seemed inadequate or unnatural to walk for long that way. Instead, I squeezed Chol's hand, the eight-year-old whose history was still unknown to us but who must already have left many, many dead behind along the Nile. He was a trouper, his feet of course in much better shape for this hike than ours, and willing to tag along with me, Bol's friend, and Ruth, whom he knew had helped to save him from the row of kneeling captives, wherever we went. Nor was he catatonic, as they might soon be.

"Am I accident-prone?" Ruth finally asked me.

I laughed, though she did not. "No, more likely a hero manqué."

"I'm sorry."

"No, *I'm* sorry," I confessed, meaning for deciding to leave the Nimule-Gulu road. Despite the bombings and crush, we probably would have come to no harm and been rescued quicker, even as a group.

Poxed with bruise-colored bites, her breasts and buttocks joggled, provoking a feeding frenzy among the bugs, and causing her to transfer Leo from her shoulders to ride crosswise in her arms as a shield who could slap some of them himself. "I'm sorriest," she concluded with finality, as we watched Chol retrieve the occasional morsel, a yam or mango, that an LRA porter as young as himself might have dropped after that group had looted a ruined *shamba*. Not that we passed too many. This wild border had never been subjugated by either the colonial order or the dictators after independence. There were no markets or police; you ate what you killed or grew and could defend.

"But I think we're in the clear," I insisted, and mentioned seeing Ya-Ya as a reward awaiting us when we got to Nairobi.

"And Attlee's family?" she countered, trailing off. Night descends fast in the tropics, and hyena tracks were scribbled on the roadway. "In the clear," she parroted me, then reached to rub my bad shoulder apologetically because I'd been trying to cheer her up. "Dismal," she added. "Mayhem!"

But at dusk on the outskirts of a deserted settlement, probably Madi Opei, we happened upon a hut that boasted an intact roof, a door that latched. Also a rat Chol killed with a rock; and another in the next *tukl;* plus an incautious mongoose, whose hip he broke with his throwing arm. Promptly all three were dangling over a twig fire as their fur was singed off and he foraged for fallen fruit and overlooked vegetables the raiders had missed. We found no pots to boil water in, or scraps of clothing—only a flat tub of broken metal to sizzle some smelly eggs and plantains on. The chickens were gone.

Like a pair of old marrieds, we sat cross-legged in our blotchy birthday suits, nibbling raw okra, drinking risky brook water. It was frustrating but sufficient to fill everybody's tummy and cut the crying a little. Having been too frightened to utter a peep this afternoon, Mig and Leo were making up for it now. Out and about with a stick for protection, I saw a leopard crossing through the mottled shadows, but did come up with three white sorghum sacks, inscribed A GIFT OF THE PEOPLE OF THE UNITED STATES, of the sort so often pilfered from aid deliveries and sold by local traders. Regrettably they were empty when I prodded them with my stick. When Chol pulled one over his head, however, I realized that, yes, we might wear these for warmth tonight. A sharp bit of metal served to cut three holes in each; this delighted Ruth, who could feel clothed.

"My shortie," she called hers. "When were sack dresses in fashion, about 'fifty-eight?"

I was less pessimistic, too. I'd be back at the Arab's in a week or less, chatting up a KLM stewardess crew at the rooftop pool across the street—although, sure, hollowed out by our ordeal. Wasn't that what you did in life: bring back Ya-Ya and Mig, and jolly some international adoption agency into placing them decently abroad, then feel hollowed out? People of Ruth's and my type defined ourselves in part by where we were. Alexandria, Nairobi, Kampala, instead of Chicago, Atlanta, Paducah, and "after it's over" didn't apply as a nostrum because it was never over. Our self-medicating self-drama would need to be further swamped.

In fact, we had one more grisly discovery. Leo was howling with colic—Ruth worried that he'd "picked up an amoeba"—while the wind whinnied outside like hyenas searching for a skeleton to crunch, yet answering his wails, and blew brush around that sounded like the footfalls of fighters creeping near. I'd grabbed a broken panga for a sense of protection, which may have lent me the courage to follow Chol to a hut we hadn't looked inside but seemed the source of unidentifiable sounds, "Animal, vegetable, or mineral?" as my mind asked, to defuse my fear. By the moon's illumination, this was inevitably not a baby mammal abandoned by its mother but a man tied by his hands to a king post, with his feet chopped off. Tourniquets had prevented him from bleeding to death, in order to prolong his misery. The stumps were suppurating.

Faint from shock, blood loss, or early gangrene, he didn't reply to my English yet understood it and indicated, when his hands were freed and his thirst relieved, that riding a bike had been his crime. Broken, it lay beside him; the LRA was known to forbid the use of such contraptions. As a teacher, he now breathed—he had had to. His stumps were bulging, coagulated pustules, but neither of us could liberate them from those infernal hide strips half-buried in dribbling flesh. Although I wanted to spare Ruth the experience, minor surgery with the point of the panga was required. I won't describe how she worked; it was our worst hands-on interlude. Then, after praying with him, we slept until the sun was high and, in the other hut, he had crossed the blessed threshold of unconsciousness.

Not just Mig and Leo were complaining and bumping about; Chol was chatting in Dinka through the door to somebody standing outside. Nobody scary would be speaking in Dinka, we reminded ourselves, if only so that our pulse rate could go down. Boys' voices: I remembered the two youngsters who had been so quick off the mark they'd outrun the whole LRA crew. Maybe they'd followed us when the coast was clear. And soon, indeed, we were hugging them and cooing as intensely as if they could somehow represent everybody who'd been lost.

Besides not being hungry, they rustled up a few bananas for us, and the ingredients for a gumbo, which we fried instead of boiled, and killed a resident cobra or two we hadn't known about. Our plasticized white canvas grain sacks made us look like the Tin Man and the Michelin Woman, but I kept wearing mine, instead of cutting it into a loincloth, in solidarity with Ruth, who was acutely worried by a touch of fever she felt Leo had. The desperately emaciated condition the priest had found him in along the Palotaka road must have weakened him.

Mig, rolling the busted bicycle around to persuade me to show him how to ride it, seemed to possess an indestructible constitution, and the oldest two flashed their fingers competitively to solve a problem in addition they had set for themselves to remind me of our classes together. Seeing that Ruth and I had survived the ambush without needing to either run or kneel must have convinced them that sticking with us was their best bet—not that they *could* have trekked back to Dinka land. But watching a vulture spiral, I was anguished, remembering the hamstrung boy holding his mangled thighs, waiting to be eaten when we and the LRA left the scene; and the nibbling already on the body of the man here who had died last night enclosed in a hut but whom we should be burying, except we hadn't the tools or strength.

The helter-skelter night vocalizations had been dispelled by gloriously sunshot corridors of color, a starburst of shapes, a millennial spectrum, radiating through the jungle. No more dreams of fighters stealing toward our *tukl* to set the thatch afire. I thought of Craig or that other CIA guy, Herbert, going back to the wife who raised show dogs in Maryland, after a hairy assignment, to play golf and cleanse his memories with Bach and Mozart in a cozy "den," while I might perhaps aspire to take over Al's desk job when he left, or the street shelter.

"Another day, another dollar," I told Ruthie. Like Nairobi's kids, ours skipped along, winging a stone at a dove or hefting a chosen stick. The plywood shell of Madi Opei's health clinic remained, next to a giant shade tree with a blackboard nailed to the trunk for lessons, and a curl of logs poignantly arrayed around to sit on, if there were any inhabitants. In the crapshoot of war, these children didn't blame us for errors of judgment. They lived—others not—and simply cocked an eye for the generous rosettes of a fingery banana tree or a well that didn't smell poisoned. Gradually the country became more hillocky, checkered with clearings for goat grazing or farming, as we trudged south. Mig was hiccuping but not feverish, and not mincing on the soles of his feet, like us.

"Okay, buster, I owe you, I'll admit," Ruth said, although I sensed that her more serious preoccupation was the loss of Makundi as an anchor in her life. "You should get yourself a little family," she added, mentioning a former priest we knew who had left the church to marry a ravishingly pretty Nuer girl and worked for secular aid groups now but maintained a joshing, side-by-side relationship with the Catholics, too. "Like Al's wife does, she would keep you at home."

Ruth was right that I was secretly afraid of floating off like a balloon, whereas she was afraid of that suicidal gene she imagined lurking in her. Cut loose from this job, both of us were going to be regarded as employable. Nothing that had gone awry would be blamed on us, just as Father Leo would not have taken flak if his exit had slammed into an ambush. The question would fall to us of what to do: often a puzzle for NGO people. The well-heeled ones apply for a post in Geneva and tour disaster sites white-collar-style. They have villas and careers.

Our two surviving older youngsters, trotting restlessly in front of our sore feet, suddenly whirled around and dived into a gully to hide. Though recognizing the Dinka word for "soldiers," we were too exhausted to conceive of any action other than waiting in the middle of the road to learn our fate. It was highest noon, but Leo's temperature was hotter than that, and he was letting us know we all were quite thirsty.

A file of ten or a dozen dispirited-looking, olive-drab-clad, adult-sized figures were approaching, holding their rifles crosswise because our own running children had alarmed them. However, noticing two *mzungus,* even so weirdly costumed, eased their concerns. This was a patrol of regulars, of respectable age, and we slumped down on a log to rest at last, hoping for an English-speaking officer with a radio, perhaps, who could summon a truck to rescue us.

They were cautious, in case we turned out to be captives set out as decoys. But Ruth put her hand on my arm as we sat waiting. "We're out of the woods!" She laughed, feelingly. In Tanzania, she said, there were refugee camps with just the nuts and bolts of helping people—no civil war going on in the vicinity. The soldiers clustered around us, registering their curiosity, but not in English. Ruth's Swahili sufficed to assure them that our two Dinka boys, Malual and Manyok, were not LRA, not to be shot. In that and rudimentary Luganda we talked of Kampala, Jinja, and Mbale, because government policy was to send troops from other Ugandan tribes—the Ganda, Luo, Batooro, Kiga, Nkole—to police in Acholi land, reducing fraternization; and they had still less interest in Sudan's wars. If not stationed here, they might have been at the Zaire or Rwandan frontier, or trying to prevent the Dodoths and Turkanas from killing each other on the Kenyan border.

"What a luxury, to be guarded!" Ruth said, rubbing her feet and encouraging the soldiers to laugh at our grain sacks if they wanted to, so as to build rapport. "I feel like a well that's refilling." They were glad to have stumbled across us anyway because it cut their walk short for today, and they shared some peanuts. But no, no radio; a private with the physiognomy of the Rwenzori Mountains was dispatched to hike back to the base and fetch the truck early. I pinched my sackcloth to remind myself that I was not actually naked. I didn't feel as if I had a "well" to fill—more like an acid spill in part of my mind—yet even so I didn't want to trade Africa yet for New Hampshire's mingy winter slush and property-tax politics, that perpetual spirit of cutting your losses. Ruth was a centripetal force. Her future seemed predictable enough, at least until Africa blindsided her again. I was more of a floater—not centrifugal, but more like a balloon. At Kitgum, when the truck got us there, we could borrow clothes and bus fare, and, in Gulu, we would situate our three Dinkas of age eight and above, Chol, Malual, and Manyok, as bona fide refugees in a U.N.-sponsored camp. Then we'd smuggle Mig and Leo (loaded with antibiotics) on toward the cities, and Ya-Ya and Al. A year from now, I might still be at the Arab's, or not.

Nibbling peanuts, Ruth drank out of somebody's canteen. "Isn't this the life of Riley?" she said, then cupped her ear, hearing the rumble of the army truck.